"There is some talk already circulating around town."

Daisy rubbed her cheek, trying to take in what this meant. "Be honest with me—how bad is it?"

"To speak bluntly, our reputations will be tarnished, and it may very well spill over onto Abigail, as well."

Her spirits sank. Was her dream of being a welcomed member of the community over so soon? She wouldn't accept that. "But surely if we just go on about our business, in time the rumors will die down."

Everett shook his head. "I wish that were true. But this sort of thing can take on a life of its own, and folks have long memories. Believe me, I know."

"Then what do you suggest we do?"

"There's only one thing we *can* do—you and I must immediately announce our engagement."

Daisy halted in her tracks and stared at him, not sure she'd heard correctly. Was he serious? The only hint of emotion she could see in his face, however, was that irritating hint of cynical amusement he wore like armor.

Books by Winnie Griggs

Love Inspired Historical

The Hand-Me-Down Family
The Christmas Journey
The Proper Wife
Second Chance Family
A Baby Between Them
*Handpicked Husband
*The Bride Next Door

Love Inspired

The Heart's Song

*Texas Grooms

WINNIE GRIGGS

is a city girl born and raised in southeast Louisiana's Cajun Country who grew up to marry a country boy from the hills of northwest Louisiana. Though her Prince Charming (who often wears the guise of a cattle rancher) is more comfortable riding a tractor than a white steed, the two of them have been living their own happily-ever-after for more than thirty years. During that time they raised four proud-to-call-them-mine children and a too-numerous-to-count assortment of dogs, cats, fish, hamsters, turtles and 4-H sheep.

Winnie has held a job at a utility company since she graduated from college. She saw her first novel hit bookstores in 2001. In addition to her day job and writing career, Winnie serves on committees within her church and on the executive boards and committees of several writing organizations, and she is active in local civic organizations—she truly believes the adage that you reap in proportion to what you sow.

In addition to writing and reading, Winnie enjoys spending time with her family, cooking and exploring flea markets. Readers can contact Winnie at P.O. Box 14, Plain Dealing, LA 71064, or email her at winnie@winniegriggs.com.

The Bride Next Door

WINNIE GRIGGS

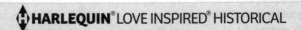

Recycling programs
for this product may
not exist in your area.

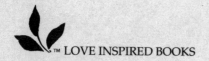 ™ LOVE INSPIRED BOOKS

ISBN-13: 978-0-373-82967-5

THE BRIDE NEXT DOOR

Copyright © 2013 by Winnie Griggs

www.LoveInspiredBooks.com

Printed in U.S.A.

Do not store up for yourselves treasures on earth, where moths and vermin destroy, and where thieves break in and steal. But store up for yourselves treasures in heaven, where moths and vermin do not destroy, and where thieves do not break in and steal. For where your treasure is, there your heart will be also.
—*Matthew* 6:19–21

To my accountability partner, Sherrie,
who helped me stay on track as I was writing this
book. And to my sister Tammy, who took the time
from her busy schedule to read the finished product
and give me her honest feedback.

Chapter One

Turnabout, Texas, April 1895

The ornery, splinter-ridden door refused to budge, no matter how hard she shoved. Or how hard she glared.

Daisy Johnson stood on the darkened sidewalk, glowering at the weathered barricade that stood between herself and her new home. She absently scratched a splinter from her thumb as she glanced down at the black-and-white dog sitting patiently at her heels. "Don't worry, Kip. I'm going to get us inside, one way or the other."

Kip gave her a supportive yip, then began scratching his side.

A noise from over to her left caught Daisy's attention. Down the street, a shadowy figure exited the livery and headed unsteadily down the sidewalk toward the hotel. Probably coming from one of the poker games the locals held there—an activity she was unfortunately all too familiar with.

Other than that, things were quiet. Which was fine by her. Kip was the only company she needed tonight.

Daisy spared a quick glance at the adjoining building, which housed the newspaper office, and thought briefly about knocking on the door to see if she could borrow something to use as a pry bar. But she discarded the thought almost before it had fully formed. Not only was the hour late, but from what she recalled about the man who owned the place, he was an uppity gent with a high-falutin accent of some sort. His attitude reminded her too much of her grandmother. Not the sort who would take kindly to being roused from sleep. Or someone she'd want to owe any favors.

Turning back to the stubbornly closed door, she jutted her chin out and tilted her hat back. No warped slab of lumber was going to get the better of her, not when she was so close to her goal.

Using her foot to shove aside one of the rotten boards she'd pried from across the door frame, Daisy jiggled the key and turned the knob again. There was just enough light coming from the glow of the nearby streetlamp to confirm the door wasn't locked. Which meant it was just stuck.

"If you think you can out-ornery me," she muttered at the door as she rolled up her sleeves, "then you better think again." With that, she took firmer hold of the knob, twisted it as far as it would go, and led with her shoulder as she rammed against the door. Kip stopped scratching and gave her a you-can-do-it bark.

The door held a moment longer, then scraped noisily open a few inches. Progress. But not enough. Kip might be able to squeeze through that opening, but not her.

Steeling herself, Daisy threw her shoulder into it one more time, grunting at the impact. With a last creak of protest, the door gave up its fight and opened wide enough to allow her to pass.

With a triumphant grin and a prickling of anticipation, Daisy retrieved her pack, tossed her bedroll up on her shoulder and met Kip's curious glance. "This is it, boy. We're home."

With a deep breath, Daisy took her first step inside the building, Kip at her heels. The room was mostly cloaked in shadows, illuminated only by what light filtered in from the streetlamp, and it took a few moments for her eyes to adjust.

As she surveyed what little she could see of the room, her grin disappeared. "Jehoshaphat!" She'd spent the night in abandoned barns that were cleaner and neater than this place.

Striding farther into the room, Daisy muttered a few unladylike epithets under her breath as she batted at cobwebs and felt things crunch beneath her boots that she wasn't ready to examine more closely.

She spied a lamp sitting on the counter and was relieved to find a bit of oil still in the base. It took several attempts, but she finally managed to get it lit and then took a closer look around.

She could hear Kip sniffling around, picking up goodness only knew what kind of scents. A couple of loud doggy sneezes confirmed that it was as dusty at his level as it was at hers.

She hadn't expected a servant-scrubbed palace, but hang it all, she'd hoped to find something in a little better condition than *this*. No wonder the previous owner had been so quick to gamble it away.

She started to close the outer door, then changed her mind. It wouldn't hurt to leave it open for a little while to help air out the place.

Daisy tromped across the room, ignoring the skittery scrambling sounds coming from just outside the circle of lamplight. Hopefully, whatever critters had taken up residence in here were on their way out. Still, she was glad for Kip's company.

The back room wasn't much better than the front. In the yellowish light of the lamp, she could see dust, debris and a smattering of rickety furniture scattered higgledy-piggledy across the space. Daisy kicked at an old sack lying in her path, then let out an explosive sneeze as a cloud of dust billowed up in her face.

Great! This was just pointy-fanged-rattlesnake perfect.

She fanned the air in front of her between sneezes. Why should the day end even a gnat-speck better than it had started?

Then she caught herself up short. *Not that I'm complaining, mind You, Lord. I know You answered my prayers in a powerful way when You took Pa's weakness for gambling and turned it to good by providing me with the deed to this building. And I truly am mighty grateful. Besides, I do know there's nothing wrong with this place that a bit of honest sweat and elbow grease won't fix up just fine and dandy. You've done Your part, and now I aim to do mine.*

Daisy looked around again. *Make that* a lot *of elbow grease.*

But that didn't scare her none. No, sir. The place was more than roomy enough for what she had in mind. She could already picture how it would look all cleaned up and put to rights. It would be so wonderful to have a place of her own, a place to set down roots and build a proper life. And to finally make some genuine friends of her very own.

And maybe, if she was very, very good, she could have a family of her very own one day, as well.

I know, Lord, baby steps. I asked for a family of my own, and instead, You gave me the seeds of one by providing a means for me to settle down in one place. I'm going to do my best to make myself an acceptable helpmeet in the eyes of some God-fearing man. I promise to look past appearance, manner and finances to see the heart of whoever You send my way.

Feeling focused and enthusiastic once more, Daisy went back to work. First order of business was to clear herself out a place to sleep. There was no way she could lie down in the midst of this gritty, grimy, cluttered mess, so if she was going to get a good night's rest, she'd best start cleaning.

She tested the soundness of a crate near the doorway, then set the lamp and bedroll down. Plopping her hat and pack beside them, she rolled up her sleeves. No time like the present to get started.

Everett Fulton forced his heavy eyelids open, peering blearily around his darkened room. The faint memory of his dream lingered a moment—childhood images of his home in England. Already it was fading, leaving him to wonder if the muffled clatter that had awakened him had been real or only part of his dream.

A moment later, another series of thuds answered the question.

Jerked to full awareness, he tossed off the covers and swiveled so that his feet hit the floor.

It sounded as if someone was rummaging around downstairs. If the not-so-stealthy intruder did any harm to his printing press…

Swiftly crossing the room, Everett paused only long enough to pull on a pair of pants and retrieve the iron poker that rested against the cold fireplace.

Just because he didn't own a gun didn't mean he couldn't defend himself.

Without bothering with a lamp, Everett stole down the stairs, carefully avoiding the fourth tread that had an annoying tendency to creak. His ears strained for some sign of just where his trespasser might be lurking.

He moved to the larger front room first, the room that housed his printing press and served as his office. A faint light filtered in from the large window that faced the street. His gaze went immediately to the bulky shadow that was his printing press. Most of the type was already laboriously set for this week's paper. He would have no compunction whatsoever in trouncing anyone who dared tamper with his work.

Everett's brow furrowed. All was quiet now, but he'd been certain the noise had come from down here. And everything seemed as he'd left it when he locked the doors and headed upstairs earlier.

Tightening his grip on the poker, he eased farther into the room. Taking a deep breath, he sprang around the corner of the press, his makeshift weapon raised. "Ha!"

But no thug crouched behind the machine's shadowy bulk.

Feeling foolish, he lowered his arm. Had he misjudged the direction the disturbance had come from? Everett turned to his desk, a sour smile tugging at his lips. If the intruder was after a cash box, he would be sadly disappointed.

Nothing.

He moved into the back room where he stored his blank paper and other supplies, but again, nothing.

Everett rubbed his neck, slowly exiting the room. Maybe he'd imagined the whole thing, after all.

Scriiittch.

He swung back around. It sounded as if something heavy were being dragged across the floor. He approached the far wall cautiously, then heard it again.

The noise was coming from the other side. Someone was in the adjoining building.

He frowned. The supposedly *vacant* adjoining building.

He'd never been inside, but understood the building didn't house anything more valuable than cobwebs and a jumble of rubbish and cast-off furnishings. What possible reason could someone have for rattling around in there in the middle of the night?

Everett shrugged and moved back toward the stairs. Other than the annoyance of having his sleep disturbed, it wasn't any of his concern.

Then he stilled. Except that there might be a story in it. Something more newsworthy than births, deaths and barn raisings for a change. Since he was already awake, it couldn't hurt to check things out. His pulse accelerated at the idea of a *real* story, a chance to resume his role as reporter rather than mere transcriber and typesetter. It had been quite a while…

Everett hurried upstairs, donned a shirt and shoes, then padded lightly down again.

He still carried the poker. Not that he intended to use it unless he had need to defend himself.

He was a reporter, after all, not a confounded hero.

Stepping onto the plank sidewalk, Everett paused a moment to listen. Somewhere in the distance, a dog barked and was answered by a second mutt. Four blocks away he could see light seeping from the windows of the livery. An ash-colored moth lazily circled the nearby streetlamp.

Other than that, everything was quiet. Enough light filtered down from the streetlamps and gauze-covered half moon that he could see the building next door easily.

He moved forward, studying the front of the run-down establishment. The boards that had barred the door were now lying on the sidewalk against the building, and the door itself gaped open.

He peered in, but it was too shadowy to make out anything but irregular shapes. However, he did notice a yellowish light emanating from the back room—the area where the sounds had come from.

Was it a squatter? Or a misguided thief?

Everett hesitated, listening to the scrapes and muffled grunts, torn between his reporter's instinct to find out the truth of the matter and the niggling voice that told him he'd be wise to arm himself with more than a poker before proceeding.

Besides, what if it was Gus Ferguson, the building's owner? Gus was a crotchety old hermit who kept to himself, except for the occasional trip to town to get supplies and indulge in a bit of drinking and poker playing. In the nine months Everett had resided in Turnabout, he'd never seen Gus look twice at the place, much less go inside. Why would the man choose this unlikely time to come here? Unless he'd decided to stop in after tonight's poker game.

Perhaps it would be best if he just quietly slipped away and forgot the whole thing.

Everett winced at the sound of falling crates. The sound of a woman crying out, however, had him through the door as if shot from a pistol. And was that a dog yapping?

He swallowed a yelp as he bumped his knee against the edge of a sagging counter. He kept going, though, albeit with somewhat impaired agility.

Charging into the back room, the first thing he spied was the rubble of storage shelves that had given way, dumping splintered lumber and unidentifiable contents in a dusty heap.

A grumbled *humph* drew his attention to a woman sitting on the floor, trying to pull her foot free of the mess.

"I'm okay, Kip. But as for this worm-ridden, rickety pile of junk, the only thing it's good for is kindling."

Everett recognized the voice before he got a good look at her face—it had a distinctive lilt to it and boasted a slight accent that he couldn't quite place, but was unmistakable.

Daisy Johnson. What in the world was the peddler's daughter doing here? She and her father had left town two weeks ago.

Miss Johnson looked up and recognized him at the same time. "Mr. Fulton. What're you doing in here?"

"Apparently rescuing a damsel in distress." Still concerned about her predicament, Everett crossed to her in long strides.

The dog seemed to take exception to his approach and assumed a stiff-legged, curled-lip stance in front of Miss Johnson.

"It's okay, Kip," she said, giving the dog a reassuring pat. Then she turned a frown on him. "I'm not a damsel. And I'm not in distress. My ankle just got caught under this mess, is all."

Did she even know what distress meant? "Let me give you a hand with that." Not bothering to wait for an answer, he heaved up on the piece her foot was trapped beneath, allowing her to free herself, all the while keeping a wary eye on the dog. And the dog returned his look, stare for stare.

Once she'd shifted her leg away from danger, he set the offending shelving back down. Then he knelt beside her, doing his best to ignore the dust and grime that surrounded him. "Allow me," he said, taking over the job of unlacing her boot.

"There's really no need," she protested, trying to push away his hands. "I can do that—"

He gave her his best don't-argue-with-me stare. "Be

still, please. You're stirring up more dust, and I'd rather not succumb to a fit of sneezing."

She paused, an abashed look on her face.

Good. He'd gotten through to her for the moment. Time to drive his point home. "It's important to make certain you're not badly injured before you try to stand. Or would you prefer I ask Dr. Pratt to take a look at you?"

His words had the opposite effect of what he'd expected. She glared at him. "There's no need to be so snippy. And no, I do *not* prefer to have you bother the doc at this late hour over a few bruises."

Snippy? Didn't the girl recognize authority when she heard it? Clenching his jaw to contain his irritation, he gently slid the worn, dirty bit of footwear, including her stocking, off her foot. He studied her ankle, unhappy with what he saw. "It's already starting to swell and darken. It might be wise to have Dr. Pratt take a look at you, after all."

"Glory be!" She brushed his hands away and smoothed down her skirts. "It's nothing more than a bad bruise." She flexed her ankle to prove her point, but he noticed the wince she couldn't quite hide. "It'll be fine by morning," she insisted.

Everett leaned back on his heels. He wasn't going to force the issue. After all, he wasn't her keeper—nor did he want to be. "Mind if I ask what you're doing in here?"

"I was trying to clear the way to the back door so I could open it up and air out the place."

Was she being deliberately obtuse? "I mean, why are you in here in the first place?"

She tilted her chin up. "Not that it's any of your business, but I'm cleaning the place up so Kip and I don't have to sleep in the middle of this rubbish and dirt."

He resisted the urge to roll his eyes. Daisy Johnson's lack of ladylike sensibilities went beyond the unrefined rustic "charm" that he'd grown to expect from the women of this backwater that circumstances had forced him to call home for the present. She was outspoken, obviously uneducated and her manner was rough and belligerent.

"It *is* my business if you wake me up from a sound sleep in the middle of the night," he countered.

At least she had the grace to blush at that. "Oh. Sorry. I wasn't thinking about the racket reaching over to you."

He stood and offered a hand to help her up. "Apology accepted. As long as you cease and desist until a more civilized hour."

"Fair enough."

He noticed another quickly suppressed wince as she put weight on the injured foot, but she didn't utter a sound.

"If you won't see the doctor," he said, keeping a hand at her elbow, "at least tell me where your father is so I can fetch him to tend to you." The sooner he could turn her over to someone else and return to the comfort of his bed, the better.

She tugged her arm out of his grasp and hobbled over to a nearby crate to sit down. He grimaced at the little cloud of dust that rose as she settled.

"I reckon he's halfway to the Louisiana border by now," she answered, reaching down to scratch her scruffy-looking dog.

Had her father abandoned her? Despite himself, Everett felt a stirring of sympathy. He spied the bedroll next to the lamp. "So you broke in here looking for a place to spend the night."

She shifted as if to find a more comfortable position for her foot, and he saw a snatch of cobweb caught in her tawny hair. He had an unexpected urge to brush it away, but quickly shook off the impulse.

"I aim to spend more than the night here," she said with a smile.

Did she intend to claim squatter's rights? Well, it was her bad luck that the building already had an owner. "Despite the way this place looks," he said, trying to let her down gently, "it's not abandoned. And I'm afraid the owner might not look favorably on your plans to take up residence."

"That's where you'd be wrong." There was a decidedly smug look to her smile. "*I'm* the owner, and I don't have a problem with it at all."

Chapter Two

Everett stared at her, feeling his momentary sympathy fade. Had he heard correctly? But there she sat, like a queen on her dusty throne. How could that be? "Last I heard, Gus Ferguson owned this place." He managed to keep his tone neutral.

"He *did*." She gave a self-satisfied smile. "Until he lost it to my father in a poker game."

A poker game? That shouldn't surprise him as much as it did. "And your father, in turn, gave it to you, I suppose."

She brushed at her skirt, not quite meeting his gaze. "Let's just say he owed it to me."

A cryptic turn of phrase, but he brushed aside his curiosity for now. There were more important matters to get to the bottom of. "If you don't mind my asking, what are your plans for the place?" If she was going to be his neighbor, he wanted some idea as to what he was going to be in for.

"I'm going to set up my business here."

Not the answer he'd expected. "What kind of business?"

From the look she gave him, he surmised some of his displeasure had come through in his tone.

"Well," she replied, eyeing him carefully, "I eventually want to open a restaurant."

She was just full of surprises. "You know how to cook?"

Her brown eyes narrowed, and her smudged chin tilted up. "You don't have to say it like that. I happen to be a great cook—everybody says so."

Just who did *everybody* include—her father and dog, perhaps? Then he took a very pointed look around him. "A restaurant—in *here?*"

"Of course I won't be able to open it right away." Her voice was less confident now. "I'll need to earn some money first so I can fix this place up and furnish it proper. And of course I'll need to buy a good stove."

She didn't seem particularly daunted by the task ahead of her. "And how do you intend to do that? Earn the money, I mean."

She shrugged. "I'm not my father's daughter for nothing. I'll figure something out."

Her father's daughter—did that mean she planned to try her luck in the poker game over at the livery?

She rotated her neck, and Everett saw signs of fatigue beneath her bravado. For the first time, he wondered about the particulars of her arrival. "If your father didn't come back to Turnabout with you, how did you get here?"

"I walked, mostly." Then she grinned proudly. "Made it in three days."

Her father had allowed her to take a three-day journey alone and on foot? Everett felt incensed on her behalf. Had the peddler given any thought at all to what might have happened? The man should be thoroughly trounced.

A suspicious rumbling from the vicinity of her stomach brought up another question. When had she last eaten?

The faint pinkening of her cheeks was the only acknowledgment she made of the unladylike noise. "Right now, though," she said quickly, "I'm just going to clean up a spot where I can spread my bedroll and get some sleep while I wait for the sun to come up."

He looked around at the layers of dust and the lack of useable furnishings. "You plan to sleep on the floor?"

"I don't see any fancy beds in here. Do you?" Her cheerful tone lacked any hint of self-pity. "Besides, I've bedded down on worse." Her pleased-with-herself grin returned. "And being as it'll be my very first night in my very own place, I expect I'll sleep very well."

She placed her hands on her skirt and levered herself up. "I'm sorry I disturbed your sleep, and I thank you for checking in on me, but you can go on back to your place now. I promise Kip and I won't be disturbing you anymore tonight."

Apparently feeling she'd dismissed him, she turned and started picking her way across the room.

Everett contemplated her words while he watched her limp toward a relatively uncluttered spot near the wall that adjoined his place. Her state of affairs wasn't really any of his concern, and she'd just made it abundantly clear she felt the same. She seemed content with her circumstances, and he had a busy day planned for tomorrow, so he should return to his bed and try to get what sleep he could before sunup.

But for some reason, he stood there a moment longer, watching her. His thoughts turned unaccountably to Abigail, his fifteen-year-old sister. What if she were in this situation? Which was a ridiculous thought, of course. Abigail was safely ensconced in a nice boarding school in Boston and would *never* find herself in a situation like this.

Still…

Daisy frowned as she heard her visitor—or was it intruder?—leave. For all his fine airs, he could be mighty rude. He'd all but said he didn't believe her claim to being a good cook, and it was obvious he didn't think she'd be able to open her own restaurant. And if that wasn't bad enough, she'd seen the way he looked down his nose at her.

Reminded her of Grandmère Longpre—one was *always* aware when she was displeased. Of course her grandmother would never dream of being impolite. The niceties of civilized society were too important to her.

Ah, well, Mr. Fulton didn't really know her yet, and she'd just roused him from his sleep. She couldn't really blame him for being in a bad mood. And she shouldn't forget that he *had* helped her out from under that shelving, so she should be grateful and more forgiving. As her father would say, never moon over *should bes* when your *have nows* are enough to get you by.

She'd just have to prove to Mr. Fulton and the rest of the townsfolk that she aimed to be a good, neighborly citizen of this community. Starting with making this place clean and inviting. Too bad she didn't have a broom and mop yet. She'd need to take care of that first thing in the morning. For now, she'd just make do as best she could.

She maneuvered an empty crate next to the space where she planned to place her bedroll, wincing at the bit of noise she made. Hopefully it hadn't been loud enough to disturb her neighbor. Again.

Once she had the crate in place, she eyed it critically, then nodded in satisfaction. "This'll make a fine table for now—just right for setting my lamp and Mother's Bible."

Kip answered her with a couple thumps of his tail.

She decided her change of clothing and the rest of the meager belongings she'd brought along with her could stay in her pack until she found an appropriate and *clean* place to store them.

She arched her back, trying to stretch out some of the

kinks. Tomorrow she'd give this place a good scrubbing, and maybe pick some wildflowers to add a bit of color. It would take a while to fix it up the way she wanted, but the cleaning and scrubbing part didn't cost anything except time and effort.

Already, she could picture it the way she would eventually fix it up—with bright curtains on freshly washed windows and a new coat of paint on the walls. She'd have a roomy pantry and sturdy shelves built in here for all her cooking supplies, and a big, shiny, new stove over on that far wall.

She grabbed her bedroll, still thinking about the red-checkered tablecloths and the ruffled curtains she'd purchase. But before she could get the makeshift bed unrolled properly, her neighbor returned, a scowl on his face. What now?

"Mr. Fulton, I'm so sorry if I'm making too much noise again. I promise—"

He shook his head impatiently, interrupting her apology. At the same time she noticed he was carrying a broom and a cloth-wrapped bundle.

He set the broom against the wall, nodding toward it. "I thought you might be able to make use of this," he said. Then he thrust the parcel her way. "I also brought this for you."

His tone was short, gruff, as if he wasn't happy. Was it with her or with himself? His accent had deepened, as well.

And more important—just what in the world had he brought her?

She gingerly unwrapped the parcel and was pleasantly surprised to find an apple, a slab of cheese and a thick slice of bread inside. "Why, thank you. This is so kind of you."

He waved aside her thanks. "It's just a few bits left

over from my dinner." He nodded toward the broom. "And that's just a loan."

That might be true, but the food seemed a veritable feast to her, and the broom would cut her work tonight in half. "Still, it's very neighborly." Just saying that word cheered her up.

But he still wore that impatient scowl. "Yes, well, I'll leave you to get settled in." He glanced at the sleeping area she'd set up and then back at her. "See that you keep the noise down."

She smothered a sigh, wondering why he had to spoil his nice gesture with a grumpy attitude. "Of course. Good night."

"Good night."

As she watched him leave this time, her smile returned. Regardless of his sour expression, Mr. Fulton had been quite kind. Perhaps she'd already made her first friend.

Bowing her head, she said a quick prayer of thanks for the unexpected meal, and for the man who'd given it to her.

Then she looked down at Kip as she broke off a bit of cheese to feed him. "Look here, boy. We have a nice meal to help us really celebrate our first night in our new home. Isn't God good?"

And, much as he tried to hide it, she was beginning to believe Mr. Fulton had some good in him, as well.

The next morning, as Everett prepared his breakfast, he could hear the sounds of his new neighbor's renewed efforts at cleaning out her building. He certainly hoped she didn't keep that racket up all day. Besides, did she really think she could single-handedly turn that musty, junk-cluttered place into a working restaurant?

Glancing out his window, he saw a pile of rubbish in their shared back lot that hadn't been there yesterday. He rubbed his jaw, impressed in spite of himself at the amount of effort she'd already expended this morning. Apparently, she planned to try to make her ambitious but improbable dream a reality.

As he stuck a fork in his slightly overcooked egg, he wondered how she'd fared after he left her last night. Had she gotten any sleep at all given her less-than-ideal accommodations?

He took a sip of coffee. Perhaps he should go over and check on her this morning. Not that her welfare was his concern, but she didn't seem to have anyone else to look out for her. And, even if it was confoundedly inconvenient, someone should make certain her ankle wasn't any worse this morning and that she had something to eat.

When he carried his dishes to the counter he spied her through the window, dragging another load of debris to toss on her trash pile. That unfortunate-looking mutt she'd had with her last night was racing from her heels to the far end of the lot and back again.

At least she didn't seem to be favoring her left foot. As for food, he waffled a few moments over whether to involve himself further in her business. He supposed, as long as he made it clear he expected her to fend for herself going forward, it wouldn't hurt to offer sustenance one more time.

He'd do the gentlemanly thing and invite her up for something to eat, or at least a cup of coffee. And maybe see if she was as optimistic about her enterprise this morning as she'd been last night.

But before he could act on his decision, he saw her reappear carrying a sack and head toward the edge of town, the dog trotting beside her.

What in the world was she up to now?

Feeling slightly deflated, Everett washed his dishes and

headed down to his office. Enough of this unproductive preoccupation with his neighbor. He had work to get to.

But over the next few hours he had trouble focusing on his work. He found his thoughts drifting to speculation as to where she'd gone off to and, to his irritation, caught himself listening for her return.

He supposed it was only natural to worry about any unprotected female heading out on her own in unfamiliar surroundings. No matter how far she'd walked to get here.

Everett was finally rewarded a couple of hours after her departure by the sound of her return. Minutes later, he could hear items being moved around and other evidence of her renewed efforts. Did she plan to work the entire day? He even thought he heard snatches of some cheerful but slightly off-key humming a time or two. It appeared that, no matter what other qualities Miss Johnson might have, she wasn't afraid of hard work.

And apparently, word of the new arrival had spread through town. There was a steady parade of folks strolling past his glass-fronted office, and stopping by his neighbor's place. With all the interest Miss Johnson was garnering, he wondered just how much work she was actually managing to get done.

He resisted the urge to walk over and see for himself. The impulse had been born of his desire to check on how she was faring after last night's rough start, but she apparently had plenty of drop-in visitors to assist her now.

Near noon, Everett was on his knees in front of his type cabinet, picking up the bits of type that had scattered when he dropped a tray. He blamed the incident on Miss Johnson, or rather the bothersome distraction she'd become. That and his interrupted sleep last night—also her fault— were the most likely culprits for his lack of focus today.

All he needed was an uninterrupted night's sleep tonight; then he'd be as efficient as ever tomorrow.

He was just putting the last piece back in place when his office door opened. He glanced up to see Adam Barr, one of the three men who'd traveled with him from Philadelphia to Turnabout last summer.

Everett pushed to his feet, at the same time pushing away his faint disappointment. He took a moment to slide the tray back into place and then greeted his visitor.

"You're early today," he said as he grabbed a rag to wipe his hands. Most days, Adam stopped by on his way back to the bank after having lunch at home with his wife, Reggie. He and Adam had an ongoing chess game that they both enjoyed and took quite seriously.

"Reggie has my afternoon planned out for me," Adam responded. "Jack's seventh birthday is tomorrow, and she wants my help planning a small surprise for him."

Jack was Reggie's nephew, and she and Adam had adopted him after their marriage last fall.

Adam headed toward the chessboard that was set up on the far end of the room with their game. "If I remember correctly, it was my move."

Everett followed him. "It was. And I'm looking forward to seeing how you'll answer my last move."

Adam sat down, studying the board. "I hear you have a new neighbor," he said as he fingered one of the pawns he'd captured.

"Word gets around fast. If you haven't heard a name yet, it's Daisy Johnson. You remember her—the daughter of the peddler who was arrested for stealing the money from the fair last year." Adam had been instrumental in getting the man cleared of the charges.

"*Falsely* arrested," Adam corrected. "Yes, I remember her. Spirited young lady, if I recall."

Everett agreed with that assessment but decided to change the subject. "So how is Reggie faring?"

"As stubborn as ever. She refuses to accept that she needs to curtail her more vigorous activities until the baby comes."

Adam set down the captured pawn and slid his bishop across the board. "There," he said as he stood. "That should keep you busy for a while."

Before Everett could study the move, the door opened and in came his new neighbor, carrying the broom he'd loaned her last night, and a small parcel.

While she still wore a dress that had seen better days, there was a pleased-with-the-world smile on her face that overshadowed her dearth of fashion sense. From the bounce in her step it appeared she'd managed to sleep just fine last night. There was no hint of cobwebs in her hair this morning; rather, it was well combed and neatly pulled back in a loose bun.

And, like a shadow, her dog was once more right beside her. In the daylight, the animal looked only marginally more presentable than he had last night. Black and white with a shaggy coat, the mutt had obviously led a less-than-pampered life. One ear was torn, and there was an old scar on one hind leg. And if Everett wasn't mistaken, the dog had one blue and one brown eye. Very disconcerting.

He took all that in within the few seconds following her entrance. It was the reporter in him, trained to notice even the smallest of details.

That quickening of his pulse—that was due to nothing more than curiosity as to what had brought her to his office.

Chapter Three

Daisy paused when she saw that Mr. Fulton wasn't alone. "I'm sorry. I didn't realize you were busy."

Mr. Fulton's visitor turned, and she smiled in recognition. "Mr. Barr! How nice to see you again."

Adam executed a short bow. "The pleasure is mine. I understand you've decided to take up residence in our fair town. Let me add my welcome to the others I'm sure you've already received."

Now *this* welcome seemed genuine. "Thank you. I'm looking forward to setting down roots here." The idea of finally having a permanent home was more than enough to carry her through all the work ahead of her.

"I'm sure I speak for my wife as well as myself when I say we'd be pleased to have you join us for supper one evening when you're available."

Her cheeks warmed in pleasure. "Why, thank you. I'd like that."

"Be sure to let me know if you need help getting settled in." Then Adam turned back to Everett. "It's time I headed home. I'll be back tomorrow, same time as usual, to see if you've figured out your next move." He tipped his hat her way. "Enjoyed seeing you, Miss Johnson. Good day."

Once he'd departed, Daisy felt her smile grow a bit more forced.

Which was totally unfair. After all, Mr. Fulton had been more than kind to her last night—in his own way, of course. But it was hard to remember that kindness when his disapproving demeanor reminded her so much of her grandmother.

"I don't allow animals in my office," he said stiffly.

He certainly wasn't making it easy for her to remember his kindness. "I gave him a bath out by the stream this morning." She did her best to keep her tone light. "And I assure you he's very well-behaved. So he won't leave tracks on your floor or bother any of your things."

"Nice to know, but I still don't allow animals in here."

She sighed, then looked down at Kip. "You heard the man, boy. You'll have to wait outside." She opened the door and, meeting the animal's gaze, tried to smile reassuringly as she pointed to the sidewalk. Kip, tail drooping, slowly exited. "I won't be long."

She turned back to Mr. Fulton and had to rein in the urge to glare outright.

But he apparently had no idea what she was feeling because he wore that infuriatingly condescending look on his face.

"You talk to that animal as if he understands you," he said.

"Because he does." She lifted her chin. "If not the words, then at least the feelings behind them. Dogs are smarter than most folks give them credit for."

Mr. Fulton strode forward. "I trust your foot is better this morning?"

The thoughtful question put her more at ease. "Yes, thank you, good as new." Then, remembering her reason for coming over, she thrust out the broom. "I wanted to bring this back in case you were needing it. I sure appreciate you loaning it to me. There was a wagonload of dirt that needed sweeping out of that place."

He accepted the cleaning implement and set it against the wall. Then he waved her to a chair in front of his desk. "So you're finished cleaning."

If only that were true. "Afraid not. It's going to take more than one day to take care of all that needs doing. But I made a good start." She took the seat he'd indicated.

"I saw you heading out for a walk this morning," he said as he took his own seat. "Checking out what our town has to offer?"

Had he been *spying* on her? "Actually, I went out and gathered up the materials to make my own broom. There's still a lot of cleaning to do, and I didn't want to wear yours down to a nub." She smiled. "Besides, me and Kip needed to get out in the fresh air and sunshine for a bit after stirring up all that dust and dirt this morning."

He raised a brow. "You're *making* a broom."

Why did he sound so surprised? "It's not difficult. The hardest part is finding a stick that's straight enough and sturdy enough to serve as the handle." She'd learned to be resourceful, not to mention frugal, in the time she'd spent traveling with her father.

Then she remembered the other reason she was here. "I spotted some dewberry vines out behind the schoolyard when Father and I were here before." She smiled, pleased with herself. "'Course, most of them won't ripen for another week or so, but there were some that were ready to pick. I gathered up a bunch and they made for a right tasty breakfast."

Something flickered in his expression, but she couldn't quite read what it was. Not that it mattered. She handed him the cloth-wrapped bundle. "And I brought you some, as well."

He didn't seem particularly eager as he accepted her gift.

"I assure you that wasn't necessary," he said. "All I did was loan you a broom."

"*And* brought me supper last night." Daisy watched him unwrap the cloth. "Anyway, it's not much. But they *are* quite tasty." She didn't believe in not returning favors. "Thank the good Lord there's a plentiful crop of them this year."

He stared at her offering for a moment without saying anything. Was something wrong?

"It's quite kind of you," he said, finally looking back up. "But shouldn't you keep them for yourself?"

Was he feeling sorry for her? That wouldn't do at all—she wanted friendship and respect, not pity. "Don't you like dewberries?" She couldn't quite keep the starch out of her tone.

"I don't believe I've ever tasted them. It's just—"

"Then it's settled," she said firmly. "I can pick more when they ripen—the vines are thick with them."

Looking for a way to change the subject, she blurted out the first thing that came to mind. "Do you have any idea what sort of business used to be in my place?"

"I haven't a clue. Someone who's been in Turnabout a lot longer than I have could probably tell you."

That confirmed something she'd already guessed. "So you're not from around here?"

He spread his hands. "I've only settled here recently. I lived in Philadelphia before that."

"Philadelphia. That's over on the east coast, isn't it?"

He nodded. "It is."

She'd seen a map of the entire country once, and the

east coast seemed a far piece from Texas. "So how'd you end up way out here?"

His expression closed off again. "Just looking for a change of scenery." He straightened a few papers on his desk. "So what do you have left to do?"

Had she gotten too nosy? Curiosity *was* a weakness of hers. "I've sorted through most of the furnishings downstairs, but I'm sorry to say most of what was in there wasn't fit for anything but firewood. There were a few pieces worth salvaging, though. And I found an old bed frame upstairs that'll be good as new once I get some new rope to string it with and some ticking. I figure I can collect some straw and then stuff me a fresh mattress. Before you know it, I'll have a proper bed to sleep on."

He shifted in his chair when she mentioned her bed. Her grandmother would chide her for being so indelicate.

She'd best change the subject again. "Do you know of anyone looking for help? I need to find a way to earn some money."

He leaned back in his chair. "What kind of work are you qualified to do?"

Something about the way he asked the question got her back up. "I can cook, clean, do laundry—I'll take just about any honest labor I can find. I'm not afraid of hard work or of getting my hands dirty."

"I haven't heard of anything, but you might want to check with Doug Blakely over at the mercantile. His store seems to be a gathering place for most of the townsfolk, so if anyone's looking, Doug's probably heard about it. In the meantime, how do you plan to get by?"

Now who was being nosy? "Don't you worry about me. I have a roof over my head, and I know how to live off the land when I need to. Besides those berries, there are plenty of edible roots and plants around here if you know what you're looking for."

"You can hardly live entirely on berries and roots for very long."

A gent like him probably didn't have any idea what it meant to go hungry for days at a time. "You'd be surprised what a body can live on when one has to. I also plan to set me up a little kitchen garden out behind my place. I'm especially eager to plant some herbs. Not only will they add flavor to my meals, but I use some in my concoctions."

"Concoctions?"

"Yes. I make balms and potions to keep on hand for cuts and burns and such. Father calls them my concoctions."

"And is that something you sell?"

"Oh, no. It's mostly for personal use, though I've given some away when I saw a need." She lifted her head proudly. "Some of those folks *have* asked to buy more from me, though." She shrugged self-consciously. "But I don't really feel right taking money for healing potions."

"It appears you are a woman of many talents." The sarcasm in his tone killed any chance that she would think he was paying her a compliment.

But she chose to ignore his lack of manners. Instead, she gave him her sunniest smile. "That's kind of you to say. And you'll see the proof of that when I open my restaurant."

Everett realized he'd been harsher with his new neighbor than the situation warranted. But she'd apparently misread his tone. He glanced down at her offering of berries, and his conscience tweaked at him again. "Speaking of a job," he said impulsively, "I can't offer you anything full-time, but I do have a proposal for you."

This time she leaned forward eagerly, apparently ready

to forgive his earlier rudeness. "What did you have in mind?"

He was beginning to rethink his impulse, but it was too late to back out now. "Since you say you're a good cook, what do you think about cooking for me?

"Really?"

Her hopeful expression brushed away the last of his hesitation. Besides, what could it hurt? "I'm the first to admit I'm not much of a cook myself, and I'm getting tired of the few dishes I've learned to prepare. I can't pay you much, say two bits a day, but if you did the marketing and cooking for me, you could also share in the meal." At least this way he wouldn't have the distraction of worrying about her not having enough to eat.

She smiled at him as if he'd just handed her the keys to the town. Did that mean she'd forgotten his earlier rudeness?

"That's more than generous," she said. "And you won't be sorry—cooking is something I'm good at. You'll see."

She folded her hands in her lap and struck what he supposed she thought of as a businesslike pose. "Just to make certain I understand what you're wanting, are you looking for me to provide three meals a day, seven days a week?"

He waved a hand. "I believe I can get by with something a little less all-encompassing. I was thinking six days a week, with Sundays off. I'll manage my own breakfast. And I'm not averse to eating the same thing twice, so if you prepare a large enough meal at noon, I can dine on leftovers for the evening meal."

"That's agreeable. When would you like me to start?"

"Is tomorrow too soon?"

"Not at all." Then she fingered her collar. "Do you have much of a larder?"

"It would probably be best if you start from scratch

and pick up anything you think you'll need. I'll leave the menus up to you. And I'll let the shopkeepers know to put your orders on my tab."

"Good. And don't worry, I know how to be frugal with my purchases."

A good quality, but he should make certain they were both working under the same definition of acceptable spending. "I will develop what I consider a reasonable budget for your weekly purchases. If there should arise a situation where you require more, we can always revisit the matter."

"Agreed." Apparently, she was finished with the businesswoman persona, because her face split into another of those delighted smiles. "Mr. Fulton, I'm beginning to think of you as my guardian angel."

Now there was something he'd never been called before. And it was definitely *not* something he aspired to be.

"Not only is this job going to give me some security," she continued, "but since you'll only need me for part of the day, I'll have time to find other odd jobs, as well."

Other jobs? Did she even realize what she was saying? "That's an admirably industrious attitude, but I imagine just getting your place in shape will take up most of your free time, at least for a while."

She waved a hand as if that was of no consequence. "I'll have to just fit that in when I can. Like I said, I need to earn some money, not just for staples, but to get my place furnished properly. Because the sooner I can open my restaurant, the better."

She was back to that again. Oh, well, far be it from him to harp on a point once he'd made it. "If you're serious about finding another job, as I said before, check down at Blakely's Mercantile."

"Thanks. I'll do that." She stood. "Now I'll get out of

your way. I know you're busy, and I have some more work to do over at my place. Besides, I've made Kip wait on me long enough."

Would the rest of her meals today consist of nothing more than a handful of berries? "I was thinking, Miss Johnson, that I might do an interview with you for the paper."

"With me?" She seemed genuinely startled at the idea.

"It's not every day someone new moves to town and sets up shop." Although that's exactly what he and his companions from Philadelphia had done less than a year ago.

He saw her hesitation and pressed further. "It would be doing me a favor. I'm always looking for something fresh to print in the paper."

Her face puckered as she contemplated his words. Then she gave him a doubtful look. "If you really think it will help you…"

He jumped in, not giving her time to change her mind. "Wonderful. Let's discuss this over supper tonight. The hotel has a small restaurant where we can go. And eating there has the added bonus of giving you an opportunity to check out your future competition." Not that he truly expected her to ever open her own restaurant.

"All right, I'll do it."

"And of course it will be my treat, since I am imposing on you for this interview."

She fingered her collar. "That's not necessary. I—"

He schooled his features in his haughtiest expression. "I assure you, for a business meal such as this, it's customary for the reporter to pay."

She studied him as if not quite believing him. But he didn't relax his expression, and she finally nodded.

"Good. I'll stop by your place at six o'clock, and we can walk to the hotel together if that's agreeable." Even though he'd concocted the idea on the spur of the moment to see that she had a meal this evening, he was fully prepared to take advantage of the opportunity to practice his reporting skills. This wouldn't be a very challenging interview subject, but at least it would give him something interesting to write about.

Then he gave her a severe look. "And please, leave your dog at home."

Chapter Four

"So let's start with where you're from. Originally, I mean."

Daisy shifted, uncomfortable with Mr. Fulton's scrutiny and with having to talk about her background. She sat across from him in the hotel dining room, trying to decide if there was some polite way for her to get out of this. After all, she'd come to Turnabout to make a fresh start, not dredge up the past.

Still, he'd been kind to her, and this was the first thing he'd actually asked from her in return. Determined to focus on his kindness, she sat up straighter and smiled. "If you're asking where I was born, it was in a little community called Bluewillow, Texas. I didn't live there long, though."

He scribbled a few strokes, then glanced up again. "Well, then, where did you grow up?"

"We traveled around a lot—Father was a peddler, even then. Most of the time, our wagon was our home. Then, when I was about four, my mother's health began to go downhill, and traveling became difficult for her. So the two of us went to live with her mother while she tried to recuperate."

"And where was that?"

"New Orleans." Daisy brushed at the tablecloth, smoothing away a wrinkle. That wasn't a part of her life she wanted to elaborate on. "Do you think the folks around here are really going to want to read about this stuff?"

His smile had a cynical twist to it. "I find that people everywhere have an infinite curiosity about the lives of others." He poised his pencil over his pad again. "How much time did you spend in New Orleans?"

"Eight years." Eight of the most smothering, uncomfortable years of her life. "Then I went back to traveling with my father."

"Only you? What about your mother?"

Daisy nudged the lamp on the table about a quarter inch, not quite meeting his gaze. "She passed on when I was eight."

"I'm sorry."

There seemed to be genuine sympathy in his voice.

"Thank you," she said. "Mother was a good person, you know, the kind who always tries to see the best in everyone. She was real pretty, too. Want to see?" Without waiting for his answer, she lifted the locket from beneath her bodice, then slipped the chain over her head. Opening the catch, she smiled at the picture, then handed it to Everett.

He studied the picture for a moment, his expression unreadable, then handed it back to her. "You're right. She was quite lovely."

Daisy carefully slipped the locket back over her head, feeling slightly disappointed at his lack of reaction. "What about you? I mean, I know you don't have a locket, but do you have any kind of pictures or likenesses of your family?"

"No. Now let's get back to the interview."

She smothered a groan. If only the meal would come so they could end his string of uncomfortable questions.

"If I'm doing the calculations properly," he continued, "it sounds as if you spent another four years with your grandmother after your mother passed on."

"That's right. Father thought it best to wait until I was older to resume traveling with him." She tried not to dwell on that.

"Understandable."

That pronouncement stung. It *hadn't* been understandable to the grieving child she'd been. To her, it had felt like a second abandonment.

But Everett was already moving on to his next question. "Once you resumed traveling with your father, did you enjoy it?"

Daisy relaxed. This was a topic she was happy to talk about. "Very much. It gave me a chance to meet lots of wonderful people and to see places I'd never have seen otherwise. There are so many interesting folk out there, and they all have their own story to tell."

"Stories? Now you sound like a reporter."

She grinned. "Not at all. I'd be too fascinated listening to what they had to say, I'd forget to write anything down."

His smile warmed for just a moment, then he seemed to come to himself, and he resumed his cynically amused expression. "If you enjoyed all that traveling, why did you decide to settle down?"

"Because I'm not twelve anymore." She leaned forward. "Because I want friends and a family of my own and to be part of a close-knit community."

"So why here?"

"Simple—because this is where there was a place that I owned the deed to." She realized how flippant that sounded. "But I'm glad that was the case," she added quickly. "Turnabout seems like a nice town with lots of friendly folk. A good place to put down roots."

"You speak as if you plan to make Turnabout your permanent home."

Hadn't he heard anything she'd told him the past twenty-four hours? "I sincerely hope so."

"You don't think you'll miss the traveling life?"

She understood why he'd ask that, but he'd learn eventually that she wasn't that girl any longer. "Not at all. I've discovered I'm more of a homebody than I thought." Assuming she found the right home. "The idea of setting down roots, creating a cozy homeplace, someday starting a family of my own—well, that kind of life has a whole lot of appeal to me."

"Does that mean that after you went back on the road with your father, you found yourself missing the life you had with your grandmother?"

She gave a snort of disagreement before she could stop herself. He was so far off the mark, it was laughable. But his raised brow indicated she might have revealed a little more than she'd intended. "My grandmother's home wasn't exactly the warm, loving household that I'm hoping to build for myself."

"Would you care to elaborate?"

She met his gaze without blinking. "No."

"I see." He stared at her a moment longer, as if trying to read answers in her face. Then he moved on. "Would you like to talk about the restaurant you hope to open someday? Or would you rather wait until you're closer to making it a reality before spreading the news of your intentions?"

Daisy was surprised but pleased that he hadn't pressed her. "Oh, I don't mind. I want folks to know what they have to look forward to." She leaned forward again, trying her best to communicate her vision. "I don't intend to make it all fancy and highfalutin. I want folks to feel comfortable and happy when they walk in. I'm going to serve hearty, homey food that fills the belly and warms the soul, because that's what I do best. And I'm going to paint the place in bright cheery colors and have flowers on all the tables."

"That's fine for this time of year, but it might be hard to do during the winter."

That was just like him to look for gray clouds in a sunny sky. To her relief, the food arrived just then, saving her from further inquisition.

At least for the moment.

Everett set his pencil and pad aside as the waitress fussed with serving their food.

The interview so far had raised as many questions about her as it had answered. The way she'd described her planned restaurant was indicative of how little business sense she had. She'd focused on feelings and cosmetics instead of a sound plan to achieve her goals.

She'd said she was looking for, among other things, a family of her own. So that indicated she was looking for a husband. Which probably meant the restaurant idea was only something to get her by until she had a man to provide for her.

She hadn't wanted to discuss her time at her grandmother's, yet she hadn't been happy traveling with her father, either. What was she really looking for? Did she even know herself? And would she be able to find it in Turnabout? Or would she only face disappointment and find herself moving on once again?

As soon as their waitress departed, and before he could resume his questions, Daisy beat him to the punch.

"So is it my turn for questions?" she asked with a teasing smile.

He raised a brow, not at all certain that would be a good idea. Better to treat her question lightly. "Are you planning to write an article for the paper, too? I thought you said you weren't good at writing things down."

"Don't worry. I'm not looking to give you competition, just trying to satisfy my curiosity." Her smile broadened. "You're not afraid to get a taste of your own medicine, are you?"

He couldn't let that veiled challenge pass. "What do you want to know?"

"How did a particular gent like you end up here in Turnabout?"

A *particular gent?* He wasn't sure what that meant. And more important, had she intended it as a compliment or criticism?

Better not to ask. "Before I came here, I was a reporter for a newspaper in Philadelphia. Unfortunately, the editor and I had a falling out. When I learned of an opportunity to actually own my own newspaper business here, I jumped at it." Mainly because that was the only option open to him at the time. There was nothing to be gained by mentioning the scandal he'd been involved in, the scandal that had cost him nearly everything. And deservedly so.

"So how'd you hear about this great opportunity? I mean, I wouldn't think most folks in Philadelphia have even heard of Turnabout."

Everett decided being on this end of an interview wasn't nearly the same as being on the other. "A friend of mine has some connections here—a granddaughter, as a matter of fact. He knew I was looking for something different, and he told me about it." He raised a brow. "Anything else?" he asked in his chilliest tone.

"Do all the folks in Philadelphia talk like you do?"

Was she being deliberately impertinent or merely trying to make conversation? "My accent, you mean?" She'd probably never heard a British accent before. "Actually, I lived in England until I was twelve."

Her hands stilled, and her eyes widened. "Oh, my goodness. You crossed the ocean when you were twelve?"

That part of his life seemed a dream now. Or should he say a nightmare? He wondered if his father had ever given him another thought once he'd sent him and his mother away.

He smiled at her reaction. "I didn't do it alone." Then he locked his gaze with hers. "And no, I'm not going to discuss my life before arriving in America with you, so you may as well move on."

She gave him an arch smile, or at least her version of one. "Keeping secrets of your own, are you? I guess we all have them." She didn't seem unduly bothered by his words. "So, moving on to another topic, what about family?"

Best to stick to the living. "I have a sister."

Her expression softened. "I always wished I had a sister or brother. Is she older or younger than you?"

"Much younger. And before you ask, she's attending a boarding school in Boston." He pointedly stabbed a chunk of potato with his fork. He'd had enough. "Now, why don't we put aside the interrogation and eat our meal before it gets cold."

She held his gaze for a few moments, and he could almost see her trying to decide whether or not to push forward. She finally nodded, and they both turned their focus on their food without another word.

After several minutes Everett relented, but there was no more talk of a personal nature. "Have you had that dog of yours very long?" he asked.

Her stiffness eased, and her smile returned. Apparently he'd found a question she didn't mind answering.

"No. As a matter of fact, we're brand-new friends. I'd

only been on the road to Turnabout for a couple of hours when Kip showed up and took to following me. I checked with folks at a couple of the farms I passed, and no one laid claim to him. Which was okay with me. He was friendly, and I was happy for the company."

He imagined a woman traveling alone would be—especially at night. He still couldn't believe her father hadn't taken the time to escort her back here. The man should be horse whipped.

"He's barely left my side since," she added as she reached for her glass.

"And you plan to keep him?"

She seemed surprised by the question. "Of course. Like I said, we're friends now. As long as Kip wants to stick around, he's welcome to do so."

Everett resisted the urge to shake his head. He could understand her wanting the animal's companionship and protection while she was on the road. But now that she was settled in and trying to establish herself, couldn't she see he would only be a drain on her limited resources?

But he'd said his piece. If she was an overly sentimental sort, then that was her problem.

The rest of the meal passed pleasantly enough. He was even forced to grudgingly admit, at least to himself, that Daisy could be a pleasant companion when she tried to be.

Later that evening, after he'd seen Daisy to her door and she'd promised to show up about nine o'clock the following morning since it was her first day, Everett returned to his own office.

He settled at his desk where he went to work transcribing his interview notes into an article. Tomorrow was Friday, one of the two days a week the paper went out. Tuesday was the other. That meant he had a long night ahead of him. Luckily, he'd already set aside space on the second page for his interview with Miss Johnson. He just had to craft his article so that it fit the allotted space.

As he wrote the article, he thought about what he'd learned from the sketchy details she'd given him. She was an optimist and a dreamer, that much was clear. And she wasn't afraid of hard work. She had a certain amount of courage, too, as evidenced by her striking out on her own, on foot, with nothing but what she could carry to start her new life with. But did she really have it in her to stick with a project like this and see it all the way through?

He was certain there was more to the story of the time she'd spent with her grandmother than she'd been willing to tell him. That hint of a story to uncover intrigued him.

Then there was her idea of opening a restaurant. That was reaching a bit high, especially for a female with no experience running a business. To make a go of it, she would need more than optimism and elbow grease. She would need financial reserves and business acumen, neither of which he saw much evidence of in her.

No, it would be much more practical if Miss Johnson took on a permanent job as cook for some family in town who needed her more than he did. And once he was satisfied he could vouch for her expertise, he would be willing to give her a recommendation to help her find such a position.

That should fulfill his obligation to see her settled properly.

Perhaps then he could get back to life as usual.

Daisy settled onto her makeshift bed, tired but pleased with the recent turn of events. It had been a long day, but she'd gotten a lot accomplished. This storeroom that still served as her bedchamber was now clean as a rain-washed wildflower. She'd crafted a broom of her own and rigged up some of the broken crates and furnishings to serve as temporary tables and chairs. She'd traded the telling of her tale for a satisfying meal, and she'd landed herself a job without having to look too hard.

All in all, a good day.

Daisy rolled over on her side. She was still having trouble figuring out Mr. Fulton. He could be so nice at times, and at others...

Even when he was being nice, he had that snippy, amused air about him that was just downright irritating.

The snooty tone he'd used when he asked if she intended to keep Kip still irked her. What she should have told him was that if given the choice between Kip's company and his, she'd likely pick Kip's.

I know that's not a very charitable thought, Lord, especially since I have him to thank for my meal and my job, but something about that man just riles me up. I can't abide a person who's constantly looking for warts rather than dimples.

She thought about that for a moment, then winced at her ungrateful attitude.

That was a poor excuse for an excuse, wasn't it, Lord? You tell us to judge not, and here I go judging again. And we both know I've got a wagonload of faults myself, so I've got no call to go throwing stones. I promise to try to do better in that regard. Just be patient with me if I slip again. And I'll add him to my prayers. He obviously has some kind of bee in his bonnet, and he could use some help to learn how to look for the good things around him. Maybe he just needs someone to show him the way.

Feeling better, she settled down more snugly on her bedroll. Starting tomorrow, Mr. Fulton was going to be a part of her daily life and she a part of his. If this was her purpose for being here, then she aimed to tackle it with all the enthusiasm at her disposal.

Mr. Fulton was going to learn how to shed some of that stiff-necked, snobbish air of his, or her name wasn't Daisy Eglantine Johnson.

Chapter Five

"Good morning, Mr. Fulton. You got those papers ready for me?" Jack Barr, Adam and Reggie's adopted son, stood in the doorway of Everett's office. Ira Peavy, the Barrs' live-in handyman and sometimes photography assistant to Reggie, stood behind him.

Everett smiled a greeting at the pair. "That, I do. Your stack is the one closest to the door."

Jack pulled a red wooden wagon into the building and started loading papers into the bed.

When he'd first opened the newspaper office, Everett had hired Jack to take care of making household deliveries to his regular subscribers. Of course, Ira Peavy usually went along, too, ostensibly to provide Jack with some company.

Everett exchanged greetings with Ira, then looked past the man to see the faint hint of the approaching dawn. He prided himself on having the paper available when his patrons started their day.

"You'll find one extra paper in your stack," he told Jack. "Mr. Cummings over on Second Street started subscribing this week."

"Yes, sir, I'll add him to the list."

As they loaded the last of the papers, Everett reached into his pocket and pulled out a coin. "Here's this week's pay."

Jack's eyes lit up. "Thanks!"

Ira placed his hand on the boy's shoulder. "We'd best be on our way if you want to get these deliveries done before school starts."

As soon as they departed, Everett grabbed the other three bundles of papers waiting by the door. In addition to the copies he printed for his subscribers, he always printed a number of extras. Those who chose not to subscribe often purchased copies when they were out running errands.

He kept some of those copies here at his office, of course, but he'd also made arrangements with the proprietors at the mercantile, hotel and railroad depot to sell copies in exchange for a small portion of the purchase price.

He stepped out on the sidewalk and exchanged greetings with Tim Hill, the town's lamplighter. Tim was in the process of turning off the streetlight outside the newspaper office, which meant Everett was right on schedule. Punctuality was a virtue he considered an indication of character.

As he walked through town delivering the bundles of papers to the appropriate locations, he took time to visit the merchants where Daisy would need to make purchases for her role as his cook. As he'd promised her, he instructed them to bill her purchases to him.

That request raised questions, naturally, but he offered up only the bare information that he had hired her to cook for him. Anything else they wanted to know about her, they'd have to ask her.

By the time he returned to his office, a light was shining in Daisy's downstairs window. So she was already up and about. Was she looking forward to her first day working for him? Or dreading it?

At precisely ten minutes after nine, Daisy walked into his office. He supposed that was as close to punctual as he should expect from her.

"Good morning, Mr. Fulton," she said by way of greeting.

Everett stood and moved around the desk as he returned her greeting. She carried a heavily laden basket on her arm, but didn't seem unduly burdened by it.

"I enjoyed doing the marketing today. There are some fine shops here, and most of the shopkeepers seem willing to negotiate a bit. And don't worry, I was very frugal with your money, but I think you'll be pleased with the results."

The woman did like to chatter. "As long as you stay within the budget we discussed, I won't have any complaints on that score."

She patted the basket. "I got a good deal on a couple of rabbits at the butcher shop. I hope you like rabbit stew. It's one of my specialties."

Was she looking for some kind of approval or praise? That wasn't really his way of doing business. "As I said, the meal planning is in your hands. I'm sure whatever you cook will be an improvement over what I've been preparing for myself."

She grinned. "Not the most enthusiastic response, but I hope to win you over with my cooking."

Surely no one could be this cheerful all the time? "I look forward to your attempts."

She spotted the small stack of newspapers near the door. "Are those your papers?"

"Of course." What else would they be? "It's this morning's edition of the *Turnabout Gazette*."

She eyed them as if not sure she wanted to get any closer. "Is that interview of me in there?"

Was she worried about how he'd portrayed her? "Yes,

it is." He crossed over and picked one up. "Would you like to have one so you can read it?"

Her cheeks reddened slightly. "I'm afraid I don't have any extra money to—"

"Consider a copy of the paper part of your pay." He always had a few copies left over at the end of the day.

"Why, thank you."

This talk of extra funds brought something else to mind. He cleared his throat. "I daresay there are other things you might need to get settled in properly, so when you are done for the day I will give you your first week's pay in advance."

Her cheeks reddened. "Oh, that's not necessary. I—"

He held up a hand. "No argument. I won't have my cook distracted by thoughts of how she'll make it through the week. And use this money wisely, because I'll do this only for the first week."

She smiled. "Thank you for your thoughtfulness."

He brushed that aside. "Now, let me show you to the kitchen." Everett took the basket from her, then waved her ahead of him up the stairs.

She stepped aside when she topped the stairs, pausing to look around. The stairway emptied into an open space that served multiple functions. To the left was the kitchen and dining area, and to the right was what passed for a sitting room or visitor area. Not that he ever had visitors up here. Beyond the sitting room were the two bedchambers, one of which currently served as more of a storage room. It did have a small bed—more of a cot, really—but he didn't expect to be hosting overnight guests anytime soon.

Everett placed her basket on the table and she moved past him, her gaze sweeping the room.

"This kitchen is nice," she said. "A bit spare but clean

and neat. It gives me hope for what my place might look like once I get it fixed up."

How bad was it over there? If what he'd seen of the ground floor was any indication, she really had her work cut out for her.

Daisy ran a hand lightly over the edge of the stove. "Yes, sir, a fine kitchen, indeed. This is a good stove. And you already have the fire stoked. Thanks!"

Everett waved his hand in an inclusive gesture. "The dishes are in the top cupboard, the pots and pans are over there, and the cooking implements are in that drawer. This door opens to the pantry. Feel free to use anything you find there."

She nodded as she peered inside.

He straightened. "I should warn you, the stove is a bit temperamental." Something he knew from his own less-than-successful attempts at making biscuits.

She closed the pantry door and smiled. "Most stoves take some getting used to. I'm just happy to have a real stove to cook on instead of a campfire."

That statement gave him pause. "But you *do* have experience with a household stove, don't you?"

"Of course. When I lived with my grandmother I spent a lot of my time in the kitchen, and I pestered the cook until she gave in and taught me all about cooking."

"So you haven't used one since you were twelve years old?"

"Not so. During the worst of winter each year, my father would find a town where we could rent rooms for about six weeks, rather than live in the wagon. To help pay for our lodging, and replenish our wares, he would find odd jobs and I'd find work in a kitchen somewhere."

That admission caught him by surprise. "So this isn't your first time to hire on as a cook?"

"Goodness, no. I told you, I know what I'm doing."

That remained to be seen. But he'd had enough of idle talk—time to return to his work. "I'll leave you to it, then. There's extra kindling and firewood for the stove in that corner. If you need anything else, you know where to find me."

He descended the stairs, accompanied by the sound of her cheerful humming. Was he going to have to put up with that all morning?

He supposed there were worse distractions he could be presented with.

Still, it didn't seem quite normal for someone to be so relentlessly cheerful all the time, especially someone with her less-than-ideal circumstances.

Before he'd made it back to his desk, his door opened and Alma Franklin walked in, looking for a paper. She glanced toward the stairway at the sound of Daisy's humming, and mentioned that she'd heard he'd hired a cook and asked how that was working out for him. Right on her heels, Stanley Landers came in, also looking for a paper, and he also commented on his new cook.

It was that way for the next hour—a steady stream of people either wanting to buy a paper or checking on notices that were already scheduled or purchasing advertisements. And all of them found a way to work Daisy's presence into the conversation. At least the townsfolk's curiosity had generated a few new sales. At this rate, he'd be sold out by noon.

Around ten-thirty, he caught the whiff of a mouthwatering aroma drifting down from his kitchen. Thirty minutes later, the aromas began to tease and tantalize his senses in earnest. Perhaps she really *was* as good a cook as she claimed to be.

When Everett finally got a break, just before noon, he

considered heading upstairs to check on Daisy. She hadn't left the kitchen all morning, and he wanted to assure himself she was handling things appropriately.

But his door opened once more and Hazel Andrews, the very prim woman who owned the dress shop, marched in with her usual brisk, no-nonsense air. "Good morning, Mr. Fulton."

"Miss Andrews." He waved her into a seat, then took his own. "What can I do for you?"

She sat poker straight in her chair, but her smile, while small, seemed genuine enough. "I was at the train station dropping off a package to ship to my sister," she said, "when Lionel told me he had a letter for you. I offered to deliver it since I had business with you, anyway."

Everett accepted the letter and placed it on his desk with barely a glance. "What kind of business?"

The seamstress looked pointedly at the letter. "I don't mind waiting if you'd like to read your letter first."

"I'll read it later." He could tell it was from his sister, and he'd prefer to save it for a time when he could read it alone to savor it.

Miss Andrews nodded. "On to business, then. I'm planning to run a sale on my dressmaking services next week. I'd like to buy an advertisement in the paper to announce it."

Everett opened his notebook and reached for a pencil. He was always happy to sell advertisements. "I can certainly accommodate you. What size were you thinking of?"

Once they'd discussed the particulars of the advertisement, Miss Andrews sat back, apparently ready for some casual conversation. "I hear you've hired your new neighbor to cook for you."

So even the straightlaced seamstress was interested in

the town's newest citizen. Everett closed his notebook and nodded. "That's right. She needed the work, and I was tired of eating my own cooking."

His visitor nodded approval. "Sounds like a practical arrangement." Then she changed the subject. "It'll be good to see that place next door all fixed up again. Any idea what Miss Johnson plans to do with the place?"

Everett repeated the same answer he'd given to everyone else this morning. "She mentioned plans to open a restaurant in the interview you'll find in today's newspaper. Other than that, you'll have to ask her."

She lifted her head and sniffed delicately. "I must say, if that aroma is from whatever Miss Johnson is preparing for you, she would likely do quite well as a restaurant cook."

The pesky creak that signaled someone was on the stairs sounded, and they both turned toward it.

"Mr. Fulton, I—" Daisy looked toward his visitor and paused. "Oh, sorry. I didn't mean to interrupt."

Everett and Miss Andrews both stood.

"Miss Johnson." The dressmaker stepped forward. "Allow me to introduce myself. I'm Hazel Andrews, owner of the dress shop down the street."

"Pleased to meet you, ma'am. I've walked by your place a few times. From what I can see through your shop window, you do beautiful work."

"Why, thank you." The seamstress studied Daisy with a critical eye. "If you'd like to come in for a fitting, I'd be glad to set up an appointment for you."

"Thank you for the offer," Daisy said with an apologetic smile. "As tempting as it sounds, I'm afraid purchasing new clothes is going to have to wait until I've taken care of other, more pressing matters."

The dressmaker tightened the strings to her handbag and nodded. "I understand." She gave Daisy a head-to-toe look. "Just keep in mind that appearances set the tone for a business relationship as well as a personal one."

Everett stiffened. Her tone had been friendly enough, but the words carried a barb. Had Daisy felt it?

Then Miss Andrews turned back to him. "I assume I can look for the advertisement to run in the next issue of the *Gazette*."

"Of course." Everett still had his mind on how her words might have affected Daisy as he gave her a short bow of dismissal. "And thank you for delivering the letter."

Once the door closed behind the dressmaker, Everett turned to Daisy. He still didn't detect any hint of distress or affront in her expression. Perhaps he'd overreacted. "Was there something you needed?"

She blinked, as if just remembering her errand. "Yes, of course. I wanted to tell you your meal is ready to be served. But there's no need to rush upstairs if you're busy. I'll just keep it warm until you're ready for it."

"Thank you. I'll join you there in a moment."

He waited until she had started up the stairs to open his letter, smiling in anticipation. Abigail's letters reflected her personality—they were chatty, exuberant and overly dramatic. He unfolded the missive and leaned back in his chair, prepared to be entertained.

Daisy set the table for the two of them and then ladled the stew into a serving bowl.

Had Miss Andrews offered to make her an appointment just to drum up business? Or did she think Daisy's clothing was really that awful? Daisy hadn't wasted time worrying about her wardrobe since she'd left her grandmother's. Function was what mattered, and the pieces she had—this skirt, two shirtwaists and her Sunday dress—had that going for them.

In fact, one of the things she'd disliked about living in her grandmother's home was the emphasis everyone placed on appearances. Daisy had vowed to leave all that behind her when she left there. Nowadays, as long as her clothing was serviceable and modest, she didn't give it much deeper consideration.

But Miss Andrews's words had given her pause. She *was* planning to be a businesswoman now. Perhaps it was time she gave such things a little more consideration.

Her musings were interrupted by the sound of Everett on the stairs.

"It smells good," he said as he entered the kitchen.

Her mood lightened at his praise. "Thanks." Then she felt the need to give a disclaimer. "I'm afraid the bread is a bit scorched, though. It may take me a couple of tries to get a feel for your oven."

"I daresay you're right. But I'm sure the rest of the meal will be fine."

Coming from him, she supposed that was praise of a sort. Daisy placed the stew and bread platter on the table. "I have apple pie for dessert. And I'm pleased to say it hardly got scorched at all."

He took his seat without comment, and she sat across from him.

When he reached for the bread platter, however, she cleared her throat. "Would you like to say the blessing before we start?"

Everett slowly drew his hand back and gave her an unreadable look. "Why don't you perform that service for us?"

Was he the sort who didn't like to pray in public? She hadn't thought of him as the reticent sort. But she nodded and bowed her head. "Heavenly Father, we thank You for this food and for all the other blessings of this day. Help us to remain mindful of where our bounty comes from and to whom our praises belong. And keep us ever aware of the needs of others. In Your name we pray. Amen."

She smiled up at him as he echoed her *Amen*. "Eat up."

The silence drew out for several long minutes as they concentrated on their food. Finally, she gave in to the urge to break the silence. "I read that newspaper of yours."

"Oh?"

"Yes, and I want to thank you for the job you did on that interview. You took my uninteresting life and made it sound, well, plumb interesting."

He seemed more amused than flattered by her comment. "That's the job of a good reporter—to find the hidden gem in any story."

"Hidden gem. I like that." She pointed her spoon at him, then quickly lowered it. "I didn't read just the interview, though—I read the entire thing. You did a fine job with all of it."

"Thank you. I suppose it *is* fine, for what it is."

"What it is?" His tone puzzled her.

"Yes—a small town, nothing-ever-happens, two-days-a-week newspaper."

"So you're not happy with it."

"As I said, it's fine for what it is." He gave her a pointed look. "Do you mind if we change the subject?"

Why was this such a touchy subject for him? But she obediently reached for another subject and said the first thing that came to mind. "I heard you mention something about a letter. It wasn't bad news, I hope." Maybe that's why he seemed so out of sorts.

He studied her as if searching for some ulterior motive behind her question. She thought for a moment that he would change the subject again.

But then he reached for his glass as he shook his head. "Not at all. It's a letter from my sister, Abigail."

Why wasn't he happier about it? "How nice. The two of you must be close."

He didn't return her smile. "She wants to come here for a visit."

His grim tone puzzled her. "Isn't that a good thing? I mean, wouldn't you like to see her?"

"Of course I would." He took a drink from his glass, then set it back down. "But, as I've told her any number of times, it's better if I go to Boston than if she comes here. Unfortunately, she doesn't see it that way."

"But if it's that important to her, perhaps you could allow her to come here just one time. You know, to satisfy her curiosity."

His exasperated look told her she'd overstepped her bounds. "For her to come here," he said, "there are significant arrangements that would need to be made—things such as finding a traveling companion and making certain she doesn't fall behind in any of her classes. Besides, Turnabout is no place for a girl like Abigail. And there aren't an abundance of activities to entertain and enlighten her here."

He broke off a piece of bread with more vigor than was absolutely necessary. "No, it's much better if I visit her."

A girl like Abigail? What did that mean? Was his sister one of those spoiled, pampered debutantes like the ones who'd graced her grandmother's parlor? Girls who never got their hands dirty or even knew what a callus looked like? But that wasn't a question she'd ask out loud. "Do you plan to do that? Go visit her, I mean."

"Of course. I traveled to Boston to see her over the Christmas holidays and will make another visit sometime this summer. She and I spend our time going to the theater, visiting museums, attending the opera and whatever else she cares to do."

Those were the kind of things they enjoyed doing together? "Don't you two ever go on picnics or take buggy rides through the countryside or just take long walks together?"

"Since my time with Abigail is limited, I always strive to make it count for something." His demeanor had stiffened, and his accent was more pronounced. "My sister is being raised as a proper lady, not a hoyden. Those activities add to both her education and her social polish. Their entertainment value is merely an added bonus."

Daisy straightened. She supposed she'd been put in her place. And she'd also gotten the distinct impression that Miss Abigail Fulton might be every bit as stuffy as her brother.

Ah, well, there wasn't much danger that they would cross paths anytime soon—not if big brother had his way.

Everett was glad when Daisy finally let the silence settle between them. He didn't care for all this prying into his personal life. Didn't she understand there were lines one just did not cross? Someone should sit her down and explain the rules of polite society. Not that he thought it would do any good.

Perhaps she would learn from their interaction.

His thoughts drifted to that prayer she'd voiced earlier. It had surprised him, in both its simplicity and sincerity. He hadn't heard anyone pray like that outside of church before. It seemed that her faith was a deeply personal one. But then again, he was beginning to see that she approached nearly everything in her life with everything she had.

If she was going to make it on her own, and try to establish a business, she'd have to learn to be more objective and circumspect in her approach.

Perhaps that was something else he could teach her.

Chapter Six

Daisy blew the hair off her forehead as she dried the last of the dishes. There was plenty of stew left over, and it would keep fine on the stove's warming plate until Mr. Fulton was ready for his evening meal.

She hung the dishrag over the basin, then looked around to check if anything else needed her attention before she headed home. Kip would be ready to go for a walk, and she was eager to get back to work fixing up her new home. But she wouldn't leave until she'd made certain she met her obligations here.

Mr. Fulton was fastidiously neat, and she was determined to leave the place as orderly as it had been when she arrived, if not more so. And she'd start by arranging his cupboards in a more logical manner. Logical from a cook's perspective, at any rate.

A freestanding cupboard on the far wall seemed to be the ideal place to store items that were seldom used. She crossed over to it and opened the doors, then smiled when she found it held only a few mismatched cups. She could certainly put it to better use than that. Satisfied, she closed the doors, then paused.

Was that a crack in the wall behind the cupboard? It was

mostly in shadow, but as she looked closer, she noticed the crack was perfectly straight.

Then her eyes widened. It was a door, painted over to match the surrounding wall. What with that and the fact that it was mostly hidden by the cupboard, it was easy to overlook.

Why had the door been so cunningly hidden? And what was behind it? It didn't appear to have been opened in quite some time. Did Everett even know it was here?

The doorknob was behind the cupboard, making it impossible for her to even try to open it. She studied it, hands on her hips, her curiosity growing. After all, who could resist the allure of a hidden door?

Removing her apron, Daisy headed downstairs.

Everett finished cleaning his printing equipment and arched his back, trying to ease the kink in his muscles. After ten months of trial and error, he finally considered himself proficient with the various aspects of the printing process, though there were some tasks he still didn't particularly enjoy. Back in Philadelphia, he'd been a respected reporter with a major paper. His job had been to write the stories—getting those stories to print had been someone else's job, and he'd rarely given it a second thought. But here he was responsible for every aspect of getting the paper out.

Which was another reason he was doing everything in his power to find another position as a reporter for a large newspaper once more.

He wiped his hands on a cloth as that squeaky stair announced Daisy was on her way down. "All done?" he asked, moving toward his desk to get her payment.

"I am." She glanced at one of his trays of print type. "How come all your letters look backward?"

"That's the way type is set for printing." He saw her puzzled look and explained further. "Think of it as looking at a reflection. The type is the mirror image of what the printed page will be."

Her expression cleared. "Imagine that. So you have to set all those letters into backward words so the print comes out frontward on the paper."

"Not the most eloquent way of explaining it, but yes."

She shook her head. "That sounds like it would be difficult to keep straight in your head. I know it would make me go all cross-eyed."

She did have a colorful way of speaking. "It *is* a tedious job. I will admit, even after several months at it, I find myself having to focus totally on what I'm doing or I'll get it wrong." It had given him a whole new appreciation for professional typesetters. He just hoped he didn't have to *be* one much longer.

But enough of this chitchat—he had work to do. "Here are your wages," he said, handing them over.

She accepted them with a thank-you, but didn't head for the door as he'd expected.

"Was there anything else?"

"I was wondering if you knew about the door in the wall behind your cupboard?"

What was she talking about? "A door? Are you certain?"

That got her back up. "I know a door when I see one."

Everett moved toward the stairs. "Show me."

She marched up ahead of him, then wordlessly waved him toward the far wall.

Everett drew closer to the cupboard, studying the wall behind it. Sure enough, there was the obvious outline of a door. How had he missed spotting it in all the time he'd lived here?

"I take it from your reaction you hadn't noticed it before." Daisy was right at his shoulder. "What do you suppose is in there?"

He glanced at her, and she had the grace to blush.

But Everett was curious now, too. "Let me just shift this over so we can find out."

Everett put his shoulder to the cupboard, waving off her offer of assistance. That done, he grabbed the doorknob and twisted. It was locked. "This cupboard was here when I moved in. I wonder…" He felt along the top of the cupboard, and sure enough, he found a key.

Daisy's eyes sparkled with excitement. "Must be something mighty important in there to keep it locked up."

Was she expecting a treasure of some sort? It was more likely to be nothing but a shallow closet. He quickly unlocked and opened the door, but instead of finding the storage space he'd expected, he faced the backside of another door.

"How strange," Daisy said, her disappointment evident. "It's not even deep enough to store a sack of flour. Maybe it's where they kept their brooms."

"It's not for storage at all." He moved aside so she'd have a clearer view. "This back wall is another door. I believe this is an upstairs access between our buildings, with a lock on both sides for privacy."

"You mean that other door opens from my side?" She studied it closer. "I haven't reached this far in my cleaning yet, but I can picture just where it might be."

She straightened. "How about that. The original owners must have been good friends to set this up."

Everett nodded, still mulling over the implications. "I believe I heard somewhere they were brothers."

"That makes sense." Daisy nodded in satisfaction.

"Their families probably did a lot of visiting back and forth."

He dusted his hands. "Either they had a falling out or the new owners valued their privacy when the buildings changed hands."

"That's a shame. Neighbors should be, well, neighborly." She tilted her head thoughtfully. "But there's no reason we can't make use of this."

What in the world was she thinking now? "Miss Johnson, I—"

"How would you feel about leaving the doors open whenever I'm over here cooking?"

Before he could respond, she quickly continued.

"With such easy access, I can work on a few things at my place while the food simmers. And I can even check in on Kip occasionally while I'm at it."

Somehow that arrangement didn't seem quite respectable. "I don't—"

But she wasn't finished. "Oh, and don't you worry, I won't skimp on the work I'm doing for you. I'll only go over to my place when I'm not needed here."

He shook his head irritably. "I don't mind you splitting your time, as long as the meals are prepared properly. But there are proprieties to be observed."

Her brow furrowed, and then she waved a dismissive hand. "I really can't see how that would be an issue. After all, I'll be over here cooking for you just about every day, and we haven't made a secret of that. What difference can it make if that door is open when I'm at work here?"

It went against the grain with him to give even the appearance of bending the rules of polite society. Still, she was making sense in a roundabout kind of way. "If I agree to this, and I haven't said I will, then I need your word that that animal of yours stays on your side of the wall."

"That won't be a problem." Her eagerness was palpable. "This would be such a big help to me in getting my place livable more quickly."

"I suppose there wouldn't be any harm in it." Though he still wasn't fond of the idea. "But only during your working hours. And it would probably be best if we don't spread the word about this easy access between our apartments. Some individuals might take it amiss." Did she understand what he was saying?

"Thank you. I promise I'll handle it just as you say. And don't worry, I'll keep my side securely locked when I'm done here for the day, just as propriety dictates."

Maybe she'd gotten the message, after all.

She straightened. "Now, I'm going right over to my place to see if I can find my door and the key that goes with it. It seems the previous residents *really* wanted to shut each other out."

"Family disputes can be among the bitterest." Everett pushed away the memory of his own father.

She was still studying the door. "If I'm recollecting the layout right, I think there's a rickety bookcase in front of the door on my end."

He knew a hint when he heard one. "I suppose you'd like me to help move it."

But she shook her head. "Oh, no, I was thinking out loud, not asking for help."

She might say that, but it would be ungentlemanly not to lend a hand after her comment. "Of course. But I'll accompany you all the same." Besides, he was curious to see what progress she'd made since the night she'd arrived.

As soon as she opened the door to her place, her dog raced up, tail wagging. He jumped up, planting his front paws on her skirts, and she gave his head an affectionate rub. "Hey, Kip, did you miss me, boy? I promise we'll go for a walk just as soon as I check something out upstairs."

The animal was every bit as foolishly cheerful as his mistress.

The front room was mostly bare but surprisingly clean. Daisy had apparently scrubbed the floors and walls until there wasn't a speck of dirt to be seen. Interesting that she'd worked on the downstairs before the living quarters upstairs.

She caught him looking around, and smiled proudly. "There's still a lot to be done, but I'm making progress. Right now I'm trying to decide if I want to buy yellow paint or blue paint for the walls. Yellow would be brighter and cheerier, but blue would be more relaxing and remind folks of the blue skies of springtime. What do you think?"

He had a feeling she wasn't talking about muted shades of those particular colors. "I favor more sophisticated colors, such as white or gray."

Daisy wrinkled her nose. "Where's the joy in that?"

Joy? What an odd thing to say about a color choice. But apparently, the question had been moot.

She moved to the stairs and her dog stayed right on her heels, seemingly determined to make up for the time they'd been apart. "I warn you," she said over her shoulder, "I haven't done much to fix up the second floor. You're liable to get a bit of dust and grime on you."

"I feel sufficiently warned," he said dryly. Just because he liked to maintain a neat appearance didn't mean he was averse to a little dirt when there was no help for it.

The upstairs wasn't as cluttered as the downstairs had been that first night, but it was every bit as dusty and unkempt. Gus had really let the place go. It made him wonder if there were soundness issues with the structure itself. Everett studied the walls and ceilings more closely. But there were no visible water marks or signs of crumbling woodwork.

He followed Daisy to the wall that adjoined his, and sure enough, once you knew where to look, the door was evident. He helped her shift the clutter away from the wall and they discovered the key still in the lock, so finding it wasn't an issue. When they opened the door they found themselves looking into his apartment.

Her smile widened to a broad grin. "This is wonderful—I'll be able to get twice as much work done now."

"Just remember, the dog stays on your side of the wall."

"Don't worry, he knows his place."

Everett very deliberately turned and headed down Daisy's stairs to make his exit. Regardless of how "neighborly" the prior tenants had been, there would be no use of that adjoining door as a shortcut access other than during her working hours.

He would not do anything to set the local tongues wagging. Regardless of how innocent a person was, perception and reputation were everything.

After Everett left, Daisy took Kip for a walk. As usual, she grabbed a cloth bag so she'd have something to hold anything edible or useable she found along the way. At the last minute, she remembered she needed to gather the stuffing for her mattress ticking, so she grabbed a larger gunnysack as well.

Once on the edge of town, she let Kip have his head and followed wherever the animal led, only redirecting him when he seemed headed for mischief.

This was only her second day here, if you didn't count the night she arrived, and already it felt familiar, comfortable. Everything was falling into place just as she'd hoped, even better than she'd thought possible.

She could build a good life here. She'd already made a few acquaintances that, in time, she hoped could bloom into true friendships.

The discovery of that door between her and Mr. Fulton's places had been exciting, something unexpected and fun. Sharing a secret with him made her feel closer to him somehow, even if he didn't feel any of that excitement himself.

Too bad her employer-neighbor seemed unable to appreciate a bit of adventure. Did he realize how much he was missing by being so guarded? He seemed to like reporting on what was happening around him much more than experiencing it.

Was that because he'd never felt swept up in the joy of letting his imagination run free, of focusing on the fun in whatever situation you were in? That was probably hard for him to do, what with his inflexible, cynical outlook on things. Instead of looking at that doorway as something fun and exciting, he'd seemed more concerned with how it might look if word got out about it. Looking for warts instead of dimples again.

Then she caught herself up on that thought.

She had no right to judge him. She had no idea what had made him the way he was. Maybe he'd never been taught how to have fun. Or maybe something had happened that made it hard for him to see the silver lining in things.

Well, if that was the case, it was up to her to show him how to relax and not hold on to his need for control so tightly.

Now, if she could just figure out how to accomplish that...

Chapter Seven

Saturday morning, Daisy arrived at Everett's office a few minutes after nine o'clock. It was a beautiful day and one that promised to be highly productive.

"Good morning," she said cheerily. "Fine day, isn't it?"

Her boss glanced up, then went back to looking at his ledger. "I suppose."

Not a very cheery response. "The butcher had some fine-dressed venison this morning," she continued. "I hope venison is something you like." She was already planning the way she would cook it up with a thick, rich onion gravy and some beets and dandelion greens seasoned with bacon on the side.

"Venison is fine."

He still seemed to be paying little attention to what she was saying. She hefted the basket and tried one more time to get something other than a distracted response. "By the way, I opened the door on my side of the wall when I left this morning. But don't you worry. I made sure Kip understands he can't cross the threshold."

This time he did look up and actually met her gaze. "You made sure…" He gave her a look that seemed to call her sanity into question. "And do you honestly think he understood?"

Maybe drawing him out hadn't been such a good idea. "He's actually pretty smart."

"There's nothing pretty about him," he said dryly.

"Mr. Fulton!"

"Sorry." His tone sounded anything but. "Just see that you reinforce that little talk you two had with some firm discipline if he doesn't appear willing to follow directions."

What would he do if she stuck her tongue out at him?

Cheered by the image that evoked, Daisy turned and headed up the stairs. As soon as she set her market basket down, Daisy opened the adjoining door. Kip was sitting there waiting on her, his tail wagging furiously. Daisy stooped down and ruffled the fur on his neck. "Hey, boy. What do you say we prove Mr. High-and-Mighty Fulton wrong? I'll pop over and visit you occasionally, but I have a job to do so you'll have to stay over here."

Kip gave a bark, which she took as agreement, so with one last pat, she stood and returned to her work. Today she was determined to conquer the eccentricities of the stove, and turn out bread rolls that were perfectly golden-brown.

Yes, sir, there would be nothing for her employer to fuss about today.

All morning, Everett heard the sounds of Daisy bustling around in his kitchen, more often than not humming or singing some cheery song. He could also hear her talking to her mutt, carrying on one-sided conversations as if the raggedy animal could actually understand her words.

He gave in to the urge to go upstairs and check on her at about ten-thirty. It only made sense, he told himself, to make certain things were going as they should with this new arrangement of theirs.

The angle of the adjoining door was such that, once his shoulders topped the second floor, he was able to see through it to her place. Her dog sat at the threshold but, as she'd promised, no part of him was across it. How had she managed to make her pet obey—especially when the food smells were so tempting?

Beyond the animal, he could see enough to tell him that she'd made quite a bit of progress since he'd been up there yesterday. Despite himself, he was impressed with how much she was getting accomplished.

The dog barked. Everett wasn't sure if it was a greeting or a warning, but it caught Daisy's attention and she turned, smiling when she spied him.

"Hello. If you've come to check on the meal, I'm afraid it'll be another hour or so until it's ready."

Feeling as if he'd been caught doing something he shouldn't—which was ridiculous—he tugged at his cuff. "Not at all. I just need to fetch something from my room."

He strode purposefully to his bedchamber, grabbed the notebook he kept by his bedside, then headed back out.

"I want to thank you again for letting me prop these doors open," she said as he neared the stairs. "I've already been able to get quite a bit of work done in my place this morning." She nodded toward the door. "As you can see, Kip is behaving himself just like I told you he would."

Everett made a noncommittal sound and, with a nod, headed back downstairs.

When she called him upstairs for the noonday meal, Everett deliberately took his time. No point appearing overeager.

"Your oven and I are getting along much better today," she said as they took their seats at the table. "You won't find nary a scorch mark on these rolls."

Again she asked if he'd like to say grace, and again he

passed the task to her. He noticed the speculative look she gave him, but he kept his expression bland. There was no reason for him to explain himself.

He didn't pray aloud, or pray much at all if you got right down to it. The clergyman who held the living on his father's estate in England had made certain he was familiar with the Bible and that he attended church services regularly. And for most of his childhood, Everett had been quite faithful to those teachings.

That had changed when he'd realized that his illegitimate status made him and his mother lesser people in the eyes of those oh-so-pious folks who surrounded him. And then he'd been summarily exiled from his home to America.

Now he knew that religion was for children and women, those who needed something spiritual to cling to as an emotional crutch.

He considered himself more of a social Christian—one who went to church service because it was expected. And to set the proper example for his younger sister.

But there was no point going into all of that with Daisy. She obviously felt quite differently.

As she passed him the platter of meat, she smiled. "I hope you like venison cooked this way. It was my father's favorite meal. I do believe he would've eaten it every day if it had been available."

Everett met her gaze as he served himself. "I find it strange that you speak of him with such affection."

"Strange how?"

"You ran off to get away from him. And worse, he didn't come after you, but rather let you travel alone and by foot, though he had to know where you were going." Such actions were unforgivable.

"My relationship with my father is complicated, but regardless of how we parted, I do still love him very much."

Was she just being tactful? "Admirable of you, it seems."

She shook her head. "You sound like you don't believe me, but it's true. It's just that, even though I love him, there are times when I don't like him very much."

She wasn't making a whole lot of sense.

Apparently, she saw the doubt in his expression. "My father always said it was my mother who kept him on the straight and narrow," she explained. "When she was around, there was no temptation strong enough to lure him away. That's what kept him sober and happy when I was little."

She pushed her food around her plate with a fork. "I tried to be a good daughter when I started traveling with him again, to take care of him and give him as much love as Mother did. But I guess I wasn't enough. He'd be okay for a while, but the yearning for drink and cards would get hold of him, and the next thing I know he'd have gambled away most of our earnings."

And she still claimed to love him? Had her affection made her so blind?

"When I learned he'd won the deed to the building next door, I tried to convince him to come with me, but he kept saying he was too set in his ways to change."

"That doesn't excuse his letting you set out on your own instead of giving you a proper escort."

She dredged her fork through her gravy. "That's not exactly how it happened."

"What do you mean?"

She still didn't quite meet his eyes. "I never gave him the chance to bring me here." She finally looked up. "We were over in Thornridge and had another of our arguments."

She looked so lost, so regretful that Everett almost reached out to touch her arm in support. But he'd never been comfortable with such emotional gestures.

"It was a small thing," she continued wistfully, "but it felt big at the time. So I told him to leave me in town to do some shopping and 'cool off' while he visited a few farms to try to make some sales. As soon as he was out of sight, I left a note with the owner of the mercantile and headed out on my own."

She traced a line on her glass with one finger. "It was cowardly of me, but I knew if I had to look him in the eye and tell him my intentions, I wouldn't be able to go."

Everett wasn't convinced. There's no way he would have let Abigail go like that, no matter how much they disagreed on matters. "He still should have headed out after you when he realized you'd gone."

"Well, first off, he may not have realized I was gone until the next day. Because if things followed their normal course, he would take whatever money he made on sales and find a card game. Which meant he'd have stayed out until the wee hours."

Is that the kind of existence she was accustomed to? How had she held on to her optimism all this time?

"When he did realize I was gone," she continued, "and got the note I left for him, he would have read my plea for him not to follow me."

Everett frowned. She'd said her relationship with her father was complicated—it seemed she hadn't been exaggerating. "So you deliberately severed ties with him."

"Not permanently. He'll come back through Turnabout in a few months. By then the break will have healed, and I'll be settled and we'll be able to meet on more comfortable terms."

There was that seemingly unquenchable optimism again.

She smiled wistfully. "Someday, I hope Father will be ready to settle down, too, and when that time comes, I'm hoping he'll move in with me."

She shifted in her chair, and her smile brightened. "Now, why don't we talk about something else. And since you asked me a personal question, I think a question for you is in order."

He wasn't sure he liked that challenging glint in her eye. "Such as?"

"Such as, why don't you like dogs?"

Everett immediately felt his guard go up. But there were worse things she could have asked. "It's not that I don't like dogs. I just have no use for them. They are overly exuberant, serve no useful purpose and are always trying to claim your attention. They are fine as hunters or herders, but why would one want a beast like that in one's home?"

"They also love you without question, provide warm companionship and never judge you, but instead reward every kind gesture with joy."

It almost sounded as if she were describing herself. "I suppose we shall agree to disagree on this."

"Have you ever let yourself just play with a dog?"

He was *not* going down that conversational path with her. "Not since I was a child." He pushed those foolish memories aside and changed the subject. "I can see why your father considered this his favorite meal. It's quite good."

To his relief, she followed his lead and the conversation stayed on safe, nonpersonal topics for the rest of the meal.

Once they stood up from the table, Everett waved toward the adjoining door. "Please don't forget to close and lock that door before you leave."

At her nod, he turned and headed downstairs. She probably thought he was being too much a stickler, but he was a firm believer that you couldn't go wrong if you followed the rules of propriety to the letter. That was what separated polite society from barbarians.

After Daisy returned to her own place, she locked the door on her side of the wall, just as she'd promised Everett she would. The man was just so rigid in his thinking, so very conscious of appearances. But it wouldn't hurt to follow his rules.

Then she turned to Kip. "Ready for our walk, boy?"

The dog's tail started wagging furiously, and he gave an excited bark.

Daisy laughed as she led the way. "How can anyone say they have no use for dogs? Especially a smart, friendly dog like you." Another example of how stuffy her boss could be.

Then again, Mr. Fulton *had* admitted to playing with a dog when he was a child. So at one time he'd known what it was to have fun. What had happened to him?

As soon as she stepped outside, Daisy pushed those gloomy thoughts aside and lifted her face to the sky, enjoying the feel of the warm sunshine, inhaling deeply of the fresh air. Did Mr. Fulton ever do this, just take a moment to enjoy what the day had to offer?

She doubted it.

As they headed toward the outskirts of town, Daisy began her usual one-sided conversation with Kip. "Remember all those berries I picked yesterday? Well, I traded them to Mr. Blakely over at the mercantile for some rope. Tonight I'm going to string it on the bed frame and make it good as new. Now if I can just gather up enough grass to finish stuffing my mattress, I can have me a proper bed. I'll sure be glad when I don't have to sleep on the floor anymore."

Kip answered with a bark.

She smiled down at him. "Don't worry. There's a new bed in the works for you, as well."

Kip gave another bark, then took off after a squirrel he spotted across the road.

Daisy watched him tree the bushy-tailed sprinter with a smile. Kip was such a good companion. Mr. Fulton would see that if he could look past his stuffy notions.

Maybe that was something she could teach him, unobtrusively of course, to repay him for all the nice things he'd done for her. Surely she could find ways to teach him to smile—genuinely smile, not flash that amused-at-the-world, snobby twist of his lips that passed for a smile.

He might appear stiff and cold, but he'd done so much to help her, whether he cared to admit it or not. She had to believe that there really was a kind heart under that don't-need-anybody exterior of his.

And she aimed to make him believe it, as well.

On Sunday, Daisy stepped out onto the sidewalk at almost the same moment as Everett left his building. "Good morning, Mr. Fulton. Are you on your way to church service, too?"

"I am."

So he *was* a churchgoer. She was relieved. Perhaps his reluctance to say grace at their meals was no more than a dislike of praying aloud.

He gave her an approving glance as he fell into step beside her, and she stood a little straighter, feeling a tiny touch of pride. The dress she wore was one that had belonged to her mother. It wasn't as fine as some of the other dresses that would no doubt grace the women filling the pews this morning, but it was one she could hold her head up proudly while wearing.

As they strolled down the sidewalk, Daisy felt a little self-conscious walking beside him. But she considered him her friend, not just her boss. Did he feel the same? "It sure is a beautiful day," she said, breaking the silence.

"So it is."

So much for starting a conversation. But he seemed perfectly at ease, and within a few moments she began to relax.

They received several greetings from the townsfolk they encountered, with Everett taking the time to introduce her to those she hadn't yet met, and Daisy suddenly caught another glimmer of what it would feel like to be an accepted part of this community. It felt every bit as good as she'd imagined it would.

"Good morning to you, Miss Johnson, Mr. Fulton." Hazel Andrews, the seamstress, had stepped out of her home to join them.

Everett tipped his hat, and the three exchanged pleasantries. Then Miss Andrews smiled Daisy's way. "That's a very fine dress you're wearing. A bit dated perhaps, but I can tell the workmanship is exceptional, and the fabric and detailing are quite lovely."

"Thank you. It belonged to my mother."

They arrived in the churchyard, and Miss Andrews excused herself to join a group of friends. Before Daisy could do more than look around, the bell began to peal, indicating it was time for the service to start.

Everett took her elbow and looked at her with a raised brow. "Shall we?"

The feel of his hand on her elbow startled her. He likely only meant to offer support as they climbed the stairs.

Once inside the church, he released her and moved toward a pew halfway down the aisle. She thought for a moment he was planning to join Adam and what was undoubtedly the rest of the Barr household, but he stopped one pew shy of them.

Daisy was uncertain whether to join him or if that would be considered presumptuous. But before she could even complete that thought, Everett was stepping aside to let her precede him into the pew.

There were already two men seated there, and they slid down to accommodate her and Everett. The gentleman to her left, an intimidatingly large man, gave her a friendly smile. "Good day, ma'am. I'm Mitchell Parker. And this—" he indicated the boyish looking gentleman to his left "—is Chance Dawson."

"So good to meet you. My name is Daisy Johnson."

There was no time for further pleasantries, since Reverend Harper was already stepping up to the pulpit.

When the choir led the congregation in an opening hymn a few moments later, Daisy was surprised by Everett's strong, deep voice. It seemed to set off echoing vibrations deep inside her, vibrations synchronized to the rhythms of her heartbeat and breathing.

She shook off the fanciful notion when Reverend Harper stepped up to the podium. His sermon dealt with finding joy in whatever your circumstances. Daisy almost felt as if God Himself were blessing her self-appointed mission to help Everett with this very thing. She wondered how well Everett was listening.

After the service, Adam and his obviously expecting wife stood and turned to greet them. Mrs. Barr focused her attention on Daisy first. "You must be Miss Johnson."

Daisy was immediately put at ease by the woman's warm and genuine smile. "Please, call me Daisy."

"And I'm Reggie." She waved a hand to include the

three other men in Daisy's pew. "These gents have a standing invitation to have Sunday luncheon with us. I hope you'll join us, as well."

Daisy was caught off guard by the invitation. "I don't…"

Reggie patted her hand. "Please, you can't say no. The invitation is entirely selfish on my part. It would be so wonderful to have another female at my table." Then she tilted her head apologetically. "Unless you already have other plans."

"No. I mean, of course I'd be happy to accept your invitation."

"Good. It'll be great to have some female company to help me hold my own against all of these men."

Adam tucked his wife's arm on his elbow. "I have never known you to have problems holding your own, my dear," he said affectionately.

Daisy felt a little stab of jealousy at the obvious love between these two. Was that something she'd ever find for herself?

She pushed that thought away. "Before I join you, I need to check on Kip—he's my dog."

"Of course. In fact, bring him along if you like." Reggie placed a hand on her son's shoulder. "We have a dog of our own, and Jack will be glad to keep an eye on him for you. Won't you, Jack?"

The boy nodded vigorously.

Reggie turned to Everett. "You'll show her where we live." It didn't sound like a question.

But Daisy was aghast at the suggestion that Mr. Fulton should act as her escort. "Oh, no, that's not necessary. If you'll just tell me where your home is, I'm sure I can find my way on my own."

Reggie waved her objection aside. "Nonsense. If Everett doesn't want to—"

"I will be happy to provide Miss Johnson with an escort." Everett's dry tone indicated he was humoring the ladies.

But it would be churlish to refuse now, so she simply nodded, and thanked him.

As they walked down the sidewalk together, she clasped her hands in front of her. "I apologize for taking you away from your friends."

"Where Reggie is concerned, it's best just to go along."

So he was on a first-name basis with Adam's wife. "Still, I feel as if you were put on the spot, and it was very kind of you to be such a good sport about it."

He gave her an odd look. Had she said too much again? When would she learn to think before she spoke?

When they arrived at her building, he didn't go in. Instead, he indicated he would be just inside his office and for her to knock on the door when she was ready.

As always, Kip greeted her as if she'd been gone for days rather than a few hours.

When she stepped back outside a few minutes later, Mr. Fulton joined her before she could so much as move toward his door. He gave Kip an annoyed look but refrained from saying anything. In return, Daisy was careful to keep her dog to her far side.

When they arrived at the Barr home, Jack and his own pet were waiting for them. Kip and the large, muddy-colored dog the boy called Buck sniffed each other, then started a friendly tussle that ended when Jack threw a stick and called out a fetch command.

"They like each other," the boy said with a broad smile.

"So it seems." Mr. Fulton's tone was noncommittal.

Reggie joined them. "I thought I heard you arrive. Please come in."

Jack gave his mother a pleading look. "Can I stay out here and play?"

"For a few minutes, but Mrs. Peavy will have the food on the table soon."

With a quick nod, he ran to the backyard, both dogs on his heels.

Reggie shook her head with a smile. "It'll be like lassoing the rain to get him inside for lunch." Then she turned back to her guests and escorted them inside.

Reggie led them to a cozy parlor where Adam and the two other gentlemen were already seated. They all rose as the ladies entered, but Reggie quickly waved them back down.

Daisy learned that Mr. Parker was one of the town's two schoolteachers, and that Mr. Dawson did some sort of mechanical work. She also learned that these were the other two men who had traveled here from Philadelphia at the same time Everett and Mr. Barr had. That must account for the bond they seemed to share.

The conversation was lively, and it wasn't long before Daisy felt at ease with these people. She was content to sit back and listen for the most part, but her hostess would have none of that.

"I read the article Everett wrote about you for the paper," Reggie said. "You seem to have led a fascinating life."

"I'm afraid most of that is due to Mr. Fulton's writing skill rather than my own accomplishments. To my way of thinking, my life has been rather ordinary."

Reggie laughed. "I suppose everyone thinks that about their own lives. I imagine it's been every bit as ordinary as that of everyone else in this room."

Daisy pondered that statement. Did that mean there were some tales to be told here? "Did Mr. Fulton interview each of you as well?" She'd sure be interested in reading those stories.

"I'm afraid none of us were as obliging as you were," Mr. Parker said dryly.

Before Daisy could dig further, Mrs. Peavy announced the meal was ready.

Meals at the Barr household were anything but formal. Jack was allowed to eat with the adults, and Ira and Mabel Peavy also joined them at the table.

Adam said a simple but heartfelt prayer before the meal, and once everyone was served, the conversation started up again. The food was delicious, and Daisy complimented Mrs. Peavy on her cooking.

"Why, thank you, dear. But I understand you're quite a cook in your own right. Planning to open a restaurant, even."

"Yes, as soon as I can get my place fixed up and acquire the equipment I need. Maybe you and I can swap recipes some time."

Mrs. Peavy gave her a broad grin. "I'd like that."

"Opening a restaurant." Chance Dawson was seated to her left, and he gave her a boyish grin. "That's something this town needs. You let me know if there's anything I can do to help you along." The young man, with his ready smiles and teasing attitude, was as different from Everett as a songbird was from a hawk.

"Thank you. I may take you up on that someday soon."

Everett sat across from her, and she noticed he was frowning at Chance. Was his stand against her opening a restaurant such that he didn't want anyone else to offer her a show of support? He glanced her way, and his expression immediately switched back to the aloof indifference she was so familiar with.

The conversation continued in a lively give-and-take

that Daisy thoroughly enjoyed. Mr. Parker was the quiet sort, but he could suddenly pipe in with a touch of dry wit that one had to be paying close attention to catch. Mr. Dawson was cocky, but his manner was charming rather than off-putting. And Reggie presided over the gathering with relaxed charm and humor. Despite what she'd said earlier, Daisy could see that Reggie needed no help in holding her own with this group.

When at last the meal was over, Reggie invited them to join her out in the garden for dessert.

But Daisy shook her head. "Thank you so much for a wonderful meal, but it's time for me to take my leave."

"You can't leave without tasting Mrs. Peavy's peach cobbler," Reggie protested. "It's her specialty."

Daisy smiled regretfully. "I'm sure it's wonderful, but I have something at home that requires my attention this afternoon."

"Well, if you must go, then I won't pout. But I've enjoyed having you here, and I insist you consider yourself part of our Sunday gatherings."

"Thank you. I would like that very much."

As she headed back toward her home, with Kip at her heels and a carefully packaged piece of cobbler in her hands that Reggie had insisted she take, she sent up a silent prayer of thanksgiving. She'd made a new group of friends and had spent the past hour feeling like a genuinely welcome part of that group. It was almost like having a family. Or rather, what she imagined a loving family would be like.

Everett watched Daisy make her exit, and was surprised to find her departure left a hole in their gathering. Did the rest of them feel that way, or just him? It was strange how

smoothly she'd fit into their Sunday afternoon gathering—
as if she'd always been part of it.

He'd kept an eye on her, unobtrusively, of course. After
all, he felt some responsibility for introducing her into
their midst.

Chance had sat next to her at lunch, and the would-be
lothario had actually flirted with her. Which was ridiculous. Despite her lack of polish, Daisy was much too mature for him. Not that it was really any of his concern. It's
just that it was unseemly. Not only was Chance younger
than Daisy—at least he seemed to be—but he was entirely
the wrong sort of man for her. Daisy needed a man who
could lend a bit of pragmatism and worldly wisdom to tem-
per her foolishly optimistic outlook on life. Chance was
basically a good person, but he was also brash and reckless and counted on his charm a little too much at times.

Everett pulled his thoughts back to the present and saw
Reggie eyeing him speculatively. What was that look for?
He tugged his cuff sharply and turned to ask Mitchell
about doing an article on the students who would be grad-
uating soon.

As for that gleam in Reggie's eyes, she obviously suf-
fered from an overactive imagination.

Chapter Eight

Later that afternoon, as Daisy stitched up the side of the ticking she'd finally finished stuffing, her mind kept wandering to the gathering at the Barrs' home. She'd really had a wonderful time.

A sound from the other side of the wall told her Mr. Fulton had made it home.

How had he felt about her intrusion into their gathering today? After all, Reggie had invited her in a way that hadn't allowed anyone else in the group to object without seeming rude. She'd felt his gaze on her often during the meal, but more often than not, whenever she'd glance his way he was looking elsewhere. Perhaps that had just been her imagination.

Daisy pushed those thoughts away as she placed the last stitch in her ticking and tied off her thread. She knotted it three times, just to make sure it would hold. Yesterday she'd laced the bed frame nice and tight, so it was ready and waiting for the mattress. Would it hold? She maneuvered the bulky mattress onto the frame, then gingerly sat on it. Nothing crashed to the floor—so far, so good.

She flopped back to really get a feel for it. Again, it held. It was a bit lumpy, but she could live with that. And spreading her bedroll on top ought to help smooth it a little. It sure would beat sleeping on the floor.

She popped back up and smiled at Kip. "Guess who's going to be sleeping in a real bed tonight?" Catching her mood, the dog gave a playful bark. "That's right, me. And look at this."

She stood and quickly crossed the room where she scooped up a colorful oval of cloth. "I've made a rag rug that'll be perfect for you to sleep on. See, I'll spread it right next to my bed, and we'll both have comfortable places to sleep tonight. What do you think?"

Kip's wagging tail marked his approval.

"I think this calls for a celebration."

She'd been hoarding a small tin of cocoa powder for just such an occasion. A cup of hot cocoa would be perfect to celebrate this little step to furnishing her new home. And she'd set aside a bone from the butcher to give Kip tomorrow, but he deserved to celebrate, as well.

She dug the cocoa tin out of her pack, then paused. A celebration was so much nicer when there was someone else to share it with. And while Kip was always great company, it would be nice to have another *person* to share this with.

Did Mr. Fulton like cocoa?

She chewed on her lip for a moment, then nodded to herself and opened the pass-through door on her side of the wall. She knocked firmly on the one that opened into his place.

After a moment of silence, there was the sound of movement and he opened the door. His face wore a cautious expression. Had she been too bold, after all?

"Is something wrong?" he asked.

"Not at all." She offered him her broadest smile. "I was in the mood for a celebration and thought I'd fix myself some hot cocoa as a treat." Daisy held up her battered tin. "I wondered if you'd like to have a cup with me?"

He frowned, almost as if upset she *hadn't* had a problem. "I thought we agreed not to use these doors for casual visits."

That was what had him glowering at her. She refused to let his mood dampen her spirits. "My apologies. Shall I close the door and go downstairs and knock on your office door?"

He held his pose a moment longer, then relaxed. "Now that the doors are open, I suppose that would be foolish. And thank you for the invitation." He opened his door wider and stepped back, signaling her to enter. "Why don't we use my stove to heat the milk?"

"I was going to use the fire pit outside, but your way sounds better." Then she looked down at her dog. "But only if you allow Kip to join us. He deserves to be part of the celebration, too."

Everett frowned. Before he could refuse, though, she jumped in with, "It's Sunday afternoon. Can't we call a truce on this day of rest? I promise if Kip does the least little thing to bother you, he and I will both go home."

He grimaced, but then nodded. "Oh, very well."

Relieved, Daisy stepped across the threshold, signaling Kip to follow her. Maybe she was already chipping away at his stuffy exterior. And winning this concession, small as it was, from the normally unbending stickler, gave her something extra to celebrate.

While Everett added additional wood to the stove, Daisy crossed the room and fetched a boiler. She added enough water to fill their two cups, then set it on the stove. "I don't have milk, but I'll add a little extra cocoa to make up for it." It would finish up the last of her stores, but she felt the occasion warranted it.

"I have some cream you're welcome to use."

She smiled, glad to see he was finally getting into the spirit of things. "That'll be lovely. I'll add it when I pour our cups."

He leaned negligently against the counter a few feet from her, and crossed his arms. She felt his eyes on her, silently studying her. Suddenly she felt nervous, self-conscious.

"So what are we celebrating?" he asked, finally breaking the silence.

It seemed a little indelicate to speak of her bed with him. But she couldn't *not* give him an answer, or worse yet, lie. So she chose her words carefully. "The fact that I won't have to spend another night sleeping on the floor."

The water in the pot started bubbling, and she slowly added in the cocoa and then the sugar, stirring to make sure it dissolved without leaving lumps.

She inhaled the rich aroma and looked over her shoulder with a smile. "Doesn't it smell wonderful?"

"It does smell good."

With one last stir, she lifted the pot and carefully poured the dark, aromatic liquid into the two cups. By the time she set the cups on the table, he was there with the cream.

"We probably ought to let that cool a minute," she said. Then she remembered Kip. "I'll be right back." She hurried back to her apartment and fetched the bones she'd set aside.

She caught Everett rolling his eyes when she placed the treat down in front of Kip, but thankfully he refrained from saying anything. Another sign that he was learning to unbend? Daisy quickly took her seat at the table.

"It should have cooled enough to drink by now. Shall we?"

They both sipped on their cocoa, and then Everett lifted his cup toward her in a salute. "Very nice."

"Thank you. Cocoa is one of my favorite tastes in the whole world, so I save it for special occasions."

He raised a brow. "That's quite a pronouncement."

"Oh, but it's true." She gave him a cheeky smile. "And I did say 'one of.'"

"Ah, so now you're qualifying it."

She grinned in response. "What about you?"

He eyed her cautiously. "What do you mean?"

"What's your favorite taste?"

He shrugged. "I haven't really given that much thought."

"Well, think about it now." Could she get him to be frivolous or whimsical for once? "Surely there's one thing you enjoy tasting above all others. A taste that's not just good in itself, but one that brings back pleasant memories."

He looked at her as if she were a child in need of humoring, then his expression changed and she could almost see a memory sneaking up on him. "Once, when I was a boy of about five or six," he said slowly, "my father and mother were both at Hellingsly—that's the estate where I grew up—and we were sitting down to a meal together. That in and of itself was a rare occurrence. Cook had fixed a special dinner, and the dessert consisted of a raspberry tart. I don't think I've tasted anything quite as delicious since."

If he'd been five or six at the time, that would have happened before he came to America. With an estate and a cook, had he come from a well-to-do background? That would account for his highfalutin manner.

But that memory he'd just shared, that had been a simple moment, a time of family and togetherness. Obviously those things had been important to him once upon a time. Perhaps, somewhere inside him, they still were.

He straightened and, as if realizing he'd revealed more than he intended, changed the subject. "I think Jack took a liking to your dog today."

Daisy smiled. "He seems like a sweet boy. It was very kind of Reggie to include me in your gathering today. I like your friends."

"I believe you can count them among your friends now, as well."

Daisy wasn't certain how to respond to that, so she countered with an observation of her own. "So you and Mr. Barr, Mr. Dawson and Mr. Parker traveled here together from Philadelphia last summer."

"We did."

"It's hard to credit it. You're all so different."

Something flickered in his expression—irritation, perhaps, there and gone in an instant. The next second he looked merely amused.

Everett took himself firmly in hand. First he'd talked about a childhood memory that had been all but forgotten until this very moment, and now he was imagining she was comparing him to Chance. Which, even if she were, was something of little consequence.

But she was waiting for a response from him, so he pulled his thoughts back to the conversation. "Not everyone who comes from the same place is the same. Philadelphia is a big city, undoubtedly larger than any place you've experienced. But even in a small town like Turnabout, there are marked differences in people. Look at Reggie, Hazel Andrews and Eunice Ortolon over at the boardinghouse. All born and raised here in Turnabout. But you'd be hard-pressed to find three more different women."

She nodded. "You're right, of course. I guess I just expected a group of friends who decided to undertake such an adventure together would be more alike in temperament. But I can see how being so different would actually work in your favor."

Everett didn't respond. Their concurrent trip here hadn't happened quite as she assumed, but he didn't feel the need to correct her assumptions. He'd already revealed too much personal information, and he didn't intend to give her more.

But he would do well to keep his guard up. For some unfathomable reason, she seemed able to get him to talk about himself more than he cared to. And he'd worked too hard putting his past behind him to have this curious woman pry it out of him, no matter how innocently. He was accustomed to being the one doing the digging and prying—he did *not* like being on the other end of an interrogation.

When Everett sat down to his noonday meal on Monday, he could tell something was up with Daisy. He'd learned to read her moods, and today she seemed more fidgety than usual. He was curious as to what put that distracted look on her face, but decided to hold his peace for the moment. Questioning her only resulted in her prying into his own private affairs.

It was almost a relief when, after they had served their plates, she cleared her throat. "I need to ask you something."

He carefully reached for his glass. "And what might that be?"

She took a deep breath, then spoke all in a rush. "I was hoping you'd be willing to let me off one day a week."

Was that all? Then he frowned. Was she feeling over-worked already? Were his strictures too much for her? Or did she just want to spend more time fixing up her own place? "Might I ask why?"

"Just like you suggested, I asked Mr. Blakely to let me know if he heard about anyone looking to hire somebody."

She was going to work for someone else? "But you have a job now."

"Of course, but I have some free hours in the afternoons and thought I'd find a way to use them to earn a bit of extra money. And this morning, Mr. Blakely mentioned that Mr. Dawson is looking for someone to take in his laundry for the next few weeks. Seems his regular laundry lady, a Miss Winters, is going away somewhere for a while." She leaned forward, her eyes sparkling with excitement.

Was that gleam for the job or for Chance?

"He also said there are other folks Miss Winters does laundry for," she continued, "and that I might be able to get several customers if I want them."

"Doing laundry is a tough job." He'd seen washerwomen at work before, and he knew it was hot, menial, enervating work.

But she waved his concerns away. "I know what I'd be getting into. It's not my favorite job by any means, but I've done it before and it's only for three weeks. And I could definitely use the extra money."

Again he reminded himself that he was not her keeper. And he was actually one of Selma Winters's customers, as well. He'd intended to ask around for someone to fill in for her, but it had slipped his mind until now. "In that case, I suppose I should hire you to do mine, too."

Daisy's hopeful expression immediately changed to a sunny smile. "Does this mean you're okay with me taking a day off to do this?"

Everett shrugged. "Far be it from me to stand in the way of your ambitions."

"Thanks." She stabbed a vegetable enthusiastically. "I was thinking I'd set aside Thursdays for the job. And I could make certain whatever I cooked on Wednesdays could carry over into a cold meal on Thursday."

It seemed she'd already put a lot of thought into this. But did she really know what she was getting into? "Are you certain you're not taking on more than you can handle?" He expanded on that so she wouldn't mistakenly believe he was taking a personal interest. "I wouldn't want you to be too worn out to cook come Friday."

"Don't you worry about me. I'm used to hard work."

He didn't doubt that for one minute. "That's all well and good, but are you set up to handle such a volume of laundry? Miss Winters has set a high standard."

"I already spoke to her. She's so relieved to have someone to fill in for her while she's away that she's offered to let me use her equipment and to give me some pointers."

Had she been that certain of his approval?

As if reading his mind, she elaborated. "Of course I told her it was all based on you letting me have that day off. Now that that's settled, I'll go see her this afternoon. She has some notes she wants to give me to make sure her customers are well taken care of."

Knowing Daisy, Miss Winters's customers had nothing to worry about. And he'd never seen anyone appear so gleeful at the prospect of tackling a mountain of laundry. It remained to be seen if she'd feel the same way once she'd finished a week's worth of laundry.

This was going to be a good test as to just how well that sunny disposition could survive real adversity.

Wednesday afternoon, Everett heard an unusual racket out behind his building and went to the window to check it out.

What in the world? Daisy was driving a horse-drawn wagon into the yard, a wagon loaded with washtubs and other laundry equipment. Had she loaded all that up on her own? Didn't she know how to ask for help?

He set his coffee down and headed for the stairs. By the time he stepped outside, she had jumped down from the seat and was moving toward the back of the wagon.

She paused a moment when she spotted him. "Oh, Mr. Fulton, I hope I didn't disturb you."

"Not at all. I'm just curious as to what you think you're doing."

Daisy continued on her way around the wagon. "I'm getting set up for laundry day tomorrow. Miss Winters is loaning me her equipment."

"Forgive my curiosity, but why didn't you just arrange to do the laundry at her place? Surely she would have let you have the use of her washhouse."

Daisy let down the tailgate of the wagon. "She offered. But I figure in order to make this work, I'm going to have to do some work the night before and the night after. That'll be much easier to do if I'm working from my own place."

So she realized it would take more than a day's work to get it all done. "How many of her customers did you agree to take care of?"

"Three other gentlemen besides you and Mr. Dawson. I also agreed to take in the wash for the mayor's family, since Mrs. Sanders hurt her foot yesterday."

Five individuals and a family of four? "It sounds as if you're going to have your hands full."

She nodded. "I've got all the work I can handle—and since it's only one day a week for three weeks, I can manage it without wearing myself down to a nub."

He joined her at the back of the wagon and helped her up into the bed. She began pushing items toward him, and he lifted them out and set them on the ground. It felt as if they'd been working as a team for some time.

"Is this one of Fred Humphries's wagons?" Fred owned

the livery stable and had several wagons and carriages that he rented out.

"It is. I traded him a dewberry cobbler and the promise of two more in exchange for the use of this rig and horse."

Everett happened to know that Fred's new wife had a reputation as an excellent cook, so Fred was no doubt just being obliging. Foolishly sentimental of him, but the livery operator had revealed a softer side of himself since his marriage.

Once the wagon was unloaded, he turned to help her down. Rather than simply giving her his hand, however, he impulsively grasped her waist and swung her to the ground. Her eyes widened in surprise, and she instinctively placed her hands on his shoulder. He liked the feel of them there, the warmth and the implied trust.

Their gazes locked. Her feet touched the ground, but for several heartbeats neither of them pulled away. The look in her eyes, the sound of her breathing, the faint scent that was so uniquely her were like silken ropes holding him in place. Was surprise the only thing she was feeling? Or was it threaded through with something stronger?

His own pulse quickened, and he felt a vein in his neck jump.

Then her dog ran up, barking, and the spell was broken. Both of them dropped their hands and took a step back.

"Thanks for your help." Daisy had stooped down to rub her dog's head, effectively hiding her expression from him. But her friendly tone sounded forced. She stood and moved to the front of the wagon, still not meeting his gaze. "I should get this rig back to the livery. I told Mr. Humphries I wouldn't keep it long."

He followed and handed her up. Their contact this time was brief and entirely businesslike. With a short nod and a stiff smile, she set the horse in motion. He watched as she expertly turned the wagon and headed off with her dog trotting alongside.

Everett didn't move. What had just happened? He'd come very close to crossing a line he had no business crossing. Not only was Miss Johnson his employee, but she'd made it very clear she planned to set down roots in Turnabout. And he planned to move on at his first opportunity.

Even if that wasn't the case, they were totally wrong for each other. And he needed to make that perfectly clear to her.

And to himself.

Daisy walked slowly back to her place. She wasn't sure exactly what had happened when he helped her down. For the merest heartbeat of time, she'd thought he might try to kiss her. What a ridiculous notion.

But what *would* have happened if Kip hadn't interrupted them? What would she have done if he *had* tried to kiss her?

Mr. Fulton wasn't at all the kind of man she'd been praying to find. She wanted to spend her life with a man who valued family and affection, who knew how to laugh and who wasn't afraid to show emotion.

Someone who liked dogs and kittens, for goodness' sake.

Best she stay focused on those things and not on how very nice it had felt to be in his arms.

Because only disappointment lay that way.

Chapter Nine

When Daisy turned the corner of the building, she was surprised to see Everett still there. How were they supposed to act toward each other now?

Kip's bark drew his attention, and she noted his cynically amused smile was back. It appeared he wasn't having any bothersome thoughts about their encounter. So why wasn't she more relieved?

She also noticed he'd been busy in her absence. "You set up my washtubs. Thanks so much, but you didn't have to do that."

As usual, he ignored her thanks. "I placed them here so they would be near the clotheslines but would drain away from them." He waved a hand. "But if you prefer to have them somewhere else, they're easy enough to move." His tone indicated he didn't think that would be particularly wise.

"No, no, this is perfect." Apparently, they were supposed to pretend that moment of awareness had never happened. Then again, perhaps for him it hadn't. Had she read more into it than had been there?

Of course she had. Why would a stuffy, undemonstrative man like Mr. Fulton want to embrace her?

He brushed his hands together, no doubt getting rid of some speck of dirt. "Is there anything else I can help you with?"

"Actually, I *could* use your help with one more thing."

He raised a brow as if he hadn't expected her to take him up on the offer. "And that is?"

She pointed toward the clotheslines he'd referred to earlier. "I checked those yesterday and they seem sturdy enough. But I'll need more line for all the clothes I'll have to hang. Miss Winters gave me some extra cord she had lying around, and I'd like to string it from that pole to the pecan tree, assuming it's long enough."

"Let's have a look."

She fetched the cord, and they determined by the simple expedient of stretching it between the two anchor points that it was indeed long enough. Everett retrieved a hammer and some nails from his place, and in a matter of minutes the task was accomplished.

Daisy stepped back and reviewed their work. It was easier than focusing on him. "Thank you for all your help. I hope it didn't put you out too much."

He merely shrugged. Didn't the man know how to accept a simple thank-you with grace?

Keep this businesslike, she reminded herself. "Would you mind bringing me whatever articles you want laundered? I've asked the others to do the same. I'm going to get everything marked and sorted tonight so I can start bright and early tomorrow."

"Marked?"

"That's one of the tips Miss Winters shared with me. It's how she keeps everything identified to a particular customer. She sews a couple of small identifying stitches on each piece—different colors or different patterns for each person. Once the clothes are ready for pick up, she removes the stitches."

He nodded approvingly. "Clever."

Of course he would appreciate such an efficient system.

Mr. Dawson came around the corner just then, toting a large sack. "Ah, here you are. No one answered my knock, and I thought I heard voices back here."

"Hello. Sorry—I should have been keeping an eye out."

"No need to apologize." He nodded a greeting to Everett. "Hope I'm not interrupting anything."

"Not at all," Daisy hastened to reassure him. "Mr. Fulton was just helping to get everything prepared for tomorrow."

"Was he, now?" Mr. Dawson gave his friend a speculative look.

But Everett's expression didn't change, and he didn't speak.

With a grin, the cheeky young man turned back to Daisy and lifted the sack. "Where would you like me to put this?"

"If that's your laundry, just set it there on the porch. I should have everything ready for you by Friday afternoon."

"That's fine. I can't tell you how glad I am to have someone fill in during Miss Winters's absence."

Everett interrupted them. "It appears you have no further need of my assistance, so if you'll excuse me, I have some things of my own to tend to."

"Of course. Thanks again for your help."

Later that evening, as Daisy sorted through and marked the mountain of laundry piled in her storeroom, she thought again about that moment when Everett, however unintentionally, had held her in his arms. Even if it hadn't meant anything to him, she *had* felt something. Was she developing feelings for Mr. Fulton, feelings beyond those of a neighbor and friend?

She wanted to find a good man to marry, of course, but that didn't mean she should fall for the first gentleman who showed her a bit of kindness. Besides, he obviously didn't have any feelings toward her other than those of an employer. It had been his own brand of neighborliness that she'd mistaken for something more.

Because, of course, he'd associated with debutantes and sophisticated ladies during his prior life in Philadelphia. She knew how poorly she compared to such women—her grandmother had always made that very clear.

She wouldn't apologize for who she was. She just aimed to find herself a man who would appreciate what qualities she did have.

And that obviously wasn't Mr. Fulton.

If that left her feeling disappointed, so be it. She'd get over it.

Everett rose bright and early the next morning. Truth to tell, he hadn't gotten a lot of sleep last night. He'd felt a restlessness, an edgy kind of disquiet that kept him from settling down. But today was a new day, and he intended to take control of his life again.

He looked out from his kitchen window and wasn't surprised to see Daisy already heating water over a fire. Two of her tubs were half-filled with water, and she was currently pouring the contents of a steaming kettle into the third. The sun was barely up. When had she found time to get so much done?

In that, at least, he intended to emulate her. Without her incessant humming and singing to distract him, he'd be able to focus and be much more productive than he'd been these past few days. Which was a good thing, because the paper was scheduled to go out tomorrow and he hadn't even started laying out the type. It wasn't like him to be this far behind schedule. Of course, that schedule was carefully structured to include time for unexpected delays, so he still had time to get the job done if nothing else interfered with his work.

But first he would bring Daisy a cup of coffee. That would keep him from being distracted by thoughts of her missing breakfast.

She greeted him cheerfully, apparently undaunted by the mountain of work before her. She thanked him profusely for the coffee, but as soon as she'd gulped it down, she turned right back to her work.

So, no idle chitchat today. Which was fine by him. He had work of his own to tackle.

Throughout the rest of the morning, Everett found himself missing the sound of Daisy's voice and her cheerful clattering about. Had her presence insinuated itself into his routine to the extent that he felt its absence?

He checked on her through the window a few times to see her variously working with the scrub board, stirring the clothes in steaming water or cranking it through the wringer.

At noon, he stepped outside and insisted she pause long enough to eat. They ate together on her porch in companionable silence. She shared bits of her sandwich with her mutt, but he didn't call her on it. And as soon as she finished eating, she thanked him and went back to work.

If he'd worried about there being any awkwardness between them after that little incident yesterday, his fears were put to rest. She was the same sunny, smiling Daisy as ever.

Daisy wiped her brow as she set the basket of wet laundry on the ground below the last bit of unoccupied clothesline. Not only was the day hot, but using kettles of boiling water had sapped a lot of her energy.

But the washing was done, and once she had this final load hung she'd be finished with this part of her job. Of course, it would soon be time to take down the earlier loads and begin ironing and folding.

It was going to be a long evening. Not that she was complaining. She'd prayed for other earning opportunities, and that's exactly what this was. With the money she earned from this job she'd be able to purchase some additional paint and lumber.

Mr. Fulton had done his part to make things easier on her. Not only had he helped her get everything set up yesterday, but he'd checked on her several times today—bringing her coffee this morning and a meal at noon. He'd even stepped out here a couple of times just to make certain she was okay. Not that he'd admitted such, but she knew.

Kip's bark alerted her that she was no longer alone. When she turned, sure enough, Everett was back.

"I see you're still at it," he said by way of greeting.

Dredging up enough energy to smile, she glanced at him over her shoulder. "Just finishing hanging up the last load." She placed the final pin on the final garment, then turned. "What time is it?"

"Just past four-thirty." He shook his head. "I still say it seems a hard way to earn a little extra money."

Why did he keep saying that? Was he trying to discourage her? "Nothing I can't manage for a few weeks."

"So now that you're done with the hanging, do you plan to take a break?"

"A very short one. The first load will be ready for me to take down in a little while. And that means I'll need to start sorting and folding." She tried not to let her tiredness show. "I can start on the ironing tonight, but I probably won't have time to finish." She gave him a hopeful look. "I can finish it while I'm cooking tomorrow, if that's okay with you."

"As long as you get your cooking done, whatever extra time you have is yours to use as you please."

"Do you mind if I set up my ironing board in your kitchen tomorrow, or would you prefer I keep all my business on my side of the wall?"

"As long as it's not in my way, do what works best for you."

"Thanks. Now, you might want to step back. When I pull the plugs on these tubs, the water will likely slosh over on anything in the vicinity."

She pulled the plug on the first tub, then moved to the second and did the same. Water came gushing out of both of them, flowing in wide, crooked rivulets toward the back of the lot.

The third tub, unlike the other two, sat flush on the ground. When she pulled the plug, not much happened.

"Looks like you'll need to bail the water out of that one," Everett observed.

"That'll take an awful long time." Not to mention more effort than she felt she could give at the moment. She could just kick herself for not thinking to elevate it a few inches off the ground before she'd filled it. Then she had an idea.

She looked to Everett hopefully. "Do you think, if I can lift the edge of this a few inches, you could shove a piece from the woodpile under it?"

Everett was affronted by her request. Did she think so little of him as to assume he'd stand by and let her lift that thing? He stepped forward, rolling up his sleeves. "I'll do the lifting, and you slide the wood underneath."

"Oh, but I don't want to—"

"Miss Johnson, I don't have all afternoon to argue this with you. Now, let's find some suitable pieces of wood, shall we?"

Once they found the appropriate pieces of wood, Everett moved to the large washtub and got his hands under the bottom edge to tilt it forward. Some of the water sloshed over the lip and, since he'd had the bad judgment to stand on the downhill side of the washtub, the already damp ground he stood on became soupy as the water flowed back his way. He winced as he thought about the damage to his shoes.

Daisy quickly shoved the first scrap of wood under the washtub. Grabbing the second piece, she quickly moved around him to slide it under the other side.

In her rush, however, she lost her footing and landed with a plop right on her backside. Her mutt ran up and managed to sideswipe Everett. Like a row of dominoes tumbling, Everett also lost his balance and pitched forward. Unfortunately, his left hand ended up partially under the tub, and to add insult to injury—literally—his body weight added more pressure to the already crushing weight.

The pain was immediate and excruciating. It was all he could do not to blister the air with his imprecations.

Through the haze of pain, he was aware of Daisy scrambling to her feet. "Oh, I'm so sorry. Your suit is—" Then she caught sight of his predicament and immediately grabbed hold of the tub and lifted it enough for him to pull his hand out.

The throbbing agony tripled. He gingerly tried to flex his fingers and was relieved when he was able to do so, albeit not without exacerbating the pain.

"That looks awful!" She stared at his hand, stopping just short of touching him. "Oh, this is all my fault."

It *felt* awful, too. But he refrained from saying so. "Please, just let me sit here a minute and catch my breath."

"Of course. You stay right where you are, and I'll go fetch Doc Pratt."

"Nonsense." He took another long breath, attempting to think clearly. He gingerly moved his hand again and tried to smother his groan. "I can tell it's not broken, so there's nothing the doctor can do for it that time won't accomplish, as well."

"Shouldn't we at least get him to look at it?" She pushed a damp wisp of hair from her forehead. "Please—it would make me feel better."

Why did she think that plea would convince him?

But somehow it did. "Very well. But you're not going to ask him to come here. It's my hand that's affected, not my feet." He stood. "I'm perfectly capable of walking to his office."

"Then I'm going with you."

Did she think he'd renege if she wasn't with him? But it wasn't worth arguing over.

"Give me a minute to change into something dry. And if you'd care to do the same—"

"Don't be such a fusspot." She sounded almost angry. "A little water and mud won't hurt anything, but not getting your hand looked at right away might."

Did she just call him a *fusspot?* And did she really expect the two of them to walk through town with mud-plastered backsides? He wasn't sure which offense he found the more egregious.

She swept out an arm with her finger pointed, like a general ordering his troops forward.

And without a word, he headed in the direction she'd pointed.

They walked the five blocks to Dr. Pratt's office in silence. Everett was acutely conscious of his undignified appearance, and of the curious looks they were getting, but Daisy seemed oblivious. He hadn't felt like such a spectacle since he'd been the subject of one of Reggie's unorthodox trials last summer.

Trying to block that out, and prove he was not a fusspot, but rather a confident and fastidious gentleman, Everett focused on keeping a steady pace and not jostling his hand.

When they finally reached the doctor's home, Daisy scurried ahead to knock on the door.

Dr. Pratt's wife let them in and immediately escorted them to the wing that served as the doctor's clinic. A moment later, Dr. Pratt was examining Everett's now painfully swollen hand.

In the end, he confirmed Everett's earlier prediction. "Nothing's broken, but it's going to hurt something terrible for the next few days. And I'm afraid you may lose the nail on your index finger." He rolled down his sleeves. "But I don't see any reason why those fingers won't heal cleanly, assuming you take good care of yourself."

"Thank you." Everett gave Daisy an I-told-you-so look, but refrained from saying it aloud.

"Is there anything Mr. Fulton can do to ease the pain in the meantime?"

The physician studied her a moment, then nodded. "I could provide him with laudanum if the pain gets to be more than he can bear, but—"

"That won't be necessary." Everett stood, ready to be done with this.

"In that case, I recommend some of this medicinal tea to help you sleep tonight." He pulled a small packet from a glass-fronted cabinet. "And it would be a good idea to wear a sling to keep that hand shielded from accidental bumps until it's less tender."

As they walked back toward their offices, Daisy patted his arm as if comforting a child. "I'll feed Kip, and then I'm going to fix you a nice dinner."

"There's no need for you to trouble yourself. I plan to eat some of the food left from earlier and then get back to work."

She eyed him uncertainly. "Do you really think you're up to that?"

Her concern was beginning to sound suspiciously like mollycoddling. That fusspot comment still rankled. Did she think he was some milksop who couldn't deal with a bit of pain? "Please don't concern yourself," he said stiffly. "Yes, I smashed some fingers on my left hand, but that's more of an inconvenience than a problem."

He saw the determination in her expression, but it was mixed with exhaustion. He wasn't about to let her add to her own workload over some misguided sense of guilt. "Don't you have some laundry-related chores to take care of?"

She nodded, but her expression remained mulish. "A little delay won't hurt anything."

By this time they'd reached her door, and he decided a firm tone was in order. "I appreciate your concern, but you take care of your business and let me take care of mine." With a short bow, he turned and entered his own office.

An hour later, Everett wasn't quite so sure of his ability to manage things, after all. His hand still throbbed painfully, and it seemed to have infected him with an unaccustomed clumsiness. It turned out typesetting was considerably more difficult to do one-handed than he'd imagined it would be.

He bumped his injured hand, and his reaction resulted in type scattered across the floor. The echoes of his frustrated growl still hung in the air when his door opened.

Daisy stood there, hesitating on his threshold, a small basket on her arm. What did she want now? "Can I do something for you?"

She stepped farther into the room, leaving the door open behind her. "I've done all I plan to do with the laundry tonight. I thought I'd check in to see how you were faring."

"I'm fine."

Her quickly suppressed wince let him know his frustration had come through in his voice. A low growl from the doorway drew his gaze. Her dog sat there, watching him balefully. Just what he needed right now—an edgy dog and an oversolicitous woman.

He turned back to Daisy and moderated his tone. "I'm doing all right, but I *am* busy right now."

She raised the basket. "I brought some willow-bark tea—it's my own special recipe. And I have an ointment that'll help deaden some of the pain." Her smile and tone had an uncertain quality to them, as if she expected to be turned away. "I know you don't like to be fussed over, but there's no point suffering any more than necessary."

Everett heaved a mental sigh. "I suppose a spot of tea would be nice about now."

He was rewarded with a generous smile as she hurried over and unpacked her basket at his desk.

He joined her there and watched as she quickly unscrewed the lid on a mason jar and poured its contents into a cup. "Here you go," she said, offering it to him. "One cup of my special medicinal tea."

He took a tentative sip and was surprised by the flavor. It had a slightly metallic tang to it, but there were notes of vanilla and some spice that was almost pleasant.

As she reached for the other item in her basket, she frowned at him. "I thought the doc told you to wear a sling."

"I think it was more a suggestion than a directive."

He could tell she wasn't pleased with his response, but to his surprise, she let it go and pulled out a small pot. "If you'll allow me, I'd like to massage this on your injured hand."

He looked at her skeptically, not sure he wanted anyone touching his still-tender digits.

"I promise I'll take it easy," she said. "But this really will help ease the pain." She dipped a flat wooden stick into the pot and scooped up the waxy-looking concoction. Then she extended her left hand expectantly, palm up.

He gingerly placed his swollen, painfully bruised hand in her palm.

She ever so gently began to spread the ointment onto his bruised skin. Her motions were deft, gentle, butterfly soft. The palm under his hand was warm and supportive.

In a matter of seconds, he began to feel a cooling sensation wherever the ointment touched, and then a blessed numbness.

She finally looked up, meeting his gaze. "How's that?"

He found himself captured by the way the soft light brought out the bronze glints in her coffee-colored eyes. "Much better, thank you."

With a pleased nod, she turned to replace the lid on her ointment pot.

He swallowed, then tried to hide his momentary discomfiture with a lighter tone. "You should go into the apothecary business rather than opening a restaurant."

She smiled but shook her head. "I enjoy cooking much more. Besides, Turnabout already has an apothecary."

She frowned as she took in the sight of the scattered type. "You're working on getting the paper ready to print."

"Of course. Tomorrow *is* Friday."

"But your hand is injured. Can't you delay the newspaper a day or so? I'm sure folks will understand when they hear what happened."

That just showed how little she understood him. "That's not necessary. I might be slower and clumsier than normal, but I'll manage. I haven't missed a deadline since I printed the first *Turnabout Gazette,* and I see no reason to start now." It was a point of pride with him to get his paper out on time, every time.

Then he grimaced. "This is no more than what I deserve for getting off schedule. I should have had most of this set by noon instead of leaving it until this evening." He wouldn't look too closely at why that had happened.

She crossed her arms in front of her chest. "If you're so set on this, then I'm going to assist you."

Everett noticed the dark circles under her eyes and the hint of weariness in the set of her shoulders. She'd had an exhausting day—she probably hadn't rested at all since they'd returned from Dr. Pratt's office. She needed to get some sleep, not help him with his work.

Besides, just how much help could an untrained female be? "I told you, I don't hold you responsible for what happened."

"But *I* do." She firmly tucked a tendril behind her ear. "I know I can't do the job as well as you, but I can be your hands. You stand next to me and tell me what needs doing, and I'll get it done."

Everett thought about all he had left to accomplish before morning and was sorely tempted. But he didn't want to take advantage of her. "I'll be working quite late."

That didn't appear to weaken her resolve. "All the more reason I should help—maybe together we can shave a few hours off that time. Besides, I've stayed up through the night before and probably will again."

Stubborn female. But all this arguing was wasting time.

He gave a short nod. "Very well. Let's see if we can make this work." He moved to one of the wall sconces. "But first we should brighten this room up." Dusk had fallen, and shadows were creeping into the room. He also opened the outer door wider and made certain the shades on the storefront windows were up. She could call him a fusspot if she liked, but he planned to take every precaution that no hint of impropriety was attached to Daisy's presence here.

Daisy moved to the other wall and lit the sconces there.

Once the room was suitably illuminated and all hint of privacy removed, Everett showed her the articles that needed to be prepped and then walked her through the process. Then he painstakingly, letter by letter, instructed her on where to place the type and which type to use.

Daisy was surprisingly dexterous and took direction well. It was equally surprising that it didn't take much longer than it usually did when he worked alone. But by the time they were done, the day's events had taken their toll on both of them. Exhaustion had turned Daisy's natural cheery outlook into a mild case of giddiness.

And he was tired enough to find it amusing.

When the last page was finally printed and placed on the drying rack, Daisy turned and stretched.

"We did it," she said, as if it had been a monumental accomplishment. Then she giggled and did a triumphant little dance step. Unfortunately, she bumped into a nearby file cabinet as she did so.

She continued giggling as Everett reached out to steady her, and suddenly she was in his embrace again. Her giggling abruptly stopped as her eyes widened in surprise, and something else. Was his reaction equally telling? Because she felt every bit as good in his arms today as she had yesterday.

Everett closed his eyes to steady himself, but that was

a mistake. His senses were immediately flooded with an awareness of her scent, her breathing, her warmth—of *her*.

After what seemed ages, but was probably only a heartbeat or two of time, they separated. There was no sign left of her giddiness, and bright spots of red stained her cheeks.

"I'm so sorry." She didn't quite meet his gaze. "I don't know what—"

"No need to apologize. We've both had a long day." Everett was glad his tone held steady. He cast a quick look at the open doorway and was relieved to see that, except for her dog, the sidewalk was deserted. It had been an accidental and totally innocent embrace, but others might not view it that way.

He put more distance between them, moving to the type cabinet. "Thank you for your help tonight, but I think I can finish the rest on my own."

"Yes, of course." She took a deep breath and looked around, as if seeking an answer from his furnishings. Then she straightened and turned an over-bright smile on him. "I'll take my leave, then."

"Of course. Good evening, and it'll be okay if you're a little late tomorrow."

She crossed to the door, her shoes beating a rapid tattoo across the floor. Out on the sidewalk, she gave her dog a quick rub. "Come on, Kip. Time to go home."

Everett followed slowly, watching to see she made it safely inside her place.

She never so much as glanced back.

Everett closed his door and then lowered the shades and turned out the lights. What was wrong with him? He wasn't interested in her in that way, yet this was the second time in as many days that he'd found himself holding her in his arms. And enjoying every minute of it.

They'd both been exhausted tonight, he'd still been in

some pain and neither was thinking clearly. It had been nothing more than that.

Still, the memory of how right she'd felt in his arms lingered with him long after he'd climbed the stairs.

Daisy stared at the ceiling as she lay in bed. What had come over her? If she was being honest with herself, that embrace hadn't been totally accidental, at least not on her part. She'd never hugged a man before—well, except for her father and that didn't count. Yet now she'd found herself in Everett's arms twice in as many days. And she was certain, just for a minute, that stuffy ole Everett had hugged her right back.

How was she going to face him tomorrow? She rolled over on her side. The trouble was, she couldn't find it in her heart to regret either incident. There had been a curious mix of strength and gentleness in his embrace, as if he wanted to both cherish and protect her. It had been a foreign and altogether wonderful feeling.

But she knew it was wrong.

Dear Lord, I'm not sure what's come over me, and I need Your help to be strong. I know You have a man in mind for me, and it can't be Everett because we're so different. I'm truly willing to wait for the right man, and I know it will happen in Your timing. I never thought of myself as fickle before, but maybe I am and that's what You're trying to show me—that it's something in me I need to work on.

She rolled over once again, and Kip let out a small whine from his spot beside her bed.

"Sorry, boy, I'll try to settle down." Kip was right. There weren't many hours left before sunup—she needed to stop this fretting and get some sleep.

She had a feeling she'd need all her wits about her tomorrow.

Chapter Ten

As usual, on paper delivery day, Everett rose before dawn. Not that he'd have gotten much sleep, anyway. This morning, however, with his hand still throbbing, he had to figure out an alternative to making the deliveries to the local merchants. He solved that problem by paying Jack and Ira a little extra to make those deliveries for him in addition to the household deliveries they normally made.

When Daisy breezed into his office, he braced himself for a bit of awkwardness, but it turned out to be an unnecessary precaution. She gave him a quick "good morning," then set a small jar on his desk. "Here's more of that ointment I used last night," she said. Then she headed upstairs without stopping for her usual chitchat.

Had her smile been a bit more forced than normal? Or was that only his imagination? He was relieved, naturally, that she'd chosen to act as if nothing had happened—wasn't he?

As he applied the ointment, he remembered how good it had felt when Daisy did that for him. Then he grimaced—he was turning into a blasted mooncalf.

He'd better focus on his work before he lost all sense of self-respect.

But by midmorning he was so off his game that he actually welcomed the distraction when Chance walked in. The greeting died on his lips, however, when he recognized the young girl accompanying him.

"Abigail!" What was his sister doing here? More important, how in the world had she gotten here?

"Hello, Everett. I've come to visit," she said unnecessarily.

That was all she had to say for herself? "Abigail Blythe Fulton! What—how—" He was having trouble deciding whether to start with questions or a severe scolding.

"I came in on the train, and your friend Mr. Dawson offered to show me to your office." She gave Chance a dazzling smile.

Chance's smile had an I'm-really-enjoying-this edge to it. "I met the train this morning because I was expecting some parts I'd ordered. They didn't arrive, but I found this young lady there, asking Zeke where your place was. When I found out she was your sister, I thought I should escort her here myself."

Did that mean she'd traveled completely unaccompanied? Everett's blood froze at the thought of what could have happened to her. He tore his eyes away from his sister long enough to nod Chance's way. "Thank you."

"You're welcome. Now, I'll leave you two to your visit." Chance tipped his hat toward Abigail. "Nice meeting you, Miss Abigail."

Abigail gave him a bright smile. "And you, as well, Mr. Dawson. You've been most kind, just like a real cowboy."

"Oh, for goodness' sake, Abigail, surely you're not still infatuated with those silly romantic notions. Not every man in Texas is a cowboy. In fact, Chance here came west with me from Philadelphia."

Abigail's lips formed a pout. "Aren't you glad to see me, even a little bit?"

Everett huffed in exasperation. "*Of course* I'm happy to see you, but that's entirely beside the point. How did you get here?"

Abigail finally had the grace to look abashed, but she rallied quickly. "By train, of course."

"Don't be impertinent."

She crossed the room to stand directly before him, hands clasped together in front of her. "Please don't be cross. After all, I made it here safe and sound, and it was *such* a grand adventure. I could almost imagine I was an adventuress, like Nellie Bly."

"That imagination of yours is going to get you into serious trouble someday, young lady." Then he pulled her to him in a hug, a fierce longing to protect her from all the ugliness in the world overtaking him. A moment later he set her away, keeping his uninjured hand on her shoulder. "Miss Haversham will be hearing from me. I don't understand how she could have let you travel all this way on your own. I pay her dearly to make certain you're well looked after." Had it been just a few days ago that he'd congratulated himself that Abigail would never be faced with a solo journey the way Daisy had?

"Don't blame Miss Haversham." Abigail's smile faltered, and she dropped her gaze. "I'm afraid I misled her."

Not surprising. "What did you do?"

She removed her bonnet, still not quite meeting his gaze. "I led her to believe you sent for me and that I needed to leave immediately."

His exasperation once more overtook his concern. "And she believed you?"

Abigail nibbled at her lower lip a moment. "The official-looking telegram I sent her was quite convincing," she finally said in a small voice.

This was too much, even for his impulsive little sister. He dropped his hand. "Abigail! Such actions are not only dishonest, they're rash and unthinking."

"I know." Abigail's expression turned to something very like a childish pout. "It was wrong, and I'm truly sorry. But it's the only way I could get away." She met his gaze full-on. "And I *had* to get away from that stifling place."

"Thinking that the ends justify the means is a slippery slope you don't want to start down, Abigail." He ran his right hand through his hair. "Regardless of whatever tales you spun for her, however, it's still unconscionable that Miss Haversham let you travel alone."

"Actually, I wasn't alone when I departed. Miss Haversham hired a very stern woman, one even you would approve of, to accompany me. But partway into our journey, the poor woman took ill. She got off the train at one of the stops in Illinois, and I decided to continue on without her."

"You decided—" Everett's blood ran cold at the idea of his overly trusting little sister traveling such a distance on a train full of who knows what kind of people, entirely alone and unprotected. "That was quite reckless. Do you have *any* idea what could have happened to you, a young girl traveling alone?"

"But my escort *couldn't* travel, and it wouldn't have been any better for me to travel back to Boston alone than to go forward. And nothing *did* happen, so all is well." She clasped her hands, her eyes pleading with him to understand. "Oh, Everett, I know lying to Miss Haversham was wrong and I promise to write her a very pretty and penitent letter of apology, and if you want to put me on a strict diet of bread and water for a month I won't complain. But truly, I could not stand to be in that place any longer. And you made Turnabout sound so wonderful in your letters. You know I've always dreamed of one day traveling to Texas."

Turnabout—wonderful? How had she possibly gotten that from his letters? "Yes, you will most assuredly write that letter of apology, a letter that you will hand deliver when you return to the school on tomorrow's train."

Abigail's whole expression crumpled. "You *can't* send me back so soon. I've only just arrived."

He refused to let himself be moved by her plea. "You are mistaken. I can, and I will."

"You don't understand. The telegram I gave Miss Haversham said I wouldn't be returning—at all. She's having all of my things packed and sent here."

Where had his sister learned such devious behavior? "That's quickly remedied. I'll send her a telegram today informing her that there's been a mistake."

Her expression turned mutinous. "If you send me back, I'll run away again."

Everett clenched his jaw in frustration. The idea of his sister pulling this dangerous stunt yet again was enough to turn his hair gray. He had to find a way to convince her to see reason. "Abigail, you only have another year and a half of school left." By that time, he would have moved someplace with more polish and refinement than Turnabout. "Once you're through with your schooling, of course you can live with me."

"A year and a half is *forever*." She moaned. "Please, don't make me go back, not right away. I promise I won't get in your way. I'll even be a help. You'll see. I can keep your place neat and clean, and do your laundry and cooking. I can even help here in the office if you like. I—"

"I didn't send you to boarding school all these years so you could turn into a household drudge."

"Then why *did* you send me to that place? It certainly wasn't to make me happy."

That gave him pause. Had she truly been so unhappy at Miss Haversham's? He quickly dismissed that thought—she was just being melodramatic. "I sent you there to make certain you received a good education and that you were surrounded by persons of breeding and good character." He absently rubbed his chin, then winced as his injured digits protested.

"What's wrong?" She saw his injury, and her demeanor immediately changed to one of concern. "Oh, my goodness, what did you do to your hand?"

He waved aside her concerns. "I smashed it yesterday. It'll be fine."

"Well, it doesn't look fine." She stepped closer and gingerly touched the back of his hand. "In fact, it looks awful. Did you have a doctor look at it?"

"I did. And he agreed with me that it'll be good as new given time." Sensing her distress, he moderated his tone. "It looks worse than it is."

"But it must be terribly painful." She straightened. "I'm more pleased than ever that I'm here. I can take care of you."

"I've been managing fine, thank you."

She tilted up her chin. "You *do* need someone to look after you."

"I don't—"

She held up a hand and cocked her head toward the stairs. "What's that?"

It took him a moment to realize she was talking about Daisy's singing.

Before he could explain, she gave him a wide-eyed look. "Everett, do you have a *woman* upstairs?"

Why did he suddenly feel self-conscious? "That's Miss

Johnson, my cook. And don't go changing the subject. We were discussing your return to Boston."

Abigail ignored the last part of his statement. "A cook. Why didn't you mention this Miss Johnson in your letters?"

"Because it's a recent development. Now, as I was saying—"

But Abigail was no longer paying attention.

"I want to meet her." Without waiting for permission, she headed for the stairs. "Besides, I want to see what the rest of your place looks like. You can continue your scolding later."

With a growl of frustration, Everett followed his too-impulsive-for-her-own-good sister upstairs. As he did so, it occurred to him to worry about what the meeting of these two impulsive and sometimes reckless females would result in.

Daisy, working at the ironing board, tensed as she heard that telltale squeak of the stairs. She took a deep breath and steeled herself to face Everett for the first time since she'd headed upstairs this morning. But the person who appeared wasn't Everett, but a slender, well-dressed young lady with ginger-brown hair and sparkling eyes.

"Hello," the young lady called out. "I'm Abigail, Everett's sister. And you must be Miss Johnson."

Everett's *sister?* When had she arrived? And why hadn't she been told the girl was coming? Surely this wasn't something that would have just slipped his mind.

She spied Everett just behind his sister, and he looked none too happy. What was going on?

Remembering her manners, Daisy set down the iron and wiped her hands on her apron. "Glad to meet you, Abigail."

She closed the distance between them. "And yes, I'm Daisy Johnson, your brother's cook and next-door neighbor."

"I'm so pleased to meet you." The girl's smile was infectious. "And also very glad to know Everett no longer has to subsist on his own cooking."

Daisy grinned. "Your brother didn't tell me you were expected, or I would have cooked something special." She cut Everett an accusing look, then wondered if he'd intended to tell her before their little encounter last night. "But don't you worry," she said, shaking off those uncomfortable thoughts. "The food might not be special but it'll be plentiful enough."

Abigail brushed at her skirt. "Don't blame Everett. My visit was a surprise."

"A surprise." Daisy cast another glance Everett's way and realized why he looked so grim. "I see. Well, I'm sure it was a lovely surprise."

Kip, lying in the doorway, let out a couple of attention-getting yips.

Abigail immediately spun toward the sound.

"That's just Kip," Daisy said. "He's probably wanting an introduction." Did Everett's sister share his dislike for dogs? "Don't worry, though," she added quickly. "Kip stays over on my side of the wall, just like your brother asked."

Abigail glanced up at her brother. "You banished this sweet animal from your home?" She shook her head sadly. "I shouldn't be surprised." Then she turned to Daisy. "Unlike Everett, I love dogs. I always wanted one of my own, but they aren't allowed at Miss Haversham's. Do you mind if I pet him?"

"Not at all. And he loves it when you scratch him behind the ears."

Abigail stooped down in front of Kip and ruffled his

fur. "Aren't you just the handsomest animal?" Then she glanced back, her expression one of childish delight. "Look, Everett, he has one blue eye and one brown eye."

"I'm aware."

The fact that he'd noticed surprised Daisy. But his dry tone, indicating he didn't find it particularly endearing, did not.

"Oh, that must be your place." Abigail was looking past Kip into the room beyond.

"It is." What did the girl think about the sparse, make-shift furnishings?

But Abigail went back to cooing over Kip, and Daisy cut a questioning glance Everett's way.

His expression had a long-suffering look. "I'm sorry if having an extra person to cook for complicates things for you. As Abigail stated, I wasn't aware she was coming until she showed up on my doorstep."

She could tell he wasn't pleased by that occurrence. "But now that she's here, surely you can look on it as a nice surprise."

"Nice is not the word I'd use. Abigail ran away from school and is refusing to go back."

Ouch. That couldn't be easy to swallow for a man who liked to be in control of everything. "Don't worry about it putting me out. It's just as easy to cook for three as two. You just enjoy your visit together, for however long it lasts. If you two want to eat alone, I can take my portion to my place and eat there." In fact, it might be better all the way around if she did.

"That won't be necessary." He cast an exasperated look his sister's way. "Besides, if I'm alone with Abigail any time soon I might end up changing my mind about letting her stay for now."

As if suddenly aware he'd said more than he intended,

Everett's expression closed off. He cleared his throat and turned to his sister. "Come on, Abigail. Let me show you where you can sleep while you're here."

The girl immediately popped up. "Whatever accommodations are available will be fine."

"That's a good thing," he said as they crossed the sitting room, "because I use the spare bedchamber for storing odds and ends. You're lucky the place came with a small bed in there."

Daisy knew him well enough now to read the affection beneath his dry tone. Regardless of how he felt about *how* his sister had traveled, he was undeniably glad to see her.

Daisy moved to the stove to check on the stew. She didn't have a good read on Abigail yet. At first glance, she could very well be the spoiled little socialite Daisy had expected. But there was a spark of something—innocence, playfulness, vulnerability—that told her Abigail might have more to her.

Had she really run off and traveled here on her own? Daisy could understand Everett's concern. So many things might have gone terribly wrong.

A moment later, Everett returned to the kitchen, alone. "Abigail is settling in," he explained. Then he cleared his throat. "I apologize again for my sister's unexpected arrival. She's always tended to act impulsively, but this is the first time she's acted with such blatant disregard for her safety."

Was he actually worried how she was taking this? "There's no need to apologize to me for your sister."

"Abigail is bright, good-hearted and generous. She's also overly trusting, impulsive and more of a child than she will admit."

Understanding dawned. He wanted to make certain she

didn't take too dim a view of his sister. "There are worse faults to have," she said with a smile.

He didn't return her smile. "If her welfare was your responsibility, you might not think so."

"I can see how her escapade would shake you up. But she's safely here now, so you should make the most of the chance to visit with her."

His irritation seemed to deepen. "It did not *shake me up.* I'm merely concerned for her safety. Undertaking such a journey, without letting anyone know what she was about, was foolhardy and reckless. It only proves how much of a child she still is."

Before Daisy could respond, the downstairs bell sounded, indicating someone had stopped by the office. Everett tugged at his cuff. "Don't let Abigail get in your way. If she becomes a bother, send her down to me."

Daisy returned to her ironing, pondering the pointed look Everett had given her before he left the room. She supposed, on the surface, her trip here bore some similarities to Abigail's. She'd slipped away, traveling on her own to a destination where she wasn't expected.

But there were important differences. She was much older than Abigail. Her trip had been shorter. And she'd covered familiar ground, so she knew what she'd be facing. So there'd been nothing foolhardy or reckless about her journey.

"Is he gone yet?"

Daisy looked up to see Abigail peeking out of her room.

"If you're speaking of your brother," she answered dryly, "he's downstairs."

"Good." Abigail strode into the kitchen with a let's-be-friends smile. "It's probably best if I give him a little time to get used to my being here before we encounter each other again."

Daisy held her gaze. "He's only looking out for you, you know."

"Oh, I know." Abigail waved a hand. "But I'm fifteen now, and he still treats me like I'm six."

"You could be sixty, and you'd still be his little sister."

The girl traced a pattern on the table. "I thought he'd be just a little glad to see me."

Daisy took pity on the forlorn-looking girl. "He is. Just give him time to get over the fright you gave him." Then she tried for a cheerier subject. "Did you really travel all the way here from Boston by yourself?"

Abigail preened a bit. "I did. And it was the grandest adventure. I know Everett won't ever look at it that way, but I've never done anything so frightening and so exhilarating in my life."

Daisy didn't know whether to consider Everett's sister brave or henwitted—perhaps she was a little of both.

Abigail sat at the table and studied Daisy. "Tell me about yourself. How long have you been working for my brother?"

What was Abigail thinking? "I moved to town about ten days ago. Your brother has been kind enough to help me get settled and find work."

"Kind—Everett?"

Daisy nodded. "I think of your brother as a very kind man, don't you?"

"Oh, yes, Everett has a very big heart. But he usually hides it well. I'm just surprised you saw it."

Daisy focused on her ironing. "Like I said, he's been good to me."

"Do you know what happened to his hand? It looks really bad."

Daisy's stomach clenched. "That was my fault."

Abigail's brow furrowed. "What happened?"

Would Everett's sister look at her differently when she heard her confession? "He was helping me empty a heavy laundry tub yesterday when Kip tripped him up, and he ended up falling in the mud and dropping the thing on his hand."

The girl's eyes rounded. "Oh, my. I'm sure that was a sight to see."

Daisy blinked. That wasn't at all the reaction she'd expected. "It wasn't funny—he was seriously injured."

"You're right, nothing funny about it at all." But the twinkle in Abigail's eyes told a different story. "He landed in the mud, you say?"

Daisy tried to keep a straight face. "Yes. And I marched him through town to the doc's office without letting him change."

Skepticism mixed with the amusement in Abigail's expression. "My *very* fastidious brother did that without a fuss?"

This time she didn't attempt to hide the grin. "I never said he didn't fuss."

"Oh, I wish I'd been here to see that." She gave Daisy an appreciative smile. "My brother may have finally met his match."

Daisy's treacherous mind went immediately to thoughts of the two embraces they'd shared, and she barely managed to make a noncommittal response.

Luckily, Abigail changed the subject. "If you just moved here, where were you before?"

It seemed Abigail had her brother's reporter instincts. "I traveled around a lot with my father. He's a peddler."

"A peddler—how exciting. So my little jaunt here would have been nothing to you."

Another unexpected reaction. "Oh, I wouldn't say that. We traveled a lot, but didn't cover nearly the territory you did on your trip. And I usually didn't do it alone." No point mentioning her little three-day walk to get here.

"Still, you must have seen some interesting sights in your travels. Up until now, I haven't spent much time outside of Boston."

"Well, you've certainly made up for it now."

"I have, haven't I? Now if I can just convince Everett to let me stay."

Daisy silently wished the girl good luck with that. She had a feeling having Abigail here would be good for Everett, and for Abigail, as well.

She also had a selfish reason to be glad Abigail was here. Because if it accomplished nothing else, Abigail's presence would give her and Everett something to focus on besides the awkward aftermath of last night's encounter.

Chapter Eleven

Saturday morning, Abigail's belongings arrived from Boston. It took the delivery boy over a dozen trips up and down the stairs to get all of her trunks and crates transported to the sitting room.

After he'd paid the boy and sent him on his way, Everett headed upstairs to see how his sister was faring with sorting and stowing her things. He could hear her and Daisy before he ever topped the stairs.

"That sure is a mighty fine collection of books," Daisy said.

"Oh, that's nothing," Abigail replied. "Everett's collection is even more impressive."

"In both quantity *and* quality," he said dryly as he topped the stairs. Daisy was in the kitchen peeling carrots while Abigail sat on the floor of the sitting room, surrounded by her newly arrived belongings. He winced when he saw her belongings cluttering every piece of furniture and most of the available floor space.

Abigail gave him a smile. "There you are. And speaking of books, where *are* yours? Don't tell me you left them behind when you moved here."

That was something he and his sister had in common:

their love of books. "Of course not. Some are in my room and the rest are in crates down in the storeroom. I just haven't gotten around to unpacking them."

"Why ever not? You've been here almost a year now."

Everett raised a brow. "Contrary to what you may think, little sister, setting up a newspaper from scratch is a lot of work, regardless of how small the town or the paper."

He moderated his tone. "Besides, I'm hoping to have a new job somewhere else soon, so I didn't see the point in unpacking more than what I needed to live."

Abigail frowned up at him. "Why would you want to do that? Move, I mean. Don't you like it here?"

He tried to strike a diplomatic tone. "It's fine for what it is—a small country town. But the big city is where we belong." He was aware of Daisy listening, and wondered what she made of that. Then he became irritated with himself for caring.

Abigail gave his arm a mock punch, bringing his thoughts back to the conversation at hand. "Don't be such a snob. Besides, if that's the way you feel, why did you come here in the first place?"

Again he had to choose his words carefully. "As I said at the time, my former editor and I had a parting of the ways, and I was ready to move on to something new. When I heard about the opportunity to open a newspaper here, that seemed like the perfect *temporary* solution."

All of which was true. Hopefully, she'd never learn the rest of the story. "It's been a good experience—it's allowed me to learn all the inner workings of the newspaper business. But I never intended for this to be a permanent stop. I'm first and foremost a reporter, and I need to be in a big city where things are happening to report on and where there is a staff of more than one person to get the paper out."

"I'm sure there are lots of things happening here."

"You know what I mean, Abigail." He glanced toward Daisy and cleared his throat. "Now, I've made up my mind about this and it's not up for discussion. So let's change the subject, shall we?"

Abigail shrugged and went back to digging through her trunks.

Luckily, Daisy spoke up. "I still say that's a wealth of books. Between the two of you, you could open your own library. The only time I've seen that many books in one place was at my grandmother's house."

Everett heard that strange note in her voice that crept in whenever she mentioned her grandmother. He'd be very interested in learning the story behind that. Strictly from a reporter's perspective, of course.

"That was one thing I *did* enjoy about my time in New Orleans," Daisy said wistfully. "Access to all those books. I haven't had many chances since then to do much reading."

She was well-read? Everett wasn't sure why that surprised him. Some of his assumptions about her shifted, realigned. He'd seen glimpses of intelligence in her, of course—intelligence she downplayed with her rustic, straightforward way of speaking.

"You're more than welcome to look through my books," Abigail offered. "You can borrow any that strike your fancy."

Daisy's face lit up, making Everett regret he hadn't been the one to make the offer.

"Why, thank you," she said. "I don't have much free time right now, but as soon as I get my place set to rights I may take you up on that offer."

Everett stared pointedly at his sister. "That's another thing you'll not find in Turnabout. There are none of the civilized entertainments you're accustomed to—no librar-

ies or bookstores, no theater or opera, not even a mani-
cured park or conservatory."

His sister's smile wavered a moment, then she rallied.
"There are several books I've been intending to reread.
And I'm certain I can treat myself occasionally by ordering new titles from a catalog. As for the rest, there must
be other amusements the locals indulge in, and I'm willing to experience new things."

"I understand they have town dances every few months,"
Daisy said, "and sometimes picnics on the ground after
church services."

Abigail perked up immediately. "Oh, that sounds like
fun! I do love picnics."

Everett shot Daisy a warning look. He was trying to
give Abigail reasons to leave, not stay. "At the moment,
you need to decide where you're going to store your things.
It all needs to fit in your room or in the storeroom—and I
warn you, I won't have you overcluttering my storeroom.
What doesn't fit will need to be gotten rid of." He gave
her a pointed look. "Unless, of course, we ship most of it
back to Miss Haversham's to await your return."

Abigail lifted her chin. "That won't be necessary. In
fact, I'm certain there are several of these items that I'll
no longer require in my new life here."

How could he make his sister see that returning to
school was the right thing to do? She obviously wasn't
going to give any of his arguments serious consideration.

Could he recruit Daisy's help? Better question—should
he?

Daisy placed the rolls on the table, then joined Everett
and his sister. Yesterday, with Abigail sitting down to lunch
with them, she had thought Everett would want to offer the
blessing, but he had again deferred to her. So today, with

only a quick glance his way for confirmation, she bowed her head and said, "Let us pray."

Once the amens were said and the bowls started around, Abigail cleared her throat and glanced at Everett. "I've been thinking about what you said earlier—about there being no source for books here. I'd imagine there are a number of people who would make use of a library if one were available."

Everett shrugged. "Perhaps. But the point is moot. I don't see that happening in the foreseeable future. So there's no point getting your hopes up."

She gave him a sideways look. "Maybe we can do something to change that."

Everett eyed her suspiciously. "What do you mean?"

"What if I opened a circulating library myself?"

Daisy got caught up in Abigail's proposal. "What a wonderful idea. It perfectly complements your brother's newspaper business. And you're right—I can't imagine folks not wanting to take advantage of such a wonderful opportunity."

"Nonsense." If one didn't notice the sternness in Everett's tone, his expression left no room for doubt. "You don't know the first thing about managing such an operation."

"Oh, but I do." Abigail didn't seem intimidated by her brother's lack of enthusiasm. "I used part of the allowance you sent me to join a circulating library near school, and I became good friends with Miss Teel, the librarian." She leaned forward. "I also spent a lot of time in the school library. Miss Abernathy, the teacher who managed the library, allowed me to help her in exchange for my getting first look at any new books that came in. So you see, I do have experience."

Daisy could tell Everett wasn't convinced, but she found

the idea of having access to all those books downright exciting.

"Assuming you could manage such an undertaking," Everett said, "where do you propose to set up this library? There's not much room downstairs, and I refuse to have folks trooping up and down the stairs to our living quarters."

Abigail gave him a breezy smile. "It wouldn't take up much room. I could start with just a couple of bookshelves along one wall, and a drawer in one of your file cabinets to keep all the records."

He shook his head. "I don't think—"

Daisy couldn't hold her tongue any longer. "That doesn't sound like much space at all. If your brother doesn't have room for it, you can use my place. After all, I plan to be one of your first customers."

Abigail rewarded her with a dazzling smile. "Do you mean it? I promise I won't take up too much space, and you can take a portion of my earnings for rent payment."

Daisy waved that offer aside. "Don't worry about that. In fact, the more I think on it, the more it seems good business sense on my part. It'll get folks used to coming in and out of my place so that when I'm ready to open my restaurant, they'll already be familiar with it."

She became aware that Everett was glowering at her, but couldn't find it in herself to be sorry. She liked Abigail's idea, as well as her enthusiasm for it, and could see no harm in it. She gave him a sideways glance, then focused back on Abigail. "Once your brother gets that sour look off his face, you might even be able to charm him into giving you an advertisement in his newspaper."

Abigail laughed delightedly, then turned to her brother. "You need to make certain you hold on to her."

Daisy's cheeks warmed as Abigail's words reminded her of those two embraces earlier in the week.

She risked a quick glance Everett's way. His expression didn't reflect anything but irritation with his sister.

That was a good thing. Wasn't it?

As Everett went downstairs, the lunchtime conversation played back in his head. He had to admit, Abigail's idea of a lending library had merit. It was resourceful, ingenious and enterprising all at the same time. He almost hated not to give her the approving go-ahead she so obviously wanted. But it wasn't a good idea to allow her to set down any sort of roots or strong ties here in Turnabout—not if he ever hoped to convince her to return to Miss Haversham's school. Which he fully intended to do.

He'd have to have a word with Daisy. She'd obviously meant well when she offered Abigail the use of her place, but she needed to learn to stay out of anything involving his sister. She wasn't the best example of biddable and ladylike behavior for his sister to follow.

And what was this about his "sour look?" Is that how Daisy and Abigail saw him? He took exception to that.

They should understand his strictures were motivated by a keen sense of purpose and responsibility. He was every bit as capable of enjoying life as the next man. He was just more circumspect in how he handled it.

Unbidden, Abigail's artless comment about making certain he held on to Daisy popped into his thoughts. It conjured up images of him literally holding on to her. He and Daisy hadn't spoken of it, of course. That would have given it more importance than it merited. But that didn't mean he hadn't thought about it, thought about it much more than he should have. And thought about how it would have felt to follow through and kiss her.

What about Daisy? Did she think about it at all? If so, in what light?

"So what's put that perplexed expression on your face?"

Everett looked up to see Adam staring at him, an amused smile playing on his lips.

How long had he been standing there?

Everett assumed his most dignified demeanor. "I wasn't expecting you to come by since it's Saturday. Are you so eager to answer my last move?"

Adam's expression indicated he knew Everett had avoided answering his question. "I just wanted to let you know that we won't be having our usual luncheon gathering after services tomorrow. Reggie's got it in her head to take a quick trip out to the cabin while she's still up to the trip. We're heading out in an hour or so."

Everett didn't understand what Reggie found so appealing about that rustic cabin of hers way out in the back of beyond. He and the others who'd traveled here from Philadelphia had spent their first night there upon their arrival in Turnabout. It was not an experience he cared to repeat.

More to the point, Reggie was less than two months from her confinement date. "Is that wise?"

"I'm not keen on it, but you know how Reggie can be when she sets her mind on something. I spoke to Dr. Pratt, and he's given the go-ahead. And of course, we'll have Mrs. Peavy with us."

Everett certainly intended to be firmer with his own wife when the time came. But this matter was really none of his business. "I wish you a good journey. I'll let Miss Johnson know."

"Thanks. Like I said, this is going to be a quick trip. We'll be back Monday afternoon, so Jack and Ira will be here to deliver the papers on Tuesday."

As Everett headed upstairs to deliver the news to Daisy,

he figured he'd take Abigail to the hotel dining room for Sunday lunch. And it would only be polite to include Daisy in the invitation, as well.

Daisy, however, had a different idea.

"Why don't we plan a picnic?"

Everett frowned. He wasn't much for eating on a blanket spread on the ground. But before he could say anything, Abigail took up the idea.

"Oh, what fun. And it'll give me the opportunity to see more of this area. I've been cooped up inside since I arrived here."

"That was only yesterday," Everett said dryly. "And I thought we'd go down to the hotel diner—"

"Oh, Everett, please," Abigail pleaded. "A picnic sounds ever so much more fun. For once, forget about being so stuffy and proper and just enjoy yourself."

Everett's mouth snapped shut, and he felt his jaw tighten. He looked from Abigail to Daisy, then tugged on his cuffs, one after the other. "Very well, if that's what the two of you prefer, then a picnic it is."

Abigail popped up from her seat and gave him an enthusiastic hug.

But it was Daisy's gaze he sought. And the warm approval he saw there made him glad he'd given in.

Sunday morning dawned sunny and warm—perfect picnic weather. Daisy had been in good spirits ever since yesterday when Everett made his unexpected capitulation about the picnic. Perhaps there was hope for him, after all.

She joined Everett and Abigail as they walked to church. Almost immediately they encountered Chance, and Abigail greeted him like an old friend. "Mr. Dawson, how wonderful to see you again."

Chance tipped his hat. "Good morning, Miss Abigail, Miss Johnson. Don't you ladies look lovely."

Abigail held out one side of her skirt and swished it, giving him a saucy smile. "Why, thank you."

Daisy noticed Everett had a very big brotherly frown on his face.

"How do you like your stay thus far?" Chance asked as he smiled Abigail's way.

"Very much, thank you."

"And will you be here long?"

"I'd like to stay indefinitely, if I can convince my brother not to exile me back to Boston."

"Abigail." There was a warning note in Everett's tone.

"Ah, big brothers," Chance said sympathetically. "I have three of them. They seem to always think they know best—whether they do or not."

Abigail gave him a broad smile. "Exactly!"

Everett didn't appear amused. "Please don't let us keep you, Chance," he said stiffly. "I'm sure our sedate pace is a bit tame for you."

While Everett's tone was polite, Daisy could hear the gritted-teeth undertones in his voice.

But Chance merely smiled. "Not at all. I'm enjoying the company of the two prettiest ladies in town."

Daisy decided it was time to give Everett something else to focus on before his expression locked in a perpetual glower. "Mr. Dawson," she said, "I understand you have a motorized carriage."

"Please call me Chance. And yes, I do. Let me know if either of you ladies would like to take a ride in it some-time." He glanced Everett's way. "And naturally, you could come along, too."

Daisy gave a mental wince. Seemed she'd made matters worse instead of better. Trying to avoid any additional opportunity for Chance to flirt with Abigail, Daisy maneuvered things so that she and Chance walked ahead, leaving Everett to escort his sister.

Chance gave Daisy an amused, knowing look, but he went along with the plan, and the rest of the stroll passed pleasantly enough.

Later, as they exited church after the service, Everett introduced Abigail to Reverend Harper.

"I'm pleased to meet you, Abigail. Your brother has become a valued member of our community. I hope you're here for a nice long visit."

Daisy wondered if the reverend would one day be able to say the same about her.

"Yes, sir," Abigail answered. "In fact, I'm hoping to make this my home."

Home. The word resonated inside Daisy with that same longing that had brought her here in the first place. Did it mean the same thing to Abigail? Right then and there, she determined to do everything she could to support Abigail's stand.

Everett suppressed a sigh. Why did Abigail insist on pressing the matter so publicly? "We haven't decided the length of her stay."

Reverend Harper looked from one to the other, then smiled indulgently. "Well, at any rate, I look forward to seeing you here again next Sunday."

"Yes, sir, I look forward to it, as well."

"Wonderful." The reverend looked up and waved someone over. "Here's my daughter, Constance. Let me introduce you."

As Abigail and the Harper girl latched on to each other like long-lost sisters, Everett found himself looking for Daisy. Was she still with that pup, Chance?

He spied her standing alone a few feet away, eyeing him with an exasperated look. What had gotten into her now?

It didn't take him long to find out.

"You have to quit glowering at your sister. Folks will think you don't like her. And so will she."

Had he been glowering? "I'm more frustrated than angry." He took a deep breath and schooled his expression. "It's important that she return to school as soon as possible. The longer she's here, the more ties she'll make."

"Would it really be so terrible if she didn't go back?"

"She needs to complete her education."

Daisy gave him an even look. "There are many important lessons to be learned outside the schoolroom. Perhaps it's time she focused on those."

"There will be time enough for that later." He could see Daisy still wasn't convinced. "And she needs to learn some discipline. What sort of lesson will she learn if she gets rewarded for her reckless actions?"

"I'm not talking about rewarding her—simply listening to her and giving her what she needs, not what she wants."

"And you think you know what she needs better than I do?"

"She needs the same thing we all do. She needs to know she is loved and wanted, that she belongs."

Abigail came rushing up just then, cutting off any response he might have made. Which was just as well, because for once he had no words.

Chapter Twelve

Daisy spread the blanket under a large oak while Everett took care of the horse and buggy. Abigail had run off with Kip to explore the meadow and nearby stream almost before the buggy had come to a complete stop.

As Daisy unpacked the basket of food, she smiled at the sound of Abigail's exclamations of delight and Kip's playful barking. These were the kind of outings a girl Abigail's age needed, not more museums and operas. Would Everett be able to see that?

He came over and stood stiffly at the edge of the blanket.

"Have a seat," she said conversationally. "I'll have the food set out in a minute."

Everett sat, but didn't seem any more at ease. He shaded his eyes as he glanced his sister's way. "What's Abigail doing?"

She paused and gave him a pointed look. "Exploring. Playing. It's what children do."

Everett frowned, still keeping his eyes on Abigail. "She's fifteen, not eight."

"She's still a child. And I'm not certain just how much playtime she's had in her life."

This time his gaze swung around to meet hers. "You know nothing about Abigail's childhood."

"And how much of it do you know?" Daisy wished the words back as soon as they left her lips. Everett's expression didn't change, but there had been the briefest flicker in his gaze that told her her words had hit their mark. "I'm sorry. I had no right—"

"Forget it. What are we having for lunch?"

It seemed the subject was closed. "Nothing fancy. Cold ham, cheese, bread, apples and lemonade. I also brought the leftover pecan pie from yesterday."

"Sounds good. I'll go let Abigail know we're ready to eat."

Daisy sighed as she watched him walk away. It was obvious Everett truly loved his sister. But it was equally obvious he had a blind spot when it came to what she needed.

A few moments later, Abigail and Kip came racing over, with Everett following behind at a sedate walk. "This is the most marvelous place," the girl said as she plopped down on the blanket. "I actually saw some turtles by the stream, and Kip chased a rabbit into the brush."

Daisy smiled. "That's what's so great about picnics— you never know what the day will bring." She started passing plates as Everett walked up. "Now, why don't we eat and then we can see what other entertainments we can find?"

Most of the conversation during lunch was led by Abigail, who kept up a constant stream of chatter about what she'd seen during her short exploration.

Daisy noticed Everett watching his sister speculatively. What was he thinking?

During a lull in the conversation, Daisy looked up at the sky and pointed. "Look, a rabbit."

Abigail immediately started looking around. "Where?"

"Up there. See that cloud? If you turn your head just a little bit, it looks like the head and ears of a rabbit." Then she grinned at the girl. "It's a game I played with my mother when I was younger. We'd see who could find the best image in the clouds. Why don't you give it a try?"

"Okay." Abigail leaned back, bracing herself on her arms, and studied the sky. Then she pointed. "There. That one looks like a lady's hat with a feather."

"Oh, I can see it. Very nice."

Abigail gave her brother a nudge. "You try, Everett. It's fun."

But Everett shook his head. "You ladies have your fun. I'll watch."

"Oh, come on, try it."

Daisy gave in to an impish impulse. "Don't bother your brother, Abigail. I don't think he understands whimsy."

Everett straightened and gave her an affronted look. She raised a brow in challenge, and their gazes locked for several heartbeats. Finally, he gave in.

"Very well. Let's see…"

Daisy didn't miss the pleased expression on Abigail's face. Did Everett notice?

A moment later, he pointed. "That one looks like a rather plump maple leaf."

"Oh, it does," Abigail exclaimed. "See, you're good at this."

Daisy smiled as she slipped a morsel of ham to Kip. The smile on Everett's face as he accepted Abigail's praise was a fine sight, indeed.

"If everyone's had enough to eat, I'll put the leftovers back in the basket so the bugs don't get at it."

Abigail immediately straightened. "Let me help."

But Daisy waved her off. "I can handle this. Why don't you show your brother that turtle you saw earlier?"

"Okay." She stood and tugged on her brother's arm. "Wait until you see it, Everett. It was the most amazing thing. But it's kind of small so you'll have to look real close."

Everett glanced Daisy's way. There was something unreadable in his eyes. Then with a nod, he turned back to his sister and allowed her to lead him toward the stream.

Daisy watched them, pleased with the way Everett was thawing, at least in regard to his sister. If nothing else, the girl would have some very pleasant memories to take back to Boston with her.

As she repacked the basket, her treacherous mind began to wonder if this thawing would seep over into other areas of his life, as well....

Monday dawned as a gray, drizzly day. The kind of day, Daisy decided, that cried out for a hearty soup. She hummed as she chopped the vegetables to add to the chicken and broth already simmering on the stove.

She glanced over her shoulder as Abigail returned upstairs and plopped down in one of the kitchen chairs.

"Is something wrong?" she asked the unhappy-looking girl.

"Everett is in one of his more grumpy moods. He's having trouble with the layout for the front page, and apparently my presence is a distraction."

Daisy hid a grin. The girl was definitely not the shy, retiring type.

"Is there something I can help *you* with?" Abigail asked hopefully.

Daisy didn't think Everett would appreciate her putting his sister to work doing things he paid her to do. "Thank you, but I have it under control."

"That's the same thing Everett tells me when I try to help him." The girl sighed dramatically. "I feel so useless."

If it wasn't raining, she'd let Abigail take Kip for a walk. "You could always pull out one of those books of yours and read for a while."

"I suppose." Abigail's tone carried a decided lack of enthusiasm. And she didn't stir from her seat.

Daisy reached for another topic. "How are you coming with your circulating library idea?"

That drew out a bit more energy. "I mentioned it to Constance yesterday, and she was very excited. She said she'd be happy to help me set everything up."

"So you two are getting along well?"

"Oh, yes." Abigail sat up straighter, her expression growing more animated. "We only talked for a few minutes after church, but I can tell already that we're going to be great friends. She invited me to join the choir so she'd have someone else her age there." Abigail's expression turned mischievous. "I told her I would, but she might regret the invitation. My music teacher absolutely despaired of ever teaching me to carry a tune."

"Surely you're exaggerating."

"Only a little. But I like to sing, and I think it'll be nice to have a new friend here."

The girl was quickly going about setting down roots, just as Everett had feared. And speaking of Everett…

"Have you convinced your brother to let you go through with your plans yet?"

Abigail's expression returned to its former gloomy state. "He still thinks I'm not up to the task."

Daisy wasn't sure she agreed with him, but she was reluctant to interfere. "That's too bad. I'm sure he's trying to do what he thinks is best for you."

"Good intentions don't necessarily equate to right thinking."

Daisy agreed, but refrained from comment.

Abigail sat up straighter. "Maybe, if I got everything all set up, he'd realize how serious I am."

Daisy kept her expression neutral. "You know your brother better than I do." Seeing Abigail's hopeful expression, she relented slightly. "Why don't you take a look at the space I offered you and decide how you want to set it up? I'm sure Kip would be glad to keep you company."

Abigail hopped up and moved to the doorway. "What do you say, Kip?" She stooped to scratch his ears. "Want to help me check things out?"

Kip stood, tail wagging enthusiastically.

Daisy smiled at the suddenly energetic pair. "I figure you can set up your library on the wall that backs up to your brother's office. There are a few pieces of make-shift furniture in my storeroom, along with some crates that were sound enough to save from the scrap heap. The layout over there is similar to the one on this side. Help yourself to anything you think you can use." Surely Everett wouldn't find anything to scold either of them about if Abigail just looked around.

"Thanks." Abigail was already moving away. "I'm sure it'll all be perfect."

Daisy added more vegetables and seasoning to the pot, then smiled as she heard Abigail rattle down the stairs. Everett's sister was so excited about her venture—almost as much as she herself was about someday opening her restaurant. Come to think of it, Everett was treating his sister's idea as dismissively as he had hers.

She frowned. Despite Everett's best efforts, Abigail was already building ties here. And if he was going to continue to leave his sister to her own devices, then surely she had a right to find a way to occupy her time. And if that resulted in her establishing her library, then surely there could be no harm in it.

Just like there'd be nothing wrong with her opening a restaurant.

Perhaps she did have reason to interfere, after all.

Chapter Thirteen

An hour later, Abigail returned with a decided spring to her step.

"What do you think?" Daisy asked. "Will the place serve your needs?"

"It'll be perfect." Abigail sat at the table, her eyes sparkling. "I'll need some actual bookcases eventually, but I can probably stack my books on trunks and crates to start with. Hopefully the mercantile will have cardstock that I can use to make my individual book and patron records. And I can find a bandbox or some such to keep my files in."

It sounded as if Abigail had given this a lot of thought. "As I said, you're welcome to use anything you find in my storeroom until you can acquire better."

"Thanks. Once I've earned a little money, I can hire someone to build shelves."

Daisy found herself admiring the girl's spirit. "So what do you see as your next step?"

"I'll need to catalog my books. Then I'll set up my system for tracking who has what. Fortunately, I already have notebooks that I should be able to make do with."

"That sounds like quite an undertaking." It was also

something Abigail could occupy herself with before setting up the physical library.

"Yes, but only to set it all up. Once I have it in place, it will be done." She leaned her elbows on the table. "Miss Abernathy and Miss Teel used different systems, but I think I prefer Miss Abernathy's. She arranged the nonfiction books by subject and the fiction books by author."

"That's similar to the way my grandmother had her books arranged."

Abigail gave her a speculative look. "I don't mean to pry, but you get this strange tone in your voice when you mention your grandmother."

The girl was perceptive. "I was never very comfortable in my grandmother's home. Everything there was very formal, very elegant and fancy. And I was anything but."

"You have something much better than all that," the girl said earnestly. "You have a natural warmth and grace about you that puts everyone at ease."

Daisy blinked at the unexpected compliment. "What a nice thing to say."

"Oh, it's true." Then Abigail grimaced. "But I know what you mean. It sounds like Miss Haversham's school. I felt as if I didn't have room to breathe, to be myself."

Daisy felt that surge of sympathetic kinship again. If only Everett could hear what his sister was saying, both the words and the tone, maybe he wouldn't be so quick to send her back.

Everett had paused halfway up the stairs, unabashedly eavesdropping when he heard Daisy talking about her grandmother. But her words, rather than satisfying his curiosity, only stirred it further.

Abigail's words, on the other hand, gave him something

else to think about. Had she truly felt so stifled? Or was it merely adolescent theatrics?

He resumed his climb. "What are you two up to?"

Daisy smiled brightly. "Just girl-talk. You're right on time—I'll have the meal on the table in a moment." She moved to the cupboard to fetch a large serving bowl.

Abigail popped up. "I'll set the table while you dish everything up."

Everett watched the easy camaraderie between his sister and Daisy with mixed emotions. He'd become less judgmental of Daisy, but he still didn't want the peddler's daughter's rough edges to rub off on his sister. He'd worked too hard to see that she turned into a young lady who would be welcome in any society drawing room.

This was yet another reason why the sooner he could move out of Turnabout and into more civilized surroundings, the better. It was time he started putting a few more feelers out to larger newspapers.

Once they were seated and Daisy had said grace with her usual down-to-earth eloquence, they dug into the meal.

Abigail passed the basket of rolls to Daisy. "I saw the pretty embroidery work hanging in your place," she said with a smile. "Did you do that yourself?"

Daisy shook her head. "Thank you, but no. That's some of my mother's work."

Everett frowned at his sister. "What were you doing at Daisy's place?"

Abigail flushed guiltily. "I was looking for something to do earlier, so I went over there to look around."

"That was presumptuous, don't you think?"

"Oh, I didn't mind," Daisy said quickly. "In fact, I think I may have suggested it."

A look passed between the two of them that gave Everett the feeling they were up to something.

"Besides," Daisy added quickly, "Kip was glad of the company."

"About that, Everett." Abigail straightened. "Why won't you let Kip over here? He seems such a well-behaved animal."

"We've had this conversation before. Animals belong outdoors, not in one's home." This was one point he intended to hold firm on. "If Daisy chooses to keep her pet in her home, that's her business, but that doesn't mean I should make an exception for my home."

"But you're being so unreasonable." Abigail gave him a mutinous look.

"Don't argue on my account, Abigail," Daisy said quickly. "It's truly no hardship for Kip to stay on my side of the wall."

Abigail huffed and then dipped her spoon in her bowl. "I still think it's unnecessarily restrictive."

Everett didn't respond, but neither did he relent. Getting attached to that dog would just be one more tie she'd mourn when she had to leave. And he knew from experience just how quickly one could grow fond of a pet. No, he would not put his sister through that.

Once the meal was over and Everett returned to his office, Daisy began clearing the table. She still had so much work to do at her own place, and she was eager to get back to it.

Abigail wandered over to one of her trunks of books. "It's kind of difficult to decide where to start."

Daisy was feeling guilty about hiding their activities from Everett. "When are you going to discuss your plans with your brother again?"

Abigail grimaced. "I'm not sure. You saw how he was with Kip. Once he makes his mind up about something, it's hard to change it." She gave Daisy a just-between-us look. "I need to pick my moment carefully."

Daisy understood the sentiment, but firmly believed there needed to be more honest communication between the siblings. "Well, you might want to give it a shot before you put too much more effort into it."

"I don't know. Maybe if he could see it first..."

"What do you mean?"

Abigail lifted a couple of books from her trunk. "Maybe I should set the stage—you know, arrange some books on the table and set up a few entries in my catalog. If Everett could actually see how well I've thought this through, and how serious I am, rather than just having him imagine it, he might be more inclined to approve the idea."

"I see." And she did. Because, behind all of Abigail's scheming, she saw a girl who was trying to earn the approval of her brother.

"So it's all right with you if I bring some of my books downstairs and set the stage for him?"

"Of course." Everett would probably think she was interfering again, but Daisy thought Abigail deserved a shot at convincing him. And, assuming Everett didn't dismiss it out of hand, perhaps it would get them talking to each other the way they had at the picnic yesterday. "Once I get done with these dishes, I'll be happy to help you."

Abigail shook her head with a smile. "Thank you, but I know you have your own projects to get to. I can take care of this."

The girl disappeared into her room, then reappeared with an armload of books. She smiled at Daisy as she headed for the adjoining door, giving Kip a friendly pat as she passed.

Daisy rubbed her cheek thoughtfully. How was Everett

going to react when he saw how far his sister had taken her idea?

Daisy froze as she heard a loud cry and a clatter. A heartbeat later she was dashing through the doorway, a prayer racing through her head. "Abigail! Abigail, are you okay?"

No answer.

When she reached the top of the stairs, Daisy found out why. Abigail lay crumpled at the foot of the stairs amid a scattering of books. Kip was at her side, whimpering and nudging her gently with his nose.

Yelling over her shoulder for Everett, Daisy raced down the stairs, her pulse thudding loudly in her ears. *Dear God, please let her be all right. Please, please, please.*

Just as Daisy reached the foot of the stairs, Abigail stirred and groaned. "Abigail, sweetheart, are you okay?"

The girl's eyes fluttered open. "I…I think so." She winced and groaned again. "What happened?"

"You must have fallen." How far had she tumbled? How badly was she injured?

"What happened?" The staccato question came from Everett as he clattered down the stairs.

Everett aged ten years in the time it took him to get to the bottom of the stairs. He knelt beside Abigail, searching her much-too-pale face for signs of pain or disorientation. If she was seriously hurt, he'd never forgive himself. "Don't try to move." He heard the gruffness in his voice but was powerless to alter it. "Daisy," he said without taking his eyes from his sister, "please get Dr. Pratt. Make sure he understands he needs to come immediately."

With a nod and a last squeeze of Abigail's hand, Daisy sprinted off.

Everett gently moved the hair from Abigail's forehead. "Tell me where you hurt."

She grimaced, and one hand fluttered. "I feel sore all over, but I think I'll be all right if you just give me a minute to sit up and take stock."

He held her down as she tried to sit up. "Lie still until Dr. Pratt has had a chance to look you over."

"Please, I'd like to sit up. Lying here is undignified, and I promise to let you know if something seems amiss."

Everett hesitated a moment, but couldn't hold firm against the tears welling in her eyes. Keeping his hand square on her back, he held ready to lend additional support if she gave him the least cause to suspect she needed it as she awkwardly maneuvered herself into a sitting position.

"Ow!"

He searched her face. "What is it? Where does it hurt?"

She cupped her left wrist in her right hand. "I think I may have injured my wrist." She smiled, but he could see the pain in her expression. "It looks like we may have matching injuries."

Before Everett could question her further, Daisy and Dr. Pratt rushed in.

The doctor set his bag down and knelt beside Abigail, across from Everett. "Hello, young lady. I understand you took a tumble."

Abigail gave him a wavery smile. "Yes, sir. Not very graceful of me, was it?"

"Don't be embarrassed. You're not the first of my patients to take such a tumble, and I dare say you won't be the last. Now, let's have a look, shall we?"

"Her left wrist is bothering her." Everett's gut was still churning. *Please God, let that be the extent of it.*

"Well, then, let's have a look at that first."

Eunice Ortolon, the woman who ran the boardinghouse, bustled in from the sidewalk. "Hello. I don't mean to intrude, but I saw Doc come by all in a rush. I hope no one's hurt."

Everett gritted his teeth as the town busybody studied them with avidly curious eyes. He really didn't have the patience to deal with that kind of distraction right now. But good manners won out. "My sister fell down the stairs," he said.

The woman placed her hand to her heart. "Oh, my goodness. The poor dear. Is there anything I can do to help?"

He shook his head. "Thank you for the kind offer, but now that the doctor is here I think we have all the help we need." He nodded dismissively and deliberately turned from her to the doctor.

Dr. Pratt stood. "At first glance she seems to have nothing worse than a sprained wrist and some bumps and bruises, but I'd like to conduct a more thorough examination." He gave Everett a pointed look. "Perhaps we can find a place where she'll be more comfortable while I do so."

Everett nodded, eager to get his sister to a place with more privacy. "Of course. We can take her to her bedchamber—no, make that mine—the bed is larger." He scooped his sister up and stood.

Abigail protested. "Really, Everett, I'm perfectly capable of walking."

"Not until Dr. Pratt has completed his examination."

"But your hand—"

"Is healing nicely. Now hush and be still."

Daisy headed for the staircase. "I'll make sure the room is ready. Doctor, if you'll just come this way."

Everett followed the two of them more slowly, careful not to jar his sister. The whole time he held her, he wanted to squeeze her tight, to protect her against other dangers.

This was the second time in a matter of days that she'd given him a fright. He was her brother and her guardian— he was supposed to protect her, but it didn't appear he was doing a very good job of it. Why did his well-ordered world seem to be crumbling around him lately?

By the time he reached his bedchamber, Daisy had the covers turned down and the pillows plumped up. Once Abigail was settled in, Dr. Pratt turned to him and Daisy. "Why don't you leave me and Miss Abigail? I'll call you when I've finished."

Everett wanted to protest. He wasn't ready to let Abigail out of his sight.

But Daisy touched his arm lightly and gave him a reassuring nod. "Let's let the doc do his job."

Everett gave a short nod. "Of course."

As he and Daisy stepped out of the room, however, he received yet another jolt of surprise. Mrs. Ortolon stood in his kitchen, eyeing the place speculatively. Apparently, rather than leave when he'd dismissed her, she had followed them upstairs.

"Is there anything I can do to help?" she asked with a bright smile.

Everett struggled to maintain his composure. "That's very thoughtful, but as I said, I think we have it under control now."

"Of course." Her gaze shifted from one to the other of them in a way that set the hair on the nape of his neck vibrating. What did that look mean? What was she thinking?

Then, with a mental groan, it suddenly hit him how compromising this must look to her. The doors between Daisy's and his living quarters were propped wide open. Daisy had entered his place from hers without hesitation, had entered *his bedchamber* without hesitation. He knew it had all been perfectly innocent, that Daisy's only thought had been for Abigail, but one could see any number of scenarios in this, and not all of them were entirely innocent.

Perhaps he was reading too much into the situation, but he didn't think so. But there was no way to go back and unring this bell now.

Mrs. Ortolon patted her hair. "I suppose I'll get out of your way. I do hope, Mr. Fulton, that you'll let me know if I can help in any way, won't you?"

"Of course." He had no doubt whatsoever that when she spread word of Abigail's accident, there would be something more to the story than the bare facts.

There was nothing he could do about that now, however, and there was still Abigail to worry about. He stared at his bedchamber door and raked a hand through his hair. How badly was she hurt? This would never have happened if she'd stayed put in Boston where she belonged.

Needing a target for his pent-up worries, he rounded on Daisy. "How did this happen?" he asked stiffly.

Daisy touched her collar. "I didn't see the actual fall, but she was carrying an armload of books and apparently tripped on the stairs."

He made a sharp, dismissive movement with his hands. "That much I already figured out. What I'm asking is, what was she doing carrying those books on your stairs in the first place?"

"She was at loose ends and decided to work toward setting up her circulating library—"

That confounded library again! "I knew you two were up to something when I saw you earlier. She's been working on this behind my back, and you knew about it." He saw the flicker of guilt in her expression. "How could you have encouraged this?"

"Actually, it's more that I didn't *discourage* it."

Did she honestly want to nitpick with him?

She waved helplessly. "I didn't think it would hurt—"

"No, you *didn't* think." He saw her wince and tried to moderate his tone. But she needed to understand that Abigail was *his* responsibility, and she shouldn't encourage her to find ways around his strictures. "Didn't it occur to you that I was deliberately negative about her little project to encourage her to return to school?"

Daisy's expression lost some of its defensiveness, and she stiffened. "Return to school? Have you heard anything at all of what your sister's told you on that subject?"

"Abigail is a child trying to get out of school. I'm thinking about what's best for her. She belongs in a more refined environment than what Turnabout can provide."

Her face colored—was it embarrassment or anger? "Do you know anything at all about what it is your sister wants out of life? Or are you only concerned with what *you* want out of her life?"

The woman was definitely out of line. "I suppose, based on your entire three days of knowing Abigail, you know better than I what's best for her."

"Apparently so."

Such unmitigated conceit. "I disagree. And I'll thank you to remember that I am her brother and guardian."

"As if you'd let either her or me forget that."

"And another thing. She shouldn't have been carting heavy books down those stairs. I wouldn't be surprised to learn that that fool dog of yours tripped her up."

"You leave Kip out of this."

"Only if you keep him out of our way."

Before she could respond, the bedchamber door opened. They dropped the argument to turn their attention to Dr. Pratt.

Everett reached him in a few quick strides. "How is she?"

The doctor closed the door behind him and waved Everett back toward the sitting room. "Her wrist is sprained and she's got a number of painful bruises and scrapes, so she'll be quite sore for the next few days. You'll want to watch her closely for signs of a concussion, but otherwise I think she'll be just fine."

Some of the tension eased from Everett's body. "Do you have any special instructions for how I should care for her?"

"I've splinted her wrist, and she should take care when using that hand for a while." He gave them a reassuring smile. "As I said, keep a close eye on her the next day or two. Fetch me immediately if she has dizzy spells or nausea or seems at all disoriented. Other than that, bring her by my office in a week so I can check her wrist."

Everett shook the physician's hand. "Thank you, Doctor. Let me show you out."

Dr. Pratt held up his hand. "No need. I know my way. I'm sure your sister is anxious to see you." He gave Everett a knowing look. "And vice versa." With a wave, Dr. Pratt moved to the stairs.

Daisy met Everett's gaze. "You go on. I have dishes to wash."

With a nod, Everett strode quickly to his bedchamber. He was already regretting the tone, if not the words, he'd used with Daisy. Should he apologize? But he was already at the bedroom door, and his need to see his sister drove everything else from his mind.

"How are you feeling?" he asked. She sat up in bed and he studied her closely, relieved to see more color in her face than the last time he'd seen her.

Abigail turned and set her feet on the floor. "Foolish and clumsy. I'm sorry I gave everyone such a scare."

He sat beside her and put an arm around her shoulder.

"I'm just glad it didn't have more serious consequences." Then he gave her a squeeze. "What in the world were you thinking?"

"I just thought, if I could show you how the library would look when it was all set up, and demonstrate my ideas for the whole process, that maybe you'd change your mind."

Had it really meant that much to her? "Abigail, I know you're perfectly capable of handling such an endeavor— that wasn't the point."

"It wasn't?"

"Of course not. I just didn't want you to put all that effort into something you won't be here long enough to enjoy."

He pulled slightly away so he could study her expression. "And was this all your idea, or did it come from Miss Johnson?"

Abigail shook her head. "Don't blame Daisy for this. It's something I wanted to do, and it wasn't her place to stop me."

He noted she hadn't really answered his question, but he let it pass. "No, that's my place. And what in the world were you thinking, carrying an armload of books down those stairs?"

Abigail's frown turned inward. "I just tripped is all. I know I was lucky it didn't turn out worse than it did, but truly, Everett, it could just as easily have happened when I was carrying something down to you on our side of the wall."

"There's no dog to get underfoot on our side of the wall."

She gave him an indignant poke. "Don't blame Kip, either. He was behind me, not in front of me. As I told you, it was just a misstep on my part."

She made as if to stand, but Everett held her shoulders down. "Where do you think you're going?"

"Dr. Pratt said that if I take things slow and easy, it's not necessary for me to stay in bed."

"He also said you'd be quite sore for the next few days. Don't you think you'll be more comfortable resting here for now?"

She gave him an exasperated look. "Don't go fussing over me. I'd be bored silly if I had to stay cooped up in here for any length of time. I'd rather be where I can have some company. Besides, this is your bed, not mine."

"I'll allow you out of this room if you promise me you won't do anything more strenuous than reading a book or writing a letter."

Abigail rolled her eyes. "You're acting like a mother hen with an injured chick."

Which wasn't too far off the mark for how he was feeling. And he certainly didn't intend to let her cajole him. "I mean it, Abigail. I want your word." He still hadn't quite recovered from the sight of her crumpled in a heap at the foot of the stairs.

"Oh, very well. But you have to promise not to smother me."

Everett stayed by her side as she made her way to the sofa. At her request, he moved one of her trunks of books close at hand so she could go through them and select some reading material.

Once he had her properly settled, he stood back, unsure what to do next. Daisy apparently had no such worries. He watched as she bustled past him and fussed over his sister. He also noticed that she studiously avoided making eye contact with him. Was she still smarting over their earlier discussion? But he'd been in the right.

Hadn't he?

Then she turned to him, her expression subdued. "I know you need to get back to your office. Don't worry about your sister. I promise to keep a close eye on her until you're done for the day."

Was that guilt speaking, or concern? Maybe a bit of both. "Thank you. Make sure you call me if you see the least sign that all is not well with her."

"Go on, Everett," Abigail said with a shooing motion. "I'll be perfectly fine."

He slowly descended the stairs, feeling uncharacteristically confused. Had he handled that wrong? Should he have given both Abigail and Daisy more encouragement and support?

It wasn't like him to be so indecisive. It must be Daisy's influence. His well-ordered life had been turned upside down, and it had all started when she arrived on the scene.

He didn't like it, not one bit.

The question was, what was he going to do about it?

Chapter Fourteen

Before Everett reached the bottom tread, his office door opened. Had some other busybody come to pry into his household's personal business?

But it was Adam.

"Hello. Back from the cabin, I see."

"Just got back an hour ago." He sobered. "We heard your sister had an accident, and Reggie sent me by to see how she was doing."

By mutual accord they moved to the chessboard. "It could have been worse. She ended up with a sprained wrist and some bumps and bruises, but Dr. Pratt thinks she'll be okay."

"Glad to hear it."

The two men took seats and stared at the board. It was Everett's move and he studied the pieces silently, but he wasn't really seeing them. He fingered a captured pawn, struggling with whether or not to ask the question foremost in his mind. Finally, keeping his gaze on the board, he cleared his throat. "What else have you heard about our bit of excitement?" Had he kept his tone as casual as he'd attempted to?

Adam grimaced sympathetically. "I suppose you're referring to Eunice's gossip about the open doors between your and Miss Johnson's living quarters."

There it was. Everett clenched his jaw. It sounded quite unsavory when expressed that way. "That door is only open when Miss Johnson is working here, and only as a convenience to her. There's nothing untoward going on."

"I didn't think there was."

Everett frowned. "But it doesn't really matter, does it?"

Adam's expression remained carefully neutral. "There are always those who will read more into a situation than is there."

Is that what this was—a *situation?* "I was afraid of that." Everett gave a crooked smile. "What do you think the chances are that it'll blow over if we just ignore it?"

Adam raised a brow. "You're the man of the world here—what do *you* think?"

The walls closed in on Everett as he tried to think of some way out of this mess. Daisy was *not* the type of woman he'd pictured himself marrying—not even close. It was hard to picture her on his arm in a society drawing room or trip to the opera.

But that was beside the point now. He had to be man enough to shield her from the wagging tongues that could shred her reputation to pieces. He was not his father.

Besides, he'd already been responsible for ruining one life through the inadvertent but reckless spread of lies. He couldn't stand by and let unfounded rumors and innuendo ruin another life, not when he could do something to prevent it.

After a long moment of silence, Adam spoke up again. "I guess the real question at this point is, what are you going to do about it?"

Everett met his gaze head-on, and the weight of his

responsibility settled squarely and with great finality on his shoulders. There was only one answer he could give. "What I have to."

Later that afternoon, Daisy heard a knock on her back door and opened it to find Everett standing there, his expression solemn—even more so than usual.

"Miss Johnson, if you have a moment, there's something I need to discuss with you."

Her imagination immediately kicked in. "Is it Abigail? Is something wrong? I checked on her just twenty minutes ago—"

He held up a reassuring hand. "Abigail's fine, or at least no worse than when the doctor left earlier. Constance Harper came by for a visit and the two have their heads together, thick as thieves."

She breathed a mental sigh of relief, then another possible reason popped into her head. "If this is about what happened, I'll admit I shouldn't have encouraged her, but—"

He shook his head. "I know you're not entirely to blame. My sister can be quite headstrong when she puts her mind to something. As her presence in Turnabout demonstrates."

His seeming change of attitude had her thoroughly confused. "Then what is it?"

He swept an arm out. "If you don't mind, I'd prefer to take a short stroll while we talk."

She stepped outside, still trying to figure out why he was here. "Do you mind if Kip joins us?" She wouldn't press him if he refused, but to her surprise, he merely nodded.

That really started her worrying as to what might be on his mind. "If it's not about Abigail, or my part in her accident, then what has put that serious look on your face?"

Rather than answering her question, he asked one of his own. "What do you know about Eunice Ortolon?"

Was that really what he wanted to talk to her about—one of their neighbors? But she obediently answered his question. "She runs the boardinghouse, doesn't she?"

"She does. She's also got a wagging tongue the likes of which would be hard to match."

Daisy gave him a mock-stern look. "A body could argue that you're indulging in a bit of gossip yourself just by saying that."

His half smile acknowledged her point. "True. But that still doesn't negate my prior statement."

Enough of this shilly-shallying. "And why should Mrs. Ortolon's chattiness interest me? Surely you're not worried over what she might say about your sister's fall? There's nothing about the accident that would reflect badly on her."

"I agree. There's nothing the woman can say that would reflect badly on *Abigail*. At least, not directly."

She could tell he was trying to make a point, but for the life of her, she couldn't figure it out. "Then what?"

"I realize things were unsettling in the first minutes after Abigail's fall and that neither of us were thinking clearly. But now that things are back to normal, try to remember all that happened in the time after the doctor and Mrs. Ortolon arrived."

She frowned as she did as he asked. There was obviously something specific he was concerned about—concerned enough to seek her out. "Well, Doc Pratt did a quick check of Abigail when he arrived. There was some discussion going on, but I was focused on your sister so I wasn't paying much attention." She met his gaze. "Is that it? Was something said that has you worried?"

Everett shook his head. "What happened next?"

She concentrated on trying to picture it all in her mind.

"Then we all went upstairs so Doc Pratt could examine her in private." This was silly. Why didn't he just tell her straight out what was on his mind?

"Yes, we all went up *your* stairs and into *my* quarters through the adjoining door."

"Yes, of course. It was the quickest way to get her to bed. And it was—" Daisy put her hand over her mouth as the full implication hit her. "Oh."

"Yes. *Oh.*"

Her cheeks heated. "But, surely…I mean." She met his gaze and was suddenly glad he had directed their steps to the less populated areas of town. "Oh, bother! It's all perfectly innocent."

"So it was. And is. But that no longer matters. You were in my bedchamber, remember, which only compounded things." His tone dripped with exaggerated patience, as if he were talking to a child. "If it were only Dr. Pratt, we could count on his discretion, but I'm afraid with Mrs. Ortolon in the mix, there will be no containing talk of this. In fact, there is some talk already circulating around town."

Daisy rubbed her cheek, trying to take in what this meant. "Be honest with me. How bad is it?"

"To speak bluntly, our reputations will be tarnished, and it may very well splash over onto Abigail, as well."

Her spirits sank. Was her dream of being a welcomed member of the community over so soon? She wouldn't accept that. "But surely, if we just go on about our business, in time the rumors will die down."

He shook his head. "I wish that were true. But this sort of thing can take on a life of its own, and folks have long memories. Believe me, I know."

"Then what do you suggest we do?"

"There's only one thing we *can* do—you and I must immediately announce our engagement."

Daisy halted in her tracks and stared at him, not sure she'd heard correctly. Was he serious? The only hint of emotion she could see in his face, however, was that irritating hint of cynical amusement he wore like armor. Did he think of this situation as a joke? "Surely there's something else we can do."

He spread his hands. "I'm open to suggestions."

She'd come to Turnabout fully intending to find herself a husband—in fact, that was something central to her desire to have a family. But this—this was as far from normal as one could get.

The last thing anyone would call Everett Fulton was the settling-down type. And to have a man—*any* man—feel forced to offer for her, well, that was a terrible thing to base a marriage on. "I'm sure, if I had time to think, I could come up with something."

"I'm afraid time is something we don't have." He held her gaze. "The gossip is already spreading. I want to put it to rest before Abigail hears anything…unsavory."

Daisy's cheeks heated all over again. "We can't let that happen."

"Then you agree to our engagement?"

Daisy stared at him, unable to give in just yet, still mentally scrambling for another option.

His expression softened into something approaching sympathy. "I know this isn't the ideal pairing for either of us, but the choice has been taken out of our hands. And I give you my word that I'll do my best to make this as painless for you as possible."

Somehow that only made her feel worse. "Not the most romantic of declarations."

He frowned. "I'm sorry I can't offer you love poems and other romantic nonsense. You need to understand that this is a matter of necessity."

Well, that made his feelings perfectly clear. "Of course." Then she grimaced. "I feel like this is all my fault, like I should be apologizing for putting you in this position."

He shrugged. "What's done is done. Placing blame serves no purpose now."

She noticed he didn't try to contradict her claim to be at fault. Did that mean he *did* blame her?

"The newspaper goes out tomorrow," he continued. "I'd like to insert a notice of our engagement. Hopefully, that will stem some of the censure. Do I have your permission?"

She took a deep breath. It seemed there was no getting out of this. "It sounds like I don't have a choice."

He gave a small smile. "Good. It'll be just a small notice. We can visit Reverend Harper tomorrow and set a date."

This was all happening too fast. Better to focus on something less frightening. "How do you think Abigail will feel about this sudden engagement?" Surely Everett's sister had higher expectations for the woman her brother would marry than a peddler's daughter.

"She'll probably be surprised, but she seems to like you well enough. All in all, I don't think she'll have any objections."

Again, not an enthusiastic endorsement.

"Rather than standing here wondering, though," he continued, "why don't we go over and tell her the news?"

By this time they had returned to her back door. "Now?"

He led the way to his own door. "Of course. If I'm going to place an announcement in the paper tomorrow, don't you think we should tell her now?"

"Yes, of course." The thought of saying it out loud to anyone, even Abigail, made it seem more real, somehow.

"If you don't mind, I'd like to avoid telling her that we're doing this because we were backed into a corner."

His brow lowered at that, and she rushed to explain. "It's not just to spare my feelings." She tucked a strand of hair behind her ear. "Though I'll admit that's part of it. But I want to spare *her* feelings, as well. I don't want her to suffer any pangs of guilt over this because of her accident. That wouldn't be fair to her."

He hesitated, then nodded. "I hadn't thought of that, but you're correct—Abigail has a keen sense of responsibility. I won't lie to her, but I don't see any reason to elaborate, either." He nodded toward the door. "Now, if you're ready, shall we?"

She nodded and preceded him inside. Were they really doing this? Or would she wake up soon and find this was all some kind of dream?

Please Lord Jesus, help me find a way through this. I'm so confused right now. I know You led me to this place for a reason, and even though it looks like I've really messed things up good this time, surely You can make it all come out right. I don't know if I'm doing the proper thing or not, but I'm counting on You to show me a way out if that be Your will.

They entered Everett's sitting room to find Abigail lounging on the sofa with a book in her lap.

"Oh, there you are." Abigail gave them a mock frown. "I'd begun to wonder where you'd gotten off to."

Everett looked around. "Where's Constance?"

"She had to go." Abigail looked from one to the other of them, and a small frown puckered her brow. "Is something wrong? You both seem so solemn."

Daisy couldn't stop the guilty flush warming her cheeks.

Everett, on the other hand, seemed as coolheaded as ever. "We have something to tell you," he said.

Abigail sat up straighter. "Bad news?"

"Actually, no." Everett took Daisy's hand. "In fact, we hope you'll think it's happy news."

Daisy stood silently beside Everett as he delivered the news to his sister. A silent prayer was running through her head. *Please, please don't let Abigail be upset by the announcement.*

But almost before Everett finished speaking, Abigail launched herself at him with a squeal of delight, leaving no doubt as to her feelings.

"Oh, Everett, I'm so happy for you. This is so unexpectedly spontaneous and romantic of you."

Everett appeared momentarily startled, but he patted his sister's back and then set her away with a smile. "I'm not certain whether to be flattered or insulted by that statement, but thank you. Now, stop flailing about—you need to be careful of your wrist."

Abigail dismissed his concerns with a wave. "Oh pishposh, my wrist can withstand a hug or two." She turned to Daisy and gave her an equally enthusiastic embrace. "I'm so happy. I've always wished for a sister, and now I'll have one. And such a wonderful one at that."

Daisy, unused to such easy and exuberant displays of affection, found herself squeezing the girl back.

Abigail gave Daisy's cheek a quick kiss then stood back, bathing them equally in the brilliance of her smile. "Isn't it marvelous that things worked out so I could be here for this? So much more exciting to hear the news firsthand than to read it in a dry letter."

Daisy mentally winced. How would the girl feel if she knew there would never have been a proposal without her being here? Not that Daisy blamed Abigail. Everett had warned her more than once to be circumspect in the use of that door, that perceptions were important. She should have paid better attention.

Everett gave his sister a pointed look. "If you think I'm going to say that this was worth you pulling that foolish running-away stunt of yours, you are very mistaken, young lady."

"Well, be that as it may, I think this was meant to be." She flounced back to the sofa and plopped down. "The three of us, living here together as a family—it will be absolutely wonderful."

Would it? Daisy sincerely hoped so, but right now she wasn't so sure.

Once Daisy had returned to her own apartment, Everett gave Abigail strict instructions to get some rest, and then he headed back downstairs. He needed to rearrange the type he'd already set in order to insert the engagement notice. He also wanted to make certain it was prominently displayed so there would be no possibility that it would be overlooked.

He rolled up his sleeves as he approached the press. The sooner he got the paper out, the sooner the worst of the rumors would die. And the better the chances that Abigail wouldn't be touched by them.

It would be a long evening, but the paper would be printed and ready to send out by dawn—even if he had to work all night to make that happen. At least his hand had healed enough that he could get the paper out on his own tonight.

But as he worked, his mind went back to the last time he'd worked on getting the paper out. The way he and Daisy had worked so well together. And how she'd ended up in his arms.

As her husband, he'd have the right to hold her like that again. It wasn't an unpleasant thought.

But then he remembered the discussion he'd just had with her. He'd expected that, once she understood the situation, she'd be eager to rescue her reputation. So her strong negative reaction to his marriage proposal had surprised him. As had his own reaction. It was only a matter of injured pride, he assured himself.

What else could it be?

That evening, as Daisy sat on her bed, brushing out her hair, she tried to make her peace with the day's events. Engaged to be married. And to Everett Fulton, no less.

What an unexpected turn her life had taken.

I know I've been praying for a husband, Lord Jesus. And I know the Bible says Your ways are not our ways and that Your plans are for our good, but I can't for the life of me figure out why You would play matchmaker this way. Surely this isn't Your plan. Everett Fulton doesn't even like me. So there has to be a way out—just show it to me and I promise to take it, no matter what.

Daisy bent down to absently ruffle Kip's fur. "I don't know what's what anymore, boy. Perhaps God is sending me a test of some sort. But if so, I can't seem to find the answer. How can Everett be the right man for me—I'm not sure if he even likes me. And it's clear he doesn't care for you. How can I marry a man who doesn't like dogs? No, he can't be the man God intends for me to marry. Which means He'll show me the way out if I'm patient."

Kip barked, but she wasn't sure if he was agreeing with her or just trying to encourage her.

She turned down the lamp and slipped under the covers. Thirty minutes later, she was still wide awake. Her conscience was prickling at her, telling her that faith required more than she had been giving lately. What if obedience in this situation meant going through with the marriage? Who was she to second-guess the hand she'd been dealt?

Oh, this was all just too confusing.

Forgive me, Lord. I said I'd look past all the outer trappings and accept whatever man You had in store for me. But then I go and get all stubborn and prideful when You put me to the test. If this is truly Your will, then so be it. I still don't understand it, but that's not a necessary part of Your plan, is it? My role is to hear and obey.

There. She'd done all she knew to do. It was in God's hands now.

Chapter Fifteen

The next morning, as Daisy walked beside Everett through town, she did her best to ignore the stares from the shop windows and passersby. The two of them were on their way to Reverend Harper's home, and she felt uncomfortably exposed.

The newspaper had gone out bright and early this morning—she wondered just how late Everett had stayed up last night working on it. She should have offered to help him get it ready. After all, much as he tried to downplay it, she knew his hand wasn't completely healed. But she'd needed time to herself last night.

So now the word should have spread that she and Everett were to be married. Had it been timely enough to offset any gossip that had begun to circulate yesterday?

"Chin up," Everett whispered. "You're doing fine."

Grateful for his unexpected we're-in-this-together tone, she straightened and pasted on a smile. She was a bride-to-be, after all. This was not the time for melancholy moods, at least, not in public.

Anna Harper, the reverend's wife, answered the door. "Good day, Mr. Fulton, Miss Johnson. Please come in."

She stepped back to allow them entry. "I understand congratulations are in order."

Everett gave a short bow. "Thank you, ma'am. And that's why we're here. We'd like to speak to the reverend about setting a date for the ceremony."

"Of course. He's in his study. Let me just let him know you're here."

Daisy tried not to fidget as she stood beside Everett in the Harpers' cozy parlor. The silence seemed to draw out forever. Finally, Mrs. Harper signaled for them to enter her husband's study.

Reverend Harper stood as they walked in. "Please have a seat. I thought I might be receiving a visit from you today."

Everett seated Daisy, then took the chair next to her. "As you've no doubt heard," he said, "Miss Johnson and I plan to be married. We'd like to make the appropriate arrangements with you for scheduling the ceremony."

"Of course. But I hope you won't mind if I ask a few questions first."

Daisy shifted nervously. What sort of questions?

But Everett seemed perfectly at ease. "Not at all."

Reverend Harper leaned forward, his hands clasped on his desk. "First, given the circumstances, I understand that the two of you may feel as if you have no choice in the matter. And I agree that this is the proper response to the situation. However, marriage is not an institution to enter into lightly or blindly. It is meant to last a lifetime, and to be a source of joy and comfort to the husband and wife."

Daisy nodded. That was exactly the kind of marriage she'd longed for. But was it what she'd be getting?

"So," Reverend Harper continued, "while it is admirable that you two want to do what is proper, I feel it incumbent on me to ask if you think this is a marriage you can sustain?"

Everett spoke up before she could even formulate a response. "Rest assured, Reverend, I fully intend to dutifully carry out my role as a husband, and to do what I can to make the partnership work."

"And you, Miss Johnson?"

Daisy lifted her chin, less than cheered by the tone of Everett's response. "I consider marriage a sacred institution, put in place and blessed by God Himself. If I utter my vows, then I will remain faithful to them."

Reverend Harper seemed satisfied. "Very well. I have one additional question for you, and this is something I ask all couples when they come to me, regardless of the circumstances. Have you taken the time to pray about this decision?"

This time, Daisy didn't hesitate. "Yes, sir. I've done lots and lots of praying since yesterday afternoon, and I truly feel this is where the Good Lord is leading me."

"Excellent." He turned to Everett. "And you?"

Everett's expression was closed, unreadable. "I have no doubt at all that this is the right thing to do, and that it is what a caring God would want."

The reverend gave him a long, searching look, obviously aware that Everett hadn't really answered his question. Then he nodded. "Have you given any thought to when you would like to hold the ceremony?"

They had discussed the time frame on the way over here. Daisy had wanted to draw out the engagement for at least a month to give herself time to grow accustomed to the idea. Everett had wanted to make it a matter of days in order to silence the gossips as quickly as possible. They'd reached a compromise of two and a half weeks.

"We would like to hold it two weeks from Saturday."

"That would be May twenty-fifth. Is that correct?"

"It is."

Reverend Harper opened a journal and made a nota-
tion, then looked back up. "I think that's everything I need
for now. But before you go, would you allow me to pray
with you?"

Daisy answered for them, not certain what Everett
would say. "Of course, Reverend."

"Then, if you will join hands and bow your heads."

Daisy hesitated, but Everett's hand closed over hers in
a warm, protective grip. She felt something tangible flash
between them in that touch, something that gave her hope
that they really could make this work.

"Lord God Almighty, watch over this couple as they
move toward building a new life together. Show them
that the seeds of this marriage, which were planted out of
necessity, if watered in love and faith and with its roots
planted firmly in Your Word, may produce the fruits of
joy. Remind them daily to honor You and each other, to
keep Your laws and to respect one another. Let them be
ever mindful that in You, all things are possible. Amen."

"Amen," Daisy repeated.

Everett's echoing response was a few seconds behind
hers. He gave her hand a little squeeze and then released it.

She found herself missing the warmth of his touch.

Everett was glad to get out into the sunshine as they
exited the Harper home. He hadn't expected to be affected
by this meeting—it had just been one more item to check
off his list. But when he'd felt the slight tremble of Daisy's
hand beneath his, he'd felt an unexpected surge of protectiveness, an overwhelming need to reassure her that all
would be well. That hand, so small and fragile, reminded
him that despite her fierce streak of independence, she

was a woman in search of a place to belong. He had just begun to try to absorb that when the words of the reverend's prayer washed over him, reminding him of the lifelong commitment he was making, and of God's place in it.

Was he really ready to surrender to that?

Once they were back out on the sidewalk, they strolled quietly for a while. It wasn't until they passed in front of Reggie's photography studio that they broke the silence.

Reggie was there, unlocking the door, and she greeted them with a broad smile. "Everett, Daisy, I heard your good news. Congratulations!"

Everett gave a short bow. "Thank you."

Daisy merely nodded. Had Reggie heard the gossip? What was she thinking?

"Did you set a date yet?" Reggie asked.

Again, Daisy held her tongue, leaving Everett to respond. "The ceremony will be two weeks from Saturday."

Reggie nodded. "No point wasting time once the decision's made."

Daisy finally found her tongue. "You're invited, of course."

"Thank you, but I'd like to come as more than a guest. I'm hoping you'll let me be your photographer." She gave them a serious look. "A milestone such as a wedding should be captured in a photograph, not just for yourself, but for future generations."

"I've never been photographed before." Daisy's voice held a note of awe.

Reggie squeezed her hand. "Then that settles it. I must take your photograph. And it'll be my wedding gift to you."

Everett started to protest, but Reggie held up a hand to stop him. "I insist." Her grin turned mischievous. "Not only will it be my wedding gift to you, but I almost feel like I owe it to you."

Daisy's brow furrowed. "Owe it to us?"

The look in Reggie's eye gave Everett a hint as to where this was going.

"When Everett first came to Turnabout," she explained, "he was kind enough to assist me with some of my outdoor photography."

Everett made an inelegant sound. Kindness had had nothing to do with it.

Reggie's grin widened as she cut him a sideways look. "I'm afraid I took advantage of him by getting him to help me pose a pig." She shook her head. "By the time we were done, your beau here was wearing more mud than the pig."

Daisy couldn't contain a laugh. "Oh, my, that must have been a sight to see."

"Yes, well," Everett said, "it was not my finest hour. And now that you put it that way, we will most definitely take you up on your offer."

"Consider it settled." Reggie placed a hand to her heart. "And I promise you'll like this picture much more than the one with Mr. Keeter's pig."

When they resumed their walk, he expected some teasing from Daisy about the pig. But instead, she had a solemn, troubled expression on her face. Was she having second thoughts about their engagement?

Finally, she turned to him. "I need to ask you something of a personal nature. I hope that's okay, seeing as we're to be wed."

He eyed her warily. "What is it?"

"Are you a God-fearing, Christian believer?"

Chapter Sixteen

Daisy's question took Everett by surprise, and he didn't answer immediately. He knew it was important that he not only be honest with her, but that he also choose his words carefully.

"If you mean, do I believe in Almighty God," he said slowly, "of course I do."

"But?" She appeared braced for a blow.

"But if you mean, do I believe that the almighty, all-knowing God concerns Himself with the everyday affairs of individuals, then I'm not so sure."

He saw the concern in her expression. "How can you believe in the God of the Bible and not believe He cares for all of us?"

"I didn't say He doesn't care. I said he doesn't concern Himself with minor affairs. Look, I go to church on Sundays, I tithe, I do my best not to lie and cheat—all in all, I feel like I'm an upstanding member of the congregation."

"Being a Christian doesn't have anything to do with what church you go to, or even if you go to church service at all." Her expression was so earnest, her eyes so expressive he couldn't look away.

"Father and I traveled around a lot," she continued.

"That meant we weren't always near a church come Sunday mornings. But I don't believe that makes me any less dear to God, or any less near to Him, either."

Her words weren't making a lot of sense—it was like she was talking in circles. "What is it you're asking me?"

"I'm talking about faith, about believing those things that are written in the pages of the Bible, even if you don't fully understand them. My father used to tell me that the test of faith is not holding fast to those teachings when everything is going well, but holding to them even when the world around you seems darkest."

He couldn't let that pass unchallenged. "You're actually setting your *father* up as an example of faith?" He knew he'd said the wrong thing, even before the hurt flashed in her eyes.

But she recovered quickly, and her chin came up. "None of us are perfect, and God doesn't demand that we *be* perfect—only that we repent when we fail and continue striving to do what's right and good."

She made it sound easy, he thought bitterly. And why wouldn't she, when it seemed to be part of her nature to see the good in every situation?

How would she feel if she'd faced the ugliness that he had?

And what kind of God would be capable of forgiving him what he'd done?

He was glad to see they had arrived back at his office. Without another word, he held the door open and indicated she should precede him.

Daisy stepped inside, still troubled by Everett's words. He was missing so much if he didn't build that personal relationship with God.

The silence between them stretched, threatening to become awkward. How were they supposed to interact with each other now that they were engaged?

Daisy pasted on a smile. "Time for me to get started on lunch." She headed for the stairs, then paused as something else occurred to her.

"Is something wrong?" Everett asked.

"I was thinking, now that we're engaged, it doesn't make sense for you to continue to pay me for cooking your meals."

Some of the tension eased from his face. Had he worried about what she'd say? "That's entirely up to you. I certainly have no problem continuing to pay you for the next two weeks, but you're right, in short order, we shall share equally in all that we own."

Something else to get used to. She was just starting to enjoy the idea of having money and belongings of her own. "True. But that brings up something else. I want you to know I don't expect you to share in the cost of my new stove and the other things I'll need for my restaurant." She fingered her collar. "Which means I'd better start looking for another job once Miss Winters returns."

To her surprise, he drew his brows down at that. "Surely you don't still intend to pursue that restaurant idea of yours?"

Daisy stiffened. "What do you mean?"

"Now that you'll be my wife, there's no need for you to find another means to support yourself. I should be able to provide financially for our household. Isn't that the reason you wanted the restaurant—to find a reliable source of income?"

"Only partly." She took a deep breath. "I like to cook and bake, especially when I can cook for folks who appreciate it."

"Be that as it may, I don't see the need to invest the kind

of money it will take to open a restaurant if we don't need to. At least not immediately. You can indulge yourself in the cooking you do for our household."

Is this what marriage to him was going to be like? Having him dismiss her thoughts and ideas out of hand if they didn't conform to his own? "Weren't you listening to me? I just said I didn't expect you to invest in my business. That's why I'm going to be looking for another job."

"Don't you think taking care of our home will keep you busy enough?" His tone indicated he was getting irritated.

"I'll manage. And don't worry, I won't skimp on your meals or the housekeeping if that's what you're worried about."

"Daisy, this is foolish. What do you hope to accomplish by wearing yourself out with all this unnecessary extra work?"

"It's something I want to do, something that'll be all my own. Just like this newspaper is all your own."

"Reporting the news is my profession, not a hobby."

So much for him believing in her as a businesswoman. "Are you telling me I *can't* do this?" What would she do if he said yes?

"No, of course not." He moved toward his desk. "Look, there will be enough adjustments for both of us with this upcoming marriage. Why don't we give ourselves a couple of weeks to see how things go and then discuss this again."

She took a deep breath, then nodded. "That sounds fair. But I warn you, I'm not going to just let this drop."

His cynically amused expression was back. "I didn't for one moment believe you would."

Later that morning, Daisy opened the oven to check on her cobbler as Abigail snagged one of the peach slices that hadn't made it into the oven.

"I think we should make some changes to this place after the two of you are married," the girl said thoughtfully between bites. "Or even better, *before* you get married."

One thing about Abigail: she seemed to have an endless supply of ideas. "What do you mean?"

"It would only make sense to take down the wall between the two living quarters. I mean, there's no need to keep separate spaces once we're a family."

Daisy paused in the act of closing the oven. She'd expected Abigail to mention new curtains or pictures for the walls, but nothing on this scale. She straightened and gave the girl a pointed look. "There's no need, as you say, but there's no pressing reason to change, either."

"But just picture it." Abigail rose and walked to the wall in question. "If we tore this out, we could transform your kitchen and sitting room areas into a proper parlor."

Abigail spread her arms to encompass her brother's sitting room. "Once we did that, we could turn this area into a dining room, big enough to accommodate guests."

Daisy smiled. Whatever Everett lacked in imagination, his sister more than made up for. "Planning dinner parties, are you?"

"It'll be nice to entertain our friends occasionally, don't you think? For instance, in Everett's letters he mentioned the Sunday lunches at the Barrs' home. Wouldn't you like to be able to repay them for their hospitality?"

That thought did evoke wonderful images of cozy gatherings with family and friends. Could she and Everett build that kind of home together? Is that something he even wanted?

Abigail stood and studied the other end of the living quarters with a finger to her cheek. "And don't you think the bedchambers are rather small? I mean, not tiny, but wouldn't you like something grander for you and Everett to share?"

Daisy shifted uncomfortably and turned back toward the stove. This was something she and Everett hadn't discussed yet. Everything had been so businesslike to this point, but they *were* getting married. Did he expect the two of them to share a bedchamber? Was that something *she* wanted?

"We could take the wall out between Everett's room and mine," Abigail said excitedly. "That would make one nice-size bedroom for the two of you. And if I moved into one of the bedchambers over on your side, that would give the two of you more privacy, as well."

Daisy was still mulling over the whole question of what Everett might or might not be expecting after the wedding. But she realized Abigail was waiting for her response. "That all sounds good in theory, but it also sounds like a lot of work and expense. I don't think it's something we should undertake right now."

"Now you sound like Everett." Abigail's tone made it clear she hadn't intended that as a compliment.

It was time to rein the girl in. "Be that as it may, there are enough other things that'll need attention between now and the wedding. There's no need to add to that list unless absolutely necessary."

She saw the argument poised on Abigail's lips and quickly added, "Why don't we find something else to talk about?"

"Oh, very well." Abigail returned to the table and rested her elbows there while she watched Daisy. "If I haven't told you so already, I want you to know I'm very excited that we're going to be sisters."

Daisy smiled. Now, there was a subject she was in perfect agreement with Abigail on. "Me, too. I always felt cheated not to have any brothers or sisters."

"I was beginning to despair that my brother would ever marry."

"Oh, come now. He's not so old as that."

"He's twenty-seven." Abigail said that as if it were ancient. "But it's not just his age. Everett always seemed too cynical to allow himself to fall in love."

Daisy was surprised—did Abigail really see her brother that way?

"But I can see now he needed just the right woman to come along and capture his heart," Abigail continued with a happy smile. "It's ever so romantic that he proposed so quickly after he met you. Tell me, was it love at first sight?"

Daisy hesitated. How much should she say? It seemed cruel to disillusion the girl. But she couldn't lie. "Abigail, please don't overly romanticize this. My engagement to your brother is more practical than romantic."

Abigail waved that aside. "That sounds like Everett, but don't let that worry you overmuch. I think in this case he's just letting himself believe that because it's what he's comfortable with. I see that little spark between the two of you, even if he won't admit it's there."

Spark? Now who was just seeing what she wanted to?

But while they were on this subject, there was one more thing Daisy felt compelled to say. "Abigail, I want you to understand that, while we both know I'm not the kind of girl your brother wanted in a wife, I promise to make him the best wife I know how to be."

Abigail sat up straighter. "I know nothing of the sort. You're exactly the kind of woman he wants *and* needs. And deep down, he knows that—he proposed to you, didn't he?"

Daisy felt she was getting in deeper and deeper. "Yes,

well, I think it may have had more to do with me being convenient than anything else. But I've prayed about it, and both of us are committed to making it work."

"Well, if he's not head over heels in love with you now, he soon will be." Abigail gave Daisy a surprisingly mature look. "I know Everett can be stuffy at times, but he truly is a good man with a kind heart. You'll be there now to make sure he doesn't take everything so seriously—including himself."

Daisy moved to the stove while she contemplated Abigail's words. She was so lost in thought that she didn't realize Everett had joined them until he spoke up.

"What is that dog doing in here?"

Daisy started and glanced over her shoulder. Sure enough, at some point Kip had stepped across the threshold and was now blissfully allowing Abigail the honor of scratching his side.

"Don't get all stiff and grumpy," Abigail said. "I lured him over here. After all, he'll be part of our family soon, too."

Everett's frown deepened. "That dog is *not* family."

"Don't be so stuffy. Of course he is. He's the family pet. And since Daisy will be moving over to this side after the wedding, and the whole place will then be one home, it seems ridiculous to let Kip have the run of only one half of it."

Daisy cast a quick glance Everett's way to see how he reacted to Abigail's statement, but could detect nothing except displeasure with his sister.

Finally, he gave a stiff nod. "Just make certain he doesn't make a mess."

"Of course." Abigail shot a triumphant look Daisy's way as she moved to the cupboard to collect the dishes for their meal, and Daisy was almost certain she saw a quick wink.

A moment later, as Abigail set the table, she assumed an innocent expression. "I was just talking to Daisy about some changes I think you should make to the place."

"Were you, now?" Everett's tone was dry. "Something more than allowing that animal to impinge on my home, I take it."

"Uh-huh."

"Well, you may as well tell me before you burst from holding it in."

Abigail explained her grand plans while Daisy busied herself at the stove. When the girl mentioned the bedroom idea, Daisy again glanced Everett's way, but again saw nothing more than an indulgent, long-suffering attitude toward his sister. Did that mean he'd taken it as a given that they would share a bedchamber? Or was he just good at hiding his reactions?

As uncomfortable a topic as it would be, she'd have to find a way to bring up the subject of future sleeping arrangements soon.

"So what do you think?" Abigail finally asked.

"I think, as usual, you are dreaming big and not giving any thought to what it takes to make those dreams a reality."

Abigail seemed undeterred. "That's what dreams are for. But you do agree it's a good idea, don't you? We'll be one family after the wedding, which means there won't be any need to keep the quarters separate."

"True. But there's no burning need to make any changes right away, either."

"Except for your bedchamber."

"Abigail, must you be so indelicate?"

The girl's only answer was an unrepentant grin. Then she continued on as if he hadn't interrupted. "It wouldn't take much to accomplish the changes, and I think you really should take care of it all before the wedding."

"Do you, now? And how do you propose I pay for all these grand plans of yours?"

"You can use the money you'd set aside for Miss Haversham's fees to take care of it. And we need to get new furnishings, as well. If we order a few essential items right away, they may have time to arrive before the wedding."

"I daresay we'll disagree on our notions of what constitutes essential."

Daisy set the meal on the table then, effectively silencing the siblings for the moment. But once they were seated and the blessing had been said, Everett turned to Daisy. "What do *you* think of my little sister's grand plans?"

Daisy tried to keep her tone noncommittal. "It sounds rather ambitious."

"That's my sister—she dreams on a grand scale."

Abigail pointed her fork from one to the other of them. "I can hear you, you know. And why would anyone want to limit their dreams to the mediocre?"

Daisy couldn't argue with that philosophy. Her own dreams of opening a restaurant might seem overly ambitious to some.

Everett still kept his gaze on Daisy. "Even so, perhaps we can do some of what she suggested."

That capitulation, the second from him in less than thirty minutes, caught Daisy by surprise. "Oh?"

Abigail's response was much more vocal and enthusiastic. "You mean it? Oh, Everett, that's marvelous. I do believe love has softened you a bit."

Daisy started. Love? Abigail couldn't be more wrong.

But Everett held up a hand. "I said we'd see about doing *some* of it. It would obviously be inappropriate for us to remove the wall between the two living quarters before the wedding."

"But—"

"That's not negotiable," he said firmly. "But, assuming Miss Johnson is amenable, perhaps we can move you over to her side of the building and work on enlarging the bedchamber over here."

Both looked to her for approval.

"Oh, Daisy, please say yes."

Daisy was still trying to figure out what he might be thinking. But she quickly nodded. "Of course. But I warn you, the bedchambers on my side are not nearly as nice as the ones over here. For one thing, there's no furniture in the extra bedroom."

Abigail dismissed Daisy's concern. "That's not a problem. I can move my things over there. In fact, I'll need to clear the room out, anyway, so the walls can come down."

Everett passed the bread platter to Daisy. "As for the rest, I suppose we can see about ordering a few more furnishings, as long as we agree on a budget and you stick to it."

Abigail clapped her hands. "This'll be so much fun. I have some fabulous ideas for what we can do."

Everett gave his sister a pointed look. "I think it would be more appropriate to let Daisy take the lead."

Abigail cast a chastened look Daisy's way. "Oh, of course, I only meant—"

"We can do it together," Daisy interjected quickly. "I would love to hear your ideas."

"You may live to regret that statement," Everett said dryly. "But I shall leave the specifics to you ladies. I'll work out a budget for you this afternoon."

Abigail turned to Daisy. "The wedding is in less than

three weeks, so we should start planning right away. How quickly can I move in with you?"

The girl certainly didn't waste time. "As soon as you like, I suppose. It's clean, but like I said, there aren't any furnishings to speak of."

"As soon as we're done with lunch, let's go look it over and figure out how we want to arrange things."

Everett frowned at his sister. "Don't nag at Daisy—it isn't ladylike. And your wrist hasn't healed yet, so don't try moving any furniture yourself. You two figure out what you want moved, and I'll either take care of it or hire someone who will."

Abigail apparently knew when to give in gracefully, so she merely nodded and turned her attention to her meal.

Later, just about the time Daisy finished the dishes, Constance topped the stairs.

"Oh, hello," Abigail greeted her friend. "Have you heard about Daisy and Everett's engagement? Isn't it wonderful?"

"It certainly is." The girl smiled shyly Daisy's way. "I offer my best wishes, Miss Johnson."

"Why, thank you, Constance." Daisy dried her hands on her apron. "If you girls don't mind keeping an eye on Kip, I need to speak to Abigail's brother."

"You mean your fiancé," Abigail corrected archly.

Daisy controlled the urge to roll her eyes. "Yes, him."

"While we're watching Kip, Constance can help me plan my move."

Constance gave Abigail a frown. "You're moving?"

"Not far…"

Daisy left the two girls chattering as she removed her apron and headed down the stairs. She was relieved to find that Everett was alone.

She cleared her throat, and he looked up questioningly. "Yes? Have you already finished planning my sister's move?"

"I left Abigail and Constance to it. Your sister seems quite excited about it, though I'm not sure I understand why."

"Abigail is always up for an adventure, no matter how small."

Daisy smiled, then quickly remembered her mission. "I was wondering if I could discuss something with you?"

He set his pen down and gave her his full attention. "Of course. What is it?"

She took to fiddling with her collar. "I'd prefer to discuss this somewhere we're less likely to be interrupted, especially by the two girls upstairs." Her cheeks warmed. "It's of a personal nature."

It was all she could do not to squirm under the look he gave her.

But he nodded and stood. "I see. And where would you suggest we have this discussion?"

"I thought perhaps we could take a walk." She hated the nervous tentativeness. "But if now is not a good time for you to get away, we can—"

"No, no. I can spare whatever time you need." He crossed the room to retrieve his coat. "Have you let Abigail know we're going out?"

Daisy nodded.

"Very well." He held open the door. "Shall we?"

As they stepped onto the sidewalk, he paused. "I'll let you decide on the direction this time."

She pointed south. "This way, I think." As they set out, she explained her choice just to make conversation. "There's an open field past the schoolhouse where Kip and I take a lot of our walks. It's also where I gather berries."

"I know the place."

"There's an old log near one of the trees that makes for a nice bench, and we could sit comfortably while we talk." It would also allow them to be openly visible, as propriety dictated, without worrying about interruptions.

They strolled along in a not uncomfortable silence, for all appearances just enjoying the sunshine and fresh air. And after a moment or two, Daisy managed to relax.

When they reached the spot she'd described, however, all that peace fled, leaving her edgy and uncertain.

Everett handed her down, but remained standing. "Now, what is this matter you wanted to discuss?"

She wasn't quite sure how to start. "It's rather indelicate."

That earned her an amused look. "Thanks for the warning. Now that I am suitably prepared, you may continue."

She cleared her throat, then decided it would be best to dive right in. "Based on our earlier discussion, it's obvious Abigail assumes you and I will be sharing a bedchamber after we're married." Her cheeks were on fire, but she was determined to keep her voice steady. "It's something we haven't discussed, though. I mean, I'd like to know if that's what you want."

There was no flash of shock or surprise in his expression, which indicated he'd probably anticipated her question. "I have no objections."

His tone held that amused edge she was coming to really dislike. And she wasn't about to let him off that easy. "That wasn't my question."

He spread his hands. "I suppose my expectation is that we treat it as any other marriage." He raised a brow. "However, if you are averse to that, or need time—"

"No." That had come out more emphatically than she'd intended, and her cheeks burned hotter at the look he gave her. "I mean, I've always wanted a large family, but I don't, I mean, if you don't—"

He touched her shoulder. "Daisy, it's okay."

This was the first time he'd called her by her first name. She rather liked the sound of it.

But then, as if coming to himself, he pulled his hand back and tugged on his cuff. "To be more precise, I believe that our sharing a room would be the best course of action, for a number of reasons."

Dare she ask him to list those reasons?

"However," he continued, "if that makes you uncomfortable—"

"No." This time her tone was more assured. "I agree that it makes sense to keep up appearances since that's the whole reason we're going through with this." Is that what she really meant? "I just didn't want you to feel as if you'd been backed into a corner. At least, not any more than you already had by circumstances."

"It's quite considerate of you to concern yourself with my feelings, but, my dear Miss Johnson, when have you ever known me to do anything I did not want to do?"

Far from an endearment, the *my dear Miss Johnson* made him sound more distant than ever. Not that she was looking for endearments.

She shook off that thought and went back to the conversation at hand. It seemed he'd already forgotten he'd been forced to propose to her. But, since he was being particularly pleasant, she wouldn't bring that up.

He tugged at his sleeve. "I understand we haven't known each other long and that this is not a union either of us desired."

She hoped her mental wince didn't show on her face. At least now she knew for certain how he felt.

"So I understand that you may need time to become

comfortable with the idea of our marriage. If I may be somewhat indelicate, as well, if you were obliquely referring to our sharing more than a room, you can rest assured that I am willing to give you some time in that arena, too."

Now what did he mean by that? Was he offering to sleep on the floor? She was mighty tempted to ask him to elaborate, but then chickened out. "Very well." She stood. "Thank you for your time. I think I know where you stand." But did she really?

"There is one more thing," she said impulsively.

"And that is?"

"Do you think it would be okay to use first names when we are addressing each other?"

She saw something flash in his expression, but couldn't identify it before it disappeared. Had she overstepped some line of propriety again?

Then he smiled. "I think that would be quite acceptable." He offered her his arm. "Shall we, Daisy?"

As they headed back to town, Everett replayed their conversation, and her expressions, in his mind. He knew he hadn't handled that as well as he should have, but he wasn't quite certain where he'd gone off track.

Of course he wanted her in his bed. He was a man, and she would be his wife. And if he were being totally honest with himself, somehow, over the time he'd spent with her, she'd gone from being an annoyance to something much dearer. He didn't love her in the romantic sense; it wasn't in his nature to do so. But without him really noticing how or when it had happened, he'd begun to enjoy her company, to feel the need to protect her, to want to gain her trust and more.

And that thought scared him more than anything else

in his life had up until now. And he wasn't ready to examine just why.

He should have known she'd tackle that particular issue head-on, the way she did every problem she faced in life. Daisy wasn't one to shy away from something just because it was uncomfortable or difficult. It could be a trying trait for those around her, but he was coming to admire her for it, as well.

Was he as honest and courageous when facing his own trials? He didn't like the answer to that question.

Because the fact that he was determined to hide his newly discovered feelings for Daisy was proof that he did not.

Chapter Seventeen

The next morning, Abigail ventured out for a walk. When she returned, she had a large parcel with her.

Daisy cast a stern eye her way. "You're not supposed to be carrying anything heavy."

"Now you sound like Everett. Don't worry. This isn't very heavy, and besides, a nice young man carried it all the way from the mercantile to our front door for me."

Not surprising. Daisy wondered if Everett was prepared for the fact that his nearly grown little sister would be attracting more and more attention from the youths of her acquaintance.

"Anyway," Abigail said with an airy wave of her hand, "look what I found at the mercantile." She quickly unwrapped her parcel and lifted out two colorful lengths of fabric. She draped each over a kitchen chair, then stepped back to give Daisy a better view.

Daisy wiped her hands on her apron and moved closer. One of the fabrics was exactly what she would expect Abigail to select. It was a sapphire-blue with thin, yellow, vertical stripes—very soft and pretty. The other, which drew her interest more strongly, was a bright, sunshiny-yellow with sprigs of vivid red, blue and purple flowers scattered across it. "They're beautiful," Daisy said, stroking the yellow print. "Are you planning to make some new dresses?"

"No, silly, this is for curtains." Abigail touched the blue-striped fabric. "This one is for my room. Blue is my favorite color." She gave it one last pat and looked up. "Now that I'm moving into a room that's not cluttered with Everett's miscellany, I wanted to do something to make it my own."

Daisy pointed to the more colorful fabric. "And this one?"

"That one's for your room," Abigail said with a very pleased-with-herself smile. "I couldn't resist. It was so bright and cheery that it reminded me of you. I hope you don't think it was too presumptuous."

Daisy was touched by the gesture. No one had done such a thoughtful thing for her since her mother passed away. "Not at all. The fabric is exactly what I would have picked myself. Thank you."

Abigail grinned. "You might want to wait to thank me until we have them up in your room. I still have to do the sewing. And with this bandaged wrist, I won't be at my best. Too bad we don't have a sewing machine here like the one at Miss Haversham's."

Daisy pulled her hand away from the fabric. "If it's too much trouble—"

Abigail waved her protests away. "Not at all. It just means I'll be slower and not able to do any fancy stitchery. But I'll just forgo the ruffles and pleating and make these curtains straight and plain for expediency's sake."

"I'm sure they'll look lovely."

"The only thing I'll promise is that they'll look better than those dull window shades we're using right now." She straightened. "I won't keep you from your cooking any longer. I have some measuring and cutting to do."

She gathered up the fabric. "By the way, I didn't see

Everett downstairs when I walked through. Do you know where he went?"

Daisy shook her head, aware of how little she knew of her husband-to-be's daily routine. "Out running some errands, no doubt. I'm sure he'll be back in time for lunch."

Everett sat quietly at the kitchen table as his sister and Daisy discussed cosmetic changes to his home. He was trying to come to terms with the fact that that's how things would be for him from now on. So much for the peaceful bachelor life he'd enjoyed all these years.

But for all of that, he was glad to see the two had developed a close relationship. Perhaps Daisy wasn't as refined as the girls his sister was accustomed to, but there were some things Abigail would do well to learn from his future wife.

Future wife. He was still having trouble getting used to that concept.

A sudden lull in the conversation gave him the opportunity to change the subject. He cleared his throat to grab their attention before they could launch into something else. "I'm glad you found something to keep you occupied, Abigail. It might interest you to know that I have prepared another pastime for you, as well."

"Oh?"

Why did she look so apprehensive? "I finally unloaded the boxes of books I had in the storeroom. They are now all neatly stacked in your library area next door. So, sister of mine," he said with mock formality, "once you are done with your curtains, if you want to spend some of your abundant spare time cataloging and preparing those volumes for use in your library, you have my permission."

Abigail popped up from her seat and gave Everett's

neck a hug. "Oh, thank you! Does this mean you approve of my idea now?"

"It means I'm resigned to the fact that you're not going to give up on it. And that you need some way to occupy your time so you won't get into further mischief."

She grinned unrepentantly. "So true. I'll start bringing my own books down, as well. I'll have the library ready for business in no time."

Everett gave her his sternest look. "You'll do nothing of the kind. Set whichever of your books you want to add to the library over there." He indicated a small table near the sofa. "I'll carry them to the bottom of the stairs for you as I have the time."

"That seems a bit—"

He didn't let her finish. "I don't want to catch you carrying anything down either set of stairs. Not until your wrist heals completely—do you understand?"

She huffed. "I understand my brother is a worrier."

He wouldn't reward her flippancy with a smile. "Abigail."

She gave an exaggerated sigh. "Yes, yes, I understand."

He didn't have a lot of confidence that she would follow his rules, but he planned to keep his eye on her.

"Another thing—I don't want you to take this as a sign that I'm resigned to having you stay here indefinitely. After the wedding, we will revisit the discussion of your return to Miss Haversham's."

Abigail lifted her chin defiantly. "Discussion, of course, is always an option."

He decided to let that remark go. When the time came, they both knew she would do as he instructed.

Then Abigail changed the subject. "I'm going to work on the new curtains this afternoon, but tomorrow I'll walk over to Constance's and see if she still wants to help with the library."

Was his little sister finally learning patience? There was a time when she'd have hopped up right then and there to recruit her friend to help with her latest scheme. Perhaps Daisy really was having a positive influence on her.

Later that afternoon, Abigail drifted downstairs and sat in the chair in front of Everett's desk. With a sigh, he set down his pen. Between Abigail and Daisy, he was hard-pressed to find two uninterrupted hours back-to-back. "Is there something I can do for you?"

"I think I should go ahead and move over to Daisy's quarters today. You can't get started tearing down that wall until I'm out of there," she explained. "And the sooner you do that, the sooner we can get it ready for after the wedding."

Everett still wasn't certain how he felt about having workmen invade his home, much less letting Daisy and Abigail loose to decorate it. With Daisy's flamboyant sense of color and Abigail's adventurous spirit, he could imagine the havoc they would wreak in his orderly inner sanctum.

But the die had been cast, and he couldn't turn back now. "That's all very well," he told Abigail. "But you can't start carting things over to Daisy's place without her permission. You can talk to her in the morning."

"Why don't I go talk to her now?"

"Because she spent the day cooking and cleaning up after us. It seems reasonable to think she would want some time to herself right now."

"Pish-posh, Everett. Why must you always try to be reasonable? I'm certain Daisy is like me and enjoys having people around her. Besides, she's practically one of the family now. She won't mind. And if now is not a good time for my move, I'm sure she'll say so."

"Don't try to cajole her, Abigail."

"I won't." Abigail gave one of her customary airy waves as she popped out of her chair. In a heartbeat, she was out the door.

Everett stood and headed for the stairs. He had no doubt that Daisy would agree to his sister's plans—it didn't seem to be in her nature to refuse such a request. Which meant he was in for several hours of moving Abigail's furnishings and belongings.

Chapter Eighteen

Just as Everett had predicted, Abigail had him rearrange her things a number of times until she pronounced herself satisfied. She also had him hang her newly constructed curtains in both her room and Daisy's.

He wasn't certain what he'd expected to see when he stepped into Daisy's bedchamber, but he found himself surprised by the almost monastic simplicity of it. The bed was covered by her bedroll only—there were no sheets or coverlets, and no pillows. A small braided rug sat on the floor next to the bed, and two large crates served as tables. One held a Bible and lamp, the other a hairbrush and a small wooden horse. Her clothing—what there was of it—hung on pegs on the wall across from her bed.

If he'd expected her to be embarrassed or apologetic, he was mistaken in that, as well. While he hung the curtains, she explained to Abigail, with some pride, how she'd made the mattress herself, as well as the braided rug that served as Kip's bed, and how the wooden horse was carved by her father and given to her as a gift when she was six.

She truly seemed content with what she had.

Was that part of the secret of her ever-present optimism? That she could find contentment in whatever her circumstances?

Could it really be so simple?

The next day, Everett contacted Walter Hendricks, the local carpenter, to take a look at his place with an eye toward doing the proposed remodeling.

"It seems a straightforward-enough project," Mr. Hendricks said. "I don't recommend taking the entire wall out, but we should be able to take down a good three-quarters of it to open up the room. My boys and I should be able to get it all done—tearing out and smoothing over—in about two and a half days."

"When can you start?"

The man rubbed his chin. "I have another small job ahead of you, but I should finish it up in the morning. Is tomorrow afternoon okay?"

Everett nodded. "The sooner, the better."

Mr. Hendricks gave him a knowing smile. "Don't worry. We'll have it all done before your new bride is ready to settle in."

Everett made a noncommittal response, and the carpenter, with a tip of his hat, took his leave.

Everett moved to the window to check on Daisy. Today was her laundry day, and she was hard at work. He thought about bringing her something to drink, but saw Abigail step outside with a glass in her hand.

It appeared his services were not required.

He headed downstairs, noting how unusually quiet the place seemed, leaving him free from distractions.

Except the memory of last week's laundry day and how it had ended.

* * *

Daisy brushed the back of her hand across her forehead, pushing the damp tendrils out of her way. It was only mid-morning, but already she felt wilted. Still, the chore seemed easier this second time around. Not only did she know what to expect now, but she'd learned from some of the mistakes she'd made last week.

One other thing that made the job feel less of a drudgery was Abigail's frequent visits, bringing her lemonade and passing the time with her easy chatter. The girl even offered to help with a few minor tasks, but Daisy quickly dismissed that notion. She didn't feel it would be right to accept full pay from her customers if she didn't do the work herself.

Though she enjoyed Abigail's company and appreciated her efforts, Daisy missed having Everett checking up on her the way he had last week. He *had* come out here first thing this morning, of course, before the last gauzy wisps of darkness had fully disappeared, to check that her tubs were all situated in a manner that would make them easy to drain later. She'd tried thanking him, and he'd merely said he wanted to avoid a repeat of what had happened last week. And that had been the last time she'd seen him today. Had he been too busy to bother, or merely too disinterested?

Daisy pushed those thoughts aside. Hadn't she told both Abigail and Everett that she wanted to handle this job on her own? She couldn't really fault him if he took her at her word, could she?

That back-and-forth argument with herself kept her mind occupied through the rest of the day. By evening, when she'd brought the last of the clothes in, separated out the items that needed ironing and folded the rest, Daisy was ready to focus on something different. She quickly freshened up, then went upstairs to find Abigail working on a sewing project.

"The *Gazette* goes out in the morning," she told the girl, "which means your brother will be working to get it printed tonight. I'm going over to lend him a hand."

Abigail immediately set her project aside. "What a great idea. I'm coming with you."

When they entered Everett's office, he was already printing the first page. "I know your hand is better," Daisy said by way of greeting, "but I thought you might want some help, anyway."

He looked up with a frown. "That's not necessary. I know you've had a hard day, and I have everything under control here."

The hint that he might be concerned for her welfare, maybe even had checked on her without her knowing, lifted Daisy's spirits. But it didn't dissuade her from her purpose. "Be that as it may, since we're to be married soon, I'd like to learn as much as I can about the family business."

Abigail grinned. "Family business—I like that. But since I'm not any good at this sort of thing, I'll take care of supper. I baked some fresh bread earlier. It's not as good as Daisy's, but it's passable. Why don't I prepare some sandwiches and bring them down here so we can eat picnic style. Then I'll watch Kip and keep you two company while you work."

Everett didn't raise any further objections, and they had a surprisingly pleasant evening. Abigail tried to teach Kip a few tricks with results that had Daisy laughing and even drew a smile or two from Everett. As with the laundry, Daisy found the job of typesetting much easier this second time around. And she and Everett developed a comfortable rhythm working together.

When Daisy headed home that evening, she was accompanied by Kip and Abigail. It somehow felt wrong to leave Everett all alone in his place. Of course, that was just as he had been before she showed up. Perhaps it was how he preferred it.

But when she lay in her bed later that night, she thought about how good it had felt while they were all together earlier. If she were a betting person, she'd wager that even Everett had enjoyed himself. Almost as if they were a true family.

The family they would be in actuality in less than two weeks. She lay there, letting that thought flow through her, settle in her mind. And in her heart. For the first time, it didn't seem so far-fetched that this was the man she'd build her life with.

Perhaps God had known what He was doing, after all.

Everett had waited until he heard Daisy's door close before he'd closed and locked his own outer door. Then he'd quickly climbed the stairs and listened for sounds that they were all upstairs. He heard the faint sound of Daisy's laughter, no doubt in response to something his sister had said.

Now, before he could retire, he had to disrupt the orderly arrangement of his bedchamber and get the room ready for tomorrow's demolition work.

While he shoved and slid various pieces of furniture to the far side of the room, he wondered at his mood. He had lived alone for most of the past dozen or so years. Why did it suddenly feel lonely over here?

Then his thoughts shifted to how deft Daisy was becoming at typesetting. He had to admit, she'd make a good partner in the running of his newspaper business. If that was something he wanted to continue.

Which, of course, he didn't. Someday soon he would get the break he needed and return to his place as a reporter in a big city.

In the meantime, though, there were worse things than being married to a woman who took a genuine interest in his work.

And on that thought, he turned down the lamp and climbed into bed.

Daisy was finishing the dishes the next afternoon when Walter Hendricks showed up with his two sons in tow. Predictably, Abigail made quick friends with the two Hendricks brothers, especially Calvin, the older son.

But once the work began in earnest, the girl quickly distanced herself from the noise and dust. "I have an errand to run," she told Daisy. "I won't be gone long."

Sure enough, when Daisy returned from her afternoon walk with Kip, she found Abigail waiting for her, her eyes sparkling with excitement. "I borrowed the furniture catalog from Mr. Blakely," she told Daisy. "I thought we could figure out what furniture we'd like to order."

Caught up in the girl's enthusiasm, Daisy eagerly pored over the catalog with her. But she was still uncomfortable with spending Everett's money, regardless of how he felt about it. She had to keep reining in the less-concerned Abigail. One item that hadn't been on her mental list, however, caught her eye. It was a large chaise lounge. The piece had simple lines but was topped with a wonderful-looking plush cushion. If she placed it in their bedchamber, it would give her a not-so-obvious alternate sleeping accommodation. At least then she wouldn't have to worry about which of them would be sleeping on the floor.

Abigail enthusiastically approved of her choice. "I knew you had a touch of the frivolous romantic in you. I was afraid for a moment that you were going to be thoroughly and boringly practical."

Abigail also insisted they order a sewing machine and some updated laundry equipment. Despite her frequent flights of fancy, the girl had a practical head on her shoulders.

After much back and forth, Daisy and Abigail finally had a list of items they both could agree on.

Abigail shook her head sadly. "I do think you're taking my brother much too literally on this budget business, but I'll defer to your wishes." She plucked the list from the table and linked her elbow with Daisy's. "Let's go place our order. The sooner we do, the sooner the pieces will arrive."

Daisy held up a hand. "Not so fast. We should discuss our selections with your brother first."

"But he said we should order whatever we wanted as long as we stayed within his budget, which, thanks to your stubbornness, we did."

"Yes, but since we *are* spending his money, to furnish and decorate *his* home, I'd like to make sure he doesn't have any objections to anything on our list." Everett had such elegant taste in everything, she was afraid she'd made some glaring mistakes in one or more of her choices.

But Abigail had no such qualms. "It's your home, too, and I assure you, Everett will be fine with whatever you decide—especially since you're his bride-to-be."

If only Abigail knew how little weight that really carried. "Still, I must insist."

Abigail gave in with good grace. "Oh, very well, if it makes you feel better. Let's see if he can look it over now."

"I think we should wait until he closes his office for the day."

"There's no telling when that will be. And what can it

hurt to check now? If he's too busy, he'll certainly let us know."

Daisy didn't doubt that for a moment. Still, she was hesitant to disturb him.

Abigail, however, was already headed for the stairs. Almost before her feet touched the ground floor, she started in with melodramatic emphasis. "Everett, Daisy and I have selected the barest minimum of furnishings needed to make our combined quarters livable."

Everett leaned back in his chair. "Have you, now?"

"Yes." Abigail rolled her eyes. "And it wasn't easy because Daisy insisted on being positively frugal—quite a trying experience."

"If she succeeded in reining in your extravagance, then my hat is off to her." He turned to Daisy. "You didn't let her run roughshod over you, did you?"

"Not at all."

"Good. Then I take it you're headed to the mercantile to place the order."

Daisy smiled. "Actually, if you have a minute I'd like your opinion before we place the order."

"I'm sure it is perfectly acceptable."

Did the man ever give a direct answer? "Still, I'd like you to take a quick look. I wouldn't want there to be any unpleasant surprises for you once the items arrive."

"And time is of the utmost essence," Abigail added dramatically.

He gave Daisy a quizzical look, then stood. "Well, in that case, I suppose I'd better have a look. I'm having trouble concentrating on my work with that infernal racket upstairs, anyway."

They spread the catalog and their list out on his desk, and Everett stood between them as they looked it over. Daisy let Abigail point things out to her brother and explain exactly why each item was a must-have purchase. But several times he interrupted his sister to turn to Daisy and get her opinion. Was he just being polite? Or did he really care what she thought?

When Abigail got to the chaise lounge, Daisy saw Everett give her a quick, speculative glance, but he didn't say anything. She tried to keep her expression neutral, but wasn't sure if she'd succeeded. Had he guessed the reason she had included it in her order? And if he had, what did he think about it?

In the end, Everett found himself surprised by the list. The practical items far outweighed the decorative. What had happened to all that colorful exuberance she tended to use in her own place? Had his strictures about sticking to the budget boxed her in too tightly?

When Abigail bemoaned the fact that Daisy had vetoed the purchase of a small dressing table for her use, something she insisted every young woman *must* have, Everett turned to his bride-to-be. "Do you agree with my sister over the importance of this item?"

Daisy shrugged. "A dressing table is a nice item to have, but I've gotten along for quite some time without one, so I think I can manage a bit longer. The other items on the list are much more important."

Everett studied the list again. "I believe there are items here that we need regardless of any renovations, so they should not be counted against the budget." He met Daisy's gaze again. "That means there are funds to cover the addition of the dressing table."

Daisy's eyes widened in surprise.

"And a chair for it, as well," Abigail added quickly.

With a nod, Everett scribbled the additions to their list. He did, however, say no to the fine-woven rug his sister thought would add just the right decorative touch to the room.

As the two ladies headed out toward the mercantile, Everett slowly returned to his desk. The chaise lounge on the list had caught his eye, especially when his sister artlessly explained how Daisy had picked it out without any prompting from her.

He had a pretty good idea why his future bride had selected it for their bedchamber. And if that's where she planned to spend her nights for the time being, then so be it. He'd told her he'd leave the sleeping arrangements to her discretion, and he was a man of his word.

If he was feeling a twinge of disappointment, then he would deal with it the way he dealt with every other disappointment in his life.

He would bury it and move on. Dwelling on disappointments and troubles only made one weak.

Chapter Nineteen

Daisy found that she actually enjoyed having Abigail living on her side of the dividing wall. Not only was the girl's chatter a welcome distraction from her own thoughts, but Abigail began to add touches of color and charm to the entire living space.

Cheery squares of fabric would appear as cloths to cover the crates she used as a table, and bits of bric-a-brac popped up in strategic locations.

"You don't mind if I put this chair in here rather than in my room, do you?" she'd say. "The light in here is much better to read by than the light in my room."

Another time it would be, "These curtains didn't work out as well as I thought they would in my room, so I put them here in the sitting room."

Abigail also began to treat the two living quarters like they were already one, going back and forth between them as if the invisible barrier Everett erected at the adjoining door didn't exist.

And random pieces of furniture from Everett's side began showing up in her place, as well. A footstool here, a wooden chair there—suddenly Daisy's place was looking much more cozy.

But she wasn't comfortable with Abigail's cavalier kidnapping of furniture from Everett's domain.

She finally put her foot down. "You need to stop bringing all these things over here."

Abigail's expression was one of wide-eyed ingenuousness. "All I'm doing is some simple rearranging of the furniture to make things more comfortable for the two of us. Don't you like it?"

"Don't pretend you don't know what I mean. Your brother and I aren't married yet, which means right now this is not part of his home, so you shouldn't treat it as if it were."

"It will be soon enough. I'm just getting a little head start." She waved airily. "But if you want me to stop rearranging until after the wedding, I suppose I can wait."

Daisy wasn't fooled. The girl hadn't offered to undo what she'd already done, just not do any additional encroaching.

Everett, however, seemed to either not notice or not care that pieces of his furniture were disappearing out from under him.

As observant as the man was, she suspected he was deliberately turning a blind eye to his sister's redecorating efforts. He was quite good at these subtle ways of showing how much he cared for her. Why couldn't he be more open about it? It would mean so much to Abigail.

And to Daisy, as well.

Chapter Twenty

On Sunday, as they strolled home from the gathering at the Barrs' home, Abigail complimented Daisy on her Sunday dress. Daisy, aware that Abigail was wearing yet another gown that was making its first appearance in Turnabout, smiled and gave the girl the history of the dress.

"How wonderful. I can tell from your tone that you must have loved your mother very much."

"I do. And I miss her very much, too."

The girl's expression turned wistful. "You're lucky. I don't remember my own mother much at all." Then she smiled. "But having an older sister like you will be almost as nice."

Daisy gave the girl's arm a little squeeze. She'd grown to love Abigail, to feel like she really was a sister. It was comforting to know that it was mutual.

Then Abigail cut her a speculative look. "But speaking of dresses, have you given any thought to a wedding gown?"

It was obvious Abigail didn't consider her current attire suitable.

But Daisy didn't have any other options. She grabbed

the side of her skirt and spread it wide. "Why, this one, of course."

"Oh, but it's your wedding. Surely that warrants a new gown."

Daisy shrugged, trying not to let the words hurt. "I'm not much of a seamstress, and even if I were, there's not much time before the wedding."

"But isn't there a dressmaker here in Turnabout? I'm sure she can take care of this for you. And if she's too busy, I can work on it myself. Please, let me help you select a new dress. I've been told I have a very good sense of style."

"I'm sure you do, but—"

"Please. It'll be fun."

"Better let her do it," Everett added dryly. "My sister considers herself a great arbiter of fashion, and she does enjoy having a new subject to work with."

Suddenly realizing that the garment she wore for her wedding would reflect not only on her, but on Everett and Abigail, as well, Daisy's resolve weakened. "If you really think I should…"

Abigail jumped on Daisy's capitulation. "Oh, this will be fun. We need to find just the right pattern to accentuate your lovely figure and height. I have some catalogs we can look at this afternoon."

As Abigail quickened her steps, Everett turned to Daisy. "I'm afraid you're in for a long afternoon of poring over pictures and discussing the advantages of one style over another."

She smiled. "I don't mind. And it was very sweet of her to offer to help."

"For all her faults, my sister is a very giving person." He studied her carefully. "But don't let that hold you hostage or make you feel you must give in if you disagree with her choices."

This time Daisy's smile was genuine. "Have you ever known me to not speak my mind?"

Daisy and Everett parted at Daisy's front door. By the time she reached the second floor, Abigail was exiting her room with two catalogs cradled in her arms.

Daisy immediately rushed forward. "Here, let me take those. Your wrist is not quite healed yet."

"You're turning into as much of a fussbudget as my brother." But Abigail handed the books over without arguing. "Why don't we go over to the other side so we can spread these out on the dining room table?" Without waiting for Daisy's response, she sashayed to the adjoining door, signaling for Kip to follow her.

Everett sat on the sofa, reading one of the papers he had mailed to him from various cities. He looked up and nodded a greeting, frowning at the dog before he went back to reading.

"I'd prefer not to have anything too fancy or froufrou," Daisy warned.

"Oh, I agree." Abigail opened the thicker of the two catalogs. "I think something with fairly simple lines would be best. That's not to say it won't be elegant, though. And it should have lace insets at the neckline and collar." She pointed to one of the pictures. "Oh, here, what do you think of this one?"

Daisy looked at the picture Abigail pointed out and was immediately captivated. The gown was truly beautiful. It had a gently scalloped neckline inset with lace that formed a throat-hugging collar. The bodice was embellished with tone-on-tone embroidery and beadwork. The long, fitted sleeves ended with a tapering point at the wrist.

"Oh, Abigail, it's beautiful, but it's much too fancy. The embroidery work alone would take hours and hours."

"True, but we can do a simpler version and still get the

same effect. I'll help the dressmaker if she hasn't the time." She turned the page. "We'll keep looking to see if we find anything we like better, though. We have all afternoon."

In the end, Daisy didn't see anything she liked more than that first dress. She turned back to it and stared wistfully. Could she really have something this lovely?

Abigail had no such doubts. "You're right—this is the one. Now let's talk about colors. Of course we'll have to work with whatever selection the seamstress has on hand— I don't think she'll have enough time to order anything. But I'm thinking a soft shade in the blue or green family would work best with your coloring."

Daisy nodded. She was calculating costs in her head. If she used all of her laundry money and some of the earnings she'd managed to set aside from her work for Everett, she might just be able to cover it. She'd have to start saving all over again, but neither Everett nor Abigail would have cause to be embarrassed if she wore this dress.

As if reading her thoughts, Everett spoke up from across the room. "Sounds like you've made a decision. You can speak to Miss Andrews tomorrow. Tell her to bill me for her services."

Daisy stiffened. She might not have much to bring with her into this marriage, but she could take care of her own wedding dress. "Thank you for the offer, but I'll handle this myself."

He raised a brow at that. "Does it really matter whose money we pay with? Soon there won't be any yours or mine—it'll be ours."

Did he really mean that? "Nevertheless, we aren't married yet. I'd prefer to keep things separate until we do."

He shrugged. "As you wish."

Daisy eyed him suspiciously. He'd given in a bit too easily. But then Abigail reclaimed her attention with animated discussions of trim options, including types of lace, beads, embroidery and other embellishments.

Daisy realized she'd have her work cut out for her if she was to keep it simple.

The next morning, Abigail insisted on accompanying Daisy to the dressmaker's shop. "I love to look at fabrics and patterns," she said by way of explanation. But Daisy suspected she didn't trust her to pick out the proper fabric by herself.

Hazel Andrews greeted them with reserved enthusiasm, but warmed considerably when she saw the picture of the dress they wanted her to make. "It's been some time since I had a gown of this caliber to work on. Not since Mrs. Pierce quit ordering new dresses." She studied Daisy with a critical eye, then nodded. "It has the perfect silhouette for you."

"We were thinking something in blue or green would be best," Abigail said.

"I agree. With an ivory trim perhaps." The dressmaker's eyes lit up. "Oh, and I have the perfect fabric for such a gown. I've stored it in the back for just such a special project as this. It's a lovely blue-green shot silk that will complement your eyes and look quite elegant."

Daisy quickly spoke up. "Please keep in mind that cost will be a factor. And that this dress will serve as my Sunday dress after the wedding. Perhaps we need to consider a more sensible fabric."

Hazel and Abigail exchanged glances, then the seamstress gave Daisy a placating smile. "Let me fetch it for you to look at before you make up your mind."

When the seamstress came out with the fabric, Daisy felt her resolve weaken. It truly was a lovely color, with a subtle sheen that made it seem almost fluid.

She touched it reverently, then pulled her hand back. "It looks mighty expensive. Perhaps you should show me something a little more practical."

"Oh, but it's your wedding dress," Abigail argued. "You should forget practical. And this fabric is perfect—you know it is."

Daisy cast a longing look at the fabric, then shook her head. "What else do you have that would be suitable?"

The seamstress didn't move. "This fabric is not as expensive as you might think. And for your wedding dress, I'm willing to give you a discount."

Daisy tried not to get her hopes up. But when the seamstress named her figure, she was pleasantly surprised. It would take most, but not all, of her carefully hoarded funds, but she *could* afford it.

And since Everett was so opposed to her restaurant idea, there was really no rush in replacing her funds.

During lunch, Abigail chattered away about the dress. Daisy figured Everett must be bored, so she filled in the conversational gaps with questions about what kind of stories he was working on for the next paper. And her interest was genuine. Even though he pretended disdain for the kind of news Turnabout provided him with, he always managed to give them a fair and interesting treatment. She liked his way of reporting, the way he found the tidbits that spoke to him and focused the light on them.

When the meal was over, Abigail jumped up. "Sorry I can't help with the cleanup, but I promised to meet Constance downstairs to work on our library as soon as lunch was over." She turned to her brother. "You'll help Daisy in my place, won't you?"

Daisy quickly protested. "That's not necessary, I—"

"Of course I will."

His response caught her by surprise. She'd never seen him wash dishes. But she supposed he must have before she came along.

As he carried a stack of dirty dishes from the table to the counter, Everett cleared his throat. "Is there anyone you'd like to invite to the wedding, other than the locals, I mean?"

What a thoughtful question. "I can't think of anyone."

"Are you certain? I understand your not wanting your father around after the way the two of you parted but, even if this is to be merely a marriage of necessity, I thought you might want to have some of your other family or friends around."

"That's very considerate of you, but unnecessary. I don't think my grandmother would be interested in coming. And Uncle Phillip and his wife are pretty much under her thumb. As for friends, my friends are all here. Traveling the way we did, I didn't have much chance to make friends on the road."

She spread her hands. "So there you have it. What about you?"

"Abigail is the only family I have that matters. As for friends outside of Turnabout, I'm not certain anyone I left behind in Philadelphia would travel over a thousand miles just to see me get married."

She smiled. "Then it seems we have similar circumstances. But we have the friends we've made here to witness our marriage vows, and I'm quite satisfied with that."

He nodded agreement, then cut her a sideways look. "I don't know what kind of relationship you wish to maintain with your father, but if you decide you want him here to walk you down the aisle, then we can try to find him before the wedding.

Did she want him here? She loved her father, but she

didn't like him very much these days. "It might be best if I just let him know about the wedding after the fact."

"Whatever you decide, I'll support you."

She was touched by that statement, by the implied concern. "Thank you, but even if I wanted him here, I'm not sure I'd know where to look."

Once Everett headed downstairs, Daisy's thoughts turned back to the issue of her father. Ever since Abigail arrived, she'd been trying to help Everett see how very important family was, how he should cherish the time he spent with Abigail, despite any other irritations or concerns he might feel.

Was she willing to follow her own advice?

Feeling convicted, she headed downstairs to ask Everett for his help in sending a telegram—in fact, a series of them—to whichever towns her father would be most likely to be visiting right now. He might not get the news in time to attend her wedding, but he'd be passing back through here in a few months, and she didn't want him to be surprised by her new status.

Halfway down the stairs, she paused as something else occurred to her. She should ask Everett for a sheet of paper, too. It was past time she wrote to her grandmother and at least attempted to mend fences there, as well.

Much to Abigail's delight, the furniture they'd ordered arrived two days before the wedding. Daisy instructed the deliverymen to place the sewing machine in her sitting room and the laundry equipment in her storeroom. The bed that had been ordered for Abigail went into her room. Everything else was carted up to Everett's living quarters.

Abigail dragged Daisy into Everett's much-enlarged bedchamber to help with arranging the new furnishings in just the right places.

Daisy felt uncomfortable as she entered what, until now, had been Everett's private domain. "I really think Everett should have some say in how the furnishings are placed."

"Don't be a goose. As if my brother gives a fig for such things. That's the lady of the house's responsibility."

Daisy raised a brow. "At the moment, that's still you."

"Don't be tiresome." Abigail nudged her arm. "We both know I'm just a placeholder for you. Now let's get to it. If we're quick, we can get it done before Everett comes up for lunch. Believe me, he'll be glad to have it all taken care of without having to be bothered with it himself."

Daisy wasn't so sure of that. She knew how organized Everett liked to be, how he liked his things arranged just so. But she supposed he could always rearrange things if he didn't like what they came up with.

As they worked, Daisy was especially careful about the placement of the chaise lounge, situating it beneath the window of what was formally the spare room. That would give them enough space between their beds for some semblance of privacy, if that was what they wanted. She also placed a small trunk nearby that would be perfect for storing the bed linens when not in use.

The dressing table and other items of furniture she let Abigail have some say in, and the girl happily tried several arrangements before she pronounced herself pleased.

When it was finally arranged, Abigail stepped back with a pleased smile. "Won't Everett be surprised when he sees what we've done?"

It was obvious how much Abigail craved her brother's approval. Why was it so hard for Everett to see it?

"Let's hope he's *pleasantly* surprised," Daisy said dryly.

"Oh, you know my brother." Abigail waved a hand airily. "It takes him a while to adjust to new things, but he'll come around in time."

Not the most encouraging of reassurances, but Daisy accepted it as the best they could hope for.

"I suppose we must wait until after the wedding to move all of your things in here, but perhaps there are one or two items you'd like to add now to give it a more womanly touch."

Daisy immediately balked. She wasn't ready to intrude on his domain just yet. "I don't know. That seems a bit presumptuous."

"Nonsense. Everett needs to get used to sharing." Abigail took Daisy's arm and gave it a gentle tug. "Come on. I'll help you pick out some things."

Despite her reluctance, Daisy allowed herself to be swayed by Abigail. In the end, they settled on one of her mother's stitch-work pieces and the toy horse.

When they stepped back and studied the final effect, Abigail smiled. "The perfect hint of a woman's touch to offset my brother's somber decor." She turned and gave Daisy an impulsive hug. "Oh, I'm so happy for Everett. You're going to be so good for him."

Daisy certainly hoped the girl was right.

When Everett came upstairs for lunch, Abigail insisted he view the newly furnished room. Daisy stayed in the kitchen, letting Abigail do the honors.

When they came back out, Abigail's face fairly glowed. "I told you he'd like it," she said to Daisy.

"Who am I to question the taste of two such well-traveled ladies?" Everett said with a straight face.

Daisy felt her own spirits rise. Was Everett actually learning to unbend enough to tease his sister?

Everett's conscience was troubling him, had been for a number of days. Daisy deserved to know his background now, before they were married. But would she go through with the wedding if she knew? Because it was vital, if they were to salvage her reputation, that the wedding take place.

That was his dilemma.

But this morning he'd decided he couldn't in good conscience *not* tell her.

So that afternoon, when Daisy stepped out of her building to take her dog for a walk, he was waiting for her.

"Oh, hello." She looked understandably surprised.

"Do you mind if I come along on your walk?"

"Not at all." She gave him a speculative look but didn't ask questions.

They strolled along in silence for a while, until he finally spoke up. "I think you have a right to know who it is you're marrying."

Daisy smiled. "I know exactly who I'm marrying—Everett Fulton, newspaper man, good neighbor, respected citizen of Turnabout. A man who is perhaps too much of a stickler and takes himself too seriously, but who has a good heart, is a loving brother, and has a strong sense of what is right and honorable and does his duty without question."

Her words took him by surprise. Was that truly how she saw him? But he pushed that question away. "What I mean is, you have a right to know my background, where I come from, so to speak."

She nodded solemnly. "I would love to hear your story, but only if you really want to share it with me."

He took a deep breath. He hadn't spoken of this to anyone before. Even Abigail didn't know the full story. "My father is a member of the English nobility, born the second son of an earl to be more exact."

His admission took Daisy by surprise, but it made sense. English nobility—no wonder he seemed so aloof at times.

But he was waiting for her response. "Does that mean you're a member of the nobility, as well?"

"Not exactly." His smile twisted. "You see, my father never married my mother. She was an actress and considered quite beneath him. Which means I was illegitimate."

Daisy wasn't sure what to say to this. But he didn't give her time to respond.

"Father set her up in a nice cottage at his country estate, and when I came along, he saw that I had tutors, nice clothes, ponies—everything the grandson of an earl should have. But I knew from the outset that I was illegitimate and had no real standing in the family. In fact, I was a bit of an embarrassment and was kept hidden away in the country."

"Oh, Everett, I'm so sorry."

He shrugged. "No need to be. As I said, I led a very easy and privileged life. My mother often returned to London to continue her acting career. I was left in the care of servants, and they all catered to me quite nicely."

This was somehow so much worse than what she'd endured from her grandmother. Daisy tried to match his matter-of-fact tone. "How did you end up in America? Did you get tired of being ignored by your parents?"

"Nothing so noble. When I turned twelve, my father's older brother died in a boating accident, making him the heir apparent. It became his duty to take a wife in order to provide the family line with a legitimate heir."

It all sounded so polite, so sterile. Is that where he got his notions of what marriage was all about?

Without any conscious decision, they had arrived at the same log in the same field where Daisy had questioned him about sleeping arrangements.

Everett handed her down then continued his story. "Father's new wife was understandably loath to share her husband with a mistress and his by-blow. So Mother and I were shipped to America, along with the funds to make sure we would be provided for. He even hired someone to make certain we settled in nicely."

Everett didn't sound particularly grateful.

"As luck would have it," he continued, "Mother was already carrying Abigail when we set sail. However, she didn't discover this until we were well underway, and eventually my sister was born after we arrived in America."

"What happened to your mother?"

"She married a playwright who drank too much and spent all her money. She died when Abigail was five."

She placed a hand over his. "I'm so sorry."

"Again, there's no reason for you to be. By that time I was on my own and making enough to get by. I'd been worried about Abigail for some time—the home my mother made for her was not the most nurturing of environments. When Mother passed on, I got her out of there—my stepfather didn't object—and I scraped together enough money to enroll her in Miss Haversham's school for girls. And I've managed to scrape up enough to keep her there ever since."

Daisy straightened. "My goodness. Your sister has been at that school since she was five?"

His posture took on a slightly defensive cast. "It was the best thing for her. We had no other relatives, at least none we could count on. And she certainly couldn't live with me, not in the places I was living back then."

"And now?"

"What do you mean?"

"Now you have a nice home. You're about to have a wife. Don't you think this is a good place for her now?"

"There's nothing for her here."

"There's you." *And me.*

"I don't want to talk about that right now."

Daisy wanted to shout at him that he never seemed to

want to talk about it. But she could sense there was more to his story, and that it wasn't an easy thing for him to tell it. So she pulled her thoughts back to the conversation at hand. "Do you ever hear from your father?"

"Not directly. Up until I turned twenty-one, his man of business sent me a letter with a small stipend each year on my birthday. He never acknowledged that Abigail was his. And for all I know, he was right. But he supported her, anyway. Because all the money he sent me went directly to Miss Haversham's to help pay Abigail's tuition."

That sounded just like him—not one to take a handout from the father who had rejected him.

"Last I heard," he added, "he had inherited the title and had two sons and a daughter by his wife."

"Your half brothers and half sister. And you've never met them?" That seemed so sad to her.

He merely shrugged.

She straightened and met his gaze. "Now I know your story, and it doesn't change any of those things I said about you."

Was that relief flashing in his expression? Had he truly been worried about how she would react?

But then his expression closed off again. "There's more." She saw his fist clench at his side. "I debated about whether or not to tell you this part."

Chapter Twenty-One

Daisy saw the uncharacteristic uncertainty on Everett's face, and she braced herself. Whatever was coming was going to be worse than what he'd already told her. She said a quick prayer that she would react properly.

He reached down and plucked a blade of grass. "It is at the heart of why I left Philadelphia last year. I did something I'm not very proud of."

"Oh?" She knew he tended to be hard on himself. Perhaps it wasn't as bad as he thought.

"I told you I was a reporter for a large newspaper there, and left because the editor and I had a major disagreement. What I didn't tell you was that he was right to fire me. I would have done the same thing in his place and not lost a minute of sleep over it."

Goodness, what in the world had he done? Still, she held her peace and let him do the talking.

"I had a lead on a story, a very big story, ripe with the kind of notoriety that sells newspapers. I'd gotten wind of rumors that a prominent local politician had taken a mistress and that the woman bore him a child. This man was married, mind you, and he and his wife had two children."

Given what she'd just learned of his own history, she

could see where such a story would have captured his attention, reporter or not.

"When I looked deeper, I found snippets of information that indicated he had covered up his affair by sending the woman and child to England." His lips curled in a self-mocking smile. "You can just imagine the irony of such a story falling in my lap. I checked the facts, and they seemed solid. And such was my fervor to expose this dishonorable dignitary that I didn't keep digging and checking as thoroughly as I usually do."

Her heart sank as she got an inkling of where this was going.

"Based on my reporting," he continued, "my editor published the stories and sold tons of papers. Everyone was happy as could be, except, of course, for this politician and his family, who kept protesting his innocence. Naturally, no one believed him—after all, they'd read the truth in a respected newspaper. So, in order to get himself and his family away from all the harsh public attention, this cheating politician gathered his wife and daughters and set sail on their private yacht for a getaway. Unfortunately, they were caught up in a storm, and the boat capsized. The politician and one daughter drowned. The wife and other child survived."

She placed a hand on his arm to show her sympathy for both the victims and him. "How awful."

He seemed not to notice her gesture. "A week later, the story I had written proved false. The carefully crafted lie and so-called proof had been engineered and fed to me by one of his political opponents. Someone who knew it was a story I couldn't resist."

"Oh, Everett, I'm so, so sorry."

"Because of my lack of objectivity, a good man and his family were publicly raked over the coals. And my actions, no matter how indirect, led to his death and that of his daughter." He stood and looked down at her. "I just thought you should know what sort of man you were yoking yourself to before it was too late for you to back out."

With that, he turned and left her there.

Daisy felt at a loss as she watched him leave. What he'd done had had terrible consequences. But she could see that he was hurting, that he was filled with remorse and self-loathing. She should have said something, done something to comfort him. But she'd failed him.

Father above, Everett is a man in need of forgiveness, both from You and from himself. I know You will forgive him if he but asks, but how can I help him to see that? Please, help me find a way.

Everett walked into his office and sat at his desk shuffling papers, but was unable to concentrate on any of it. Telling Daisy had been the right thing to do, the honorable thing. But that hadn't made it any easier.

She now had to choose between marrying a man who had done this truly unforgivable thing, or live with a tarnished reputation. What was she thinking? It had been cowardly of him to leave so abruptly, but reliving that nightmare had scraped his feelings raw, and he couldn't bear to see loathing or rejection in her eyes.

He had attended the funeral, had seen the politician and his daughter laid to rest. The sight of those two caskets had been convicting. The sight of the grieving widow and surviving daughter had wrenched something deep inside him.

He'd stood in the back of the crowd, not wanting his presence to bring further pain to this family. But somehow the widow had seen him. For one endless moment, their eyes had locked across that cemetery lawn and he'd felt her pain. When she finally looked away—turned her back on him—he'd walked away.

Would Daisy turn her back on him, as well?

His door opened and Daisy marched in, her dog at her heels. Her eyes were flashing with some strong emotion and he surged to his feet, bracing himself for the worst.

"It wasn't very gentlemanly of you to walk off that way without me."

He tried to read her expression. "My apologies."

"Apology accepted." She lifted her chin. "I just wanted to let you know that I ran into Adam on my way here and, since I haven't heard back from my father, I asked him to walk me down the aisle Saturday. He agreed."

Was that her way of telling him she intended to go through with the wedding? But did that mean she'd just taken the better of two unappealing options? "Adam is a good choice."

"Glad you approve." She smiled. "And for the record, though he is remarkably thickheaded and obtuse, I think my husband-to-be is also a good choice. Those things I said about him earlier still stand."

And with that, she spun around and walked away.

Everett slowly sat back down. She was going through with it, *wanted* to go through with it. The flood of emotions surging into him almost made him dizzy. There had been no loathing, no rejection in her eyes when she looked at him. There had been anger, yes, but something else, too, something amazingly like affection.

How could that be? Deep down he knew he wasn't a very likable person, even when one didn't know his secrets. Yet she saw something good in him. What was it she had said about him? *A man who is perhaps too much of a stickler and takes himself too seriously but who has a good heart, is a loving brother, has a strong sense of what is right and honorable, and does his duty without question.*

He wasn't sure he really was that person, but suddenly he very much wanted to be.

Daisy's wedding day dawned bright and clear. The sky was dotted here and there with wispy clouds that posed no danger of rain and only served to intensify the blue of the sky behind them.

Daisy stood at the back of the church with Adam and Reggie, waiting for her cue to walk down the aisle. This was it. In a few short moments, she would speak the vows that would tie her life irrevocably to Everett's. It was a scary thought, but exciting, too.

At least she was properly attired for the occasion—Everett would have no reason to apologize for her appearance. She looked down at her skirt, gently touching the luxurious fabric, admiring the scalloped hem and lace trim.

The gown Hazel and Abigail had created for her was just about the finest she'd ever seen, much less worn. And that included gowns she'd seen in her grandmother's drawing room and in Abigail's catalogs.

Abigail had played the role of sister of the bride with relish. She insisted on arranging Daisy's hair, piling it all up fancy with a few ringlets cascading down. And there was a coronet of flowers in her hair. The girl had also picked a bouquet of lovely wildflowers, along with roses from Reggie's garden.

She felt like a princess. And an impostor.

Everything about today would be perfect, if only she was marrying someone who loved her. Was this truly the answer to her prayers? Or was it rather the penance she must pay for not listening to Everett's concerns over their use of that door?

Everett had been so good about not making her feel he was angry or unhappy with the circumstances that had brought them to this. But she knew he had to feel some amount of frustration.

Would they be able to get past that?

Reggie was keeping an eye on the preacher, looking for the signal that it was time to start. Then, as if picking up on Daisy's nervousness, she turned and gave her a smile. "You look mighty fine, fine enough to fit in in my grandfather's parlor back in Philadelphia. Don't you agree, Adam?"

"That, she would. In fact, I can only remember one bride who looked lovelier." He winked at his wife, and Daisy was surprised to see a faint blush stain Reggie's cheeks. Would she and Everett ever share those kind of special moments?

Reggie looked into the sanctuary again, then turned with a smile. "All right, they're all set."

Daisy's heart stuttered, as if she'd been caught in the act of something improper. Adam tucked her arm under his elbow and smiled down at her. "Shall we?"

She pushed away the last minute wave of panic, and nodded.

Adam's smile took on an understanding edge, and he patted her hand. "Deep breath. Smile. Eyes straight ahead. You'll do fine."

She smiled gratefully, lifted her head and signaled she was ready.

All heads turned to face her as she stepped into the aisle, but Daisy's gaze sought and then locked onto Everett's. She saw his eyes widen just a bit as he took in her appearance. His obvious approval gave her a little boost of confidence.

Then Adam gave her arm a squeeze, and they were

moving forward. The walk down the aisle seemed both infinitely long and unbelievably short. Then Adam was releasing her and handing her off to Everett.

The cynicism that seemed a natural part of his expression appeared to be curiously absent now. Instead, it was replaced by something softer yet stronger at the same time. She responded with a shy smile.

When he took her hand, there was a moment of connection, of intense awareness, that almost made her jump. She could tell he felt it, too. Was it because of the occasion? Or something more?

His hold was warm, strong, possessive. But as before, there was protectiveness and tenderness, as well. She was suddenly filled with a sense of peace, of *rightness*. This was meant to be. Did Everett feel that, too?

Reverend Harper's words broke the spell, and both Everett and Daisy faced forward. But she remained acutely conscious of the man at her side, and the warm comfort of his hand holding hers so protectively.

She stood through the entire ceremony as if watching it from a distance, as if it were happening to someone else. The only thing grounding her was the feel of his hand holding hers.

To her surprise, Everett had a ring to place on her finger at the appropriate time. As he slipped it on her finger, she stared down at it, a simple gold band with a small, square-cut, blue stone set on prongs. She was enchanted by just how perfect it was, how very right it looked on her finger.

She looked up and found Everett watching her, and for once there was no guarded quality in his expression. Just warm encouragement, and something more primitive that she didn't quite understand but didn't fear. And that was the very best wedding present he could have given her.

When the vows had been recited and Reverend Harper

pronounced them man and wife, Everett bent down to give her a kiss. It was sweet and warm and altogether breathtaking. And over much too soon.

Then they were turning to face the congregation. The first person Daisy saw was Abigail, and she was surprised to see the girl had a tear trickling down her cheek, but her smile was beautifully joyful.

Then Everett was leading her down the aisle in firm, sure steps. And from every side, Daisy saw smiles of shared happiness and approval.

Had this marriage had the unexpected effect of giving her a firmer standing in the community?

She pushed that thought aside—that wasn't the kind of thing one should contemplate about one's marriage.

As they stepped out on the church steps, Daisy blinked a moment in the brightness of the sunshine. Then she blinked again in surprise. A flower-festooned motorized carriage was waiting for them, with Chance sitting in the driver's seat.

Reggie had offered to hold a reception for them at her home after the wedding, and Daisy would have been fine with making the short trip there on foot. But such a thoughtful, romantic gesture from Everett caught her off guard, and her pulse quickened in pleasure at what he'd done. When she turned to thank him, though, it was obvious from his expression that he was as surprised as she was.

Before Daisy could say anything, Abigail rushed up and gave Daisy a hug. "We're truly sisters now. I'm so happy." Then she stepped back. "Do you like the conveyance? I thought you should be transported from the church in style."

"It's very thoughtful. Thank you."

"Yes, thank you, Abigail." Everett turned to Daisy. "Shall we?"

The reception was set up in Reggie's beautiful and expansive backyard. To Daisy's surprise, there was a grand turnout. She and Everett greeted guests as they arrived until Daisy felt she must have shaken every hand in town.

As Everett circulated among the guests, his gaze kept drifting back to his wife. There was no trace of the peddler's daughter in her today. This Daisy would fit in any society ballroom or parlor. It was partly the dress, of course. But it was more than that. There was a sort of natural grace to her, a genuine friendliness that shone through from within.

Perhaps fate had dealt him a winning hand, after all.

He was making his way to Daisy's side to offer her a cup of punch when Reggie waylaid him. "I'm ready to photograph you and your bride. I'll fetch Daisy if you'll find your sister." She pointed toward a large oak that shaded one side of her lawn. "I've got the camera set up over there."

Everett finally tracked down Abigail. She and Constance were chatting with Jack, who was keeping an eye on Kip and Buck. By the time they reached Reggie, Daisy was already there.

Reggie had set up her camera so that the tree would serve as a backdrop for the picture. "Let's get a photograph with just the bride and groom first," she instructed. "If the two of you would stand right there."

She fussily arranged Daisy's dress, having her hold her flowers just so. Then she stood back, studying them. A grin teased the corners of her mouth. "You are married now. You can stand closer together. And don't be afraid to hold hands."

Everett didn't need to be told twice. Holding his wife's hand had become one of his favorite pastimes.

"Perfect. Now if you'll just hold it there for a few minutes… Okay. Now you'd mentioned wanting to get a picture of the two of you with Abigail."

Daisy nodded. "Yes. A family picture."

"In that case," Abigail interjected, "Kip should be in the picture, too."

Everett frowned. "That animal is not part of the family."

"Come now," Reggie said, "posing with an animal will be just like old times for you."

"What's this?" Abigail looked from Reggie to Everett.

Before either Reggie or Everett could elaborate, Daisy jumped in. "I'll tell you about it later."

With a nod, Abigail stood between the two of them, with Kip right in front of her.

A few minutes later, Reggie straightened. "Beautiful. I'll deliver them to you as soon as they're ready."

Daisy was glad when the reception began to break up. It had been a lovely gathering, but she was ready to return home. Except she was also a little anxious, too. At least Abigail would be there to act as a sort of buffer, to keep things feeling normal and familiar.

But to her surprise, Abigail gave her and Everett farewell hugs.

"You two go on without me," she said. "I've already packed a bag, and I'll be spending the night at the Harpers' home with Constance. And Jack has volunteered to keep an eye on Kip for you tonight, with his parents' permission, so Kip is staying right here. That means you will have the house entirely to yourselves."

Daisy couldn't quite make herself look at Everett, who remained maddeningly silent. "That's very sweet of you, but it's really not necessary," she said weakly.

"Of course it is." Abigail gave her an arch smile. "You two may not have been able to take a honeymoon trip, but as newlyweds you should have some privacy on your first night together." She made a shooing motion with one hand. "So go along, and I'll see you at church tomorrow morning."

Any further protest would raise brows, so Daisy merely nodded. Would Abigail's absence make this first night easier or more awkward?

And what in the world was Everett thinking?

Chance and his motor carriage were still there, waiting to take them home. Chance stepped forward and doffed his hat as he gave a sweeping bow. "Shall we be on our way?"

Daisy would have rather walked—anything to slow things down a little. But Everett handed her up, and within minutes they were stepping down in front of their home.

Now what?

Chapter Twenty-Two

Everett took her elbow—there was that spark again—and led her to the door. He opened it, and Daisy preceded him inside.

It was only four o'clock in the afternoon, so it was nowhere near time to retire for the evening. Daisy didn't know which was worse—waiting for night to fall, or how she was going to feel when it actually *was* time to retire for the evening.

She gave him her best attempt at a smile. "I'm going upstairs to change out of this fine dress and back into my everyday clothes. Then I'll see about fixing us some supper."

He released her arm. "Don't rush the meal on my account. I'm not very hungry at the moment, and there's some paperwork down here I need to get to."

Is that how he planned to spend the afternoon of their wedding day? But she merely nodded and headed for the stairs.

Daisy opened the door and stepped into the bedchamber she was supposed to share with Everett now. She'd been in here before, when the new furniture arrived, but somehow it looked and felt different now.

Her belongings, meager as they were, were all here—thanks to Abigail.

Her mother's Bible lay on the bedside table, and her silver hairbrush, which had also belonged to her mother, was on the dressing table. The dressing screen stood discreetly in what had once been a second bedroom.

The sight of her everyday shoes on the floor right next to Everett's seemed almost unbearably intimate.

A few minutes later, when she hung her dress in the wardrobe, she studied Everett's clothes hanging neatly there. His things were so refined, so impeccable. And her clothing, with the exception of this beautiful gown, was sadly lacking in comparison.

It was just one more reminder of how mismatched they were.

To give him credit, however, Everett hadn't made her feel unworthy, at least, not lately.

She quickly pulled out one of her serviceable homespuns. She was who she was—no point wishing she was someone else. Time for this Cinderella to head back to the kitchen.

Everett hadn't watched Daisy as she climbed the stairs earlier, but he'd been very aware of her every movement. He knew this was difficult for her, but she seemed to be holding up well. His wife was a woman of strong character.

His wife—it was really and truly done now. It might not be the marriage he'd planned for himself, but he could already see there was much to like in this arrangement.

As for this sudden awkwardness between them, it was normal for a new bride to be nervous—that had to be all it was. Because surely she knew she had nothing to fear from him. He intended to let her set the tone for the physical part of their relationship. More than likely, she planned to sleep on the chaise tonight. But he was confident that in time she would grow more comfortable with him and the idea of sharing the marriage bed. After all, she had said she'd like to have children.

He determinedly pushed those thoughts away and tried to focus on his paperwork. But later, when she called him up to supper, he realized he'd gotten very little accomplished.

During the meal, Everett tried to engage her in idle conversation, but was only partly successful. Though she responded to his comments, she seemed nervous and her gaze more often than not slid away from his. He'd never seen her so flustered before.

Finally, he decided there was only one thing he could do to settle her nerves. He cleared his throat. "I have some things I need to finish downstairs. Don't wait up on me."

Her gaze flew to his and held, her eyes widening in surprise. Was there a hint of disappointment mixed in with the relief? Or was that just wishful thinking?

Whatever the case, it would be a very long evening.

Once he left, Daisy finished cleaning the kitchen, still unable to recapture that sense of peace she'd had earlier. He'd noticed, she was sure. No doubt that had been responsible for his eagerness to leave the room once the meal was over.

The house felt so empty without Abigail and Kip. Perhaps, when those two boisterous beings returned tomorrow, things would feel more comfortable, more normal again.

Finally, the last dish was dried and put away, the table was wiped down until it practically sparkled, and the floor was swept.

There was nothing left for her to do but retire for the night. And perhaps the quicker she got to it, the better. The thought of preparing for bed with Everett in the room was enough to spur her to action.

Daisy entered the bedchamber and quickly went through her nightly rituals. When she was ready to retire, her gaze shifted from the bed to the chaise and back again. This was it—time to decide where she would sleep tonight.

The need to make this decision had been lurking in the back of her mind all day—which no doubt accounted for the state of her nerves—and she still wasn't certain what to do.

He was leaving the choice entirely up to her, and she knew he wouldn't press her. What did she want to do? What did *he* want her to do?

Father above, I don't know what I should do, or even what I want to do. I would like to be a proper wife to my husband, but I'm not sure if he'd welcome me or think me presumptuous. And am I really ready to take such a step? We've only known each other a short time.

But is this a matter of time, or a matter of closeness? Because I do feel I know his character.

She turned to the bed, her pulse quickening. But her feet wouldn't take that first step.

Yes, she knew his character, but she didn't know his heart.

At the last minute her courage failed her, and she scurried to the chaise and quickly added the pillow and coverlet from the trunk. As she burrowed under the covers, she knew herself to be a coward.

And she suspected she wouldn't get a wink of sleep tonight.

Everett quietly opened the door, not sure what he would find on the other side. She'd left a lamp lit for him with the wick turned down low.

Her soft breathing told him she was asleep. And that she had chosen the chaise. He felt an unexpected twinge of disappointment. But he didn't blame her. He really hadn't shown her any of the tender emotions a sentimental woman like her would expect from the man she married. He wasn't sure he even had it in him to give it to her. The best he could hope for was that she would grow accustomed to him.

He prepared for bed as quietly as he could, accompanied by the sound of her soft breathing. Something about that sound got under his skin and quickened his pulse. It brought back the memory of the kiss they'd shared at the end of the wedding ceremony—sweetly chaste but firing a hunger for more, bringing out all of his protective, and possessive, instincts.

He'd promised to give her however much time she needed, but how many nights would it take before she was comfortable enough with their marriage to give up the chaise?

Perhaps sharing a few more of those kisses would speed the process.

As he slipped into bed, the sound of her breathing seemed to fill the room, a strangely seductive lullaby.

It was going to be a long night.

Daisy woke to find the sun already up. She couldn't believe she'd slept straight through the night. She bolted upright, but a quick glance at the bed across the room told her she was alone. It was neatly made, with nary a wrinkle visible. Had he even slept in his bed last night?

She made quick work of her morning ablutions, then dressed and stepped out of the bedchamber.

Everett was in the kitchen, stoking the stove.

"I'm sorry I overslept. I'll have breakfast ready in two shakes."

"No need to rush. We have lots of time before church service starts."

Daisy joined him in the kitchen and pulled out the skillet, taking a mental inventory of what was in the pantry.

As she counted eggs and measured flour, Everett moved to the adjoining door and opened it, and the inner door as well. He stood staring into Daisy's former living quarters for what seemed a very long time. What in the world was he thinking about?

Finally, he moved back toward the kitchen, but left the doors open. Obviously there was no reason to keep them closed now.

"I do believe Abigail was correct," he said. "We may not be here much longer, but opening up this wall while we *are* here would make sense."

Daisy's heart dropped. Was he still so determined to move away from Turnabout? Couldn't he see what a wonderful life they could build here?

A small furrow appeared on his brow. "Do you have some reservations? If you'd rather not, we don't have to change a thing."

"Oh, no, I think it's a wonderful idea. It would definitely make this place feel more like one home instead of two."

"But?"

She took a deep breath. "I just hoped you'd changed your mind about moving."

His jaw tightened. "You knew before we agreed to this marriage that that was my plan."

"I'm not accusing you of hiding anything. I just hoped you'd come to appreciate what you have here more."

"Well, that was a false hope."

She tried to lighten the mood with a change of subject.

"I think we should celebrate our first morning as man and wife with a special breakfast. What do you say we add an extra egg to the skillet, and have some griddle cakes and strawberry preserves as well?"

Everett accepted her change of subject without protest. "That sounds good. And while you're working on that, I'll fix the coffee."

Just like a happily married couple.

Too bad it was all an act.

Chapter Twenty-Three

As soon as they arrived in the churchyard, Abigail left Constance's side and hurried over. She gave them both exuberant hugs and arch smiles before rushing inside to join the choir.

As Daisy walked into the church, the same church where yesterday she'd spoken her marriage vows, she had the feeling everyone was looking at her differently today. And she supposed she *was* different. She had a new name, a new status, a new family.

After the service, they again had their midday meal at the Barrs' home. Before they sat down at the table, though, Reggie led them into the study where the wedding pictures were displayed on a small table.

Daisy stepped forward eagerly and was immediately entranced by what she saw.

The first picture was the one Reggie had taken of her and Everett alone. Daisy couldn't stop staring at the way Everett looked in the picture, as if he were actually proud to be standing next to her. There was something reassuring and uplifting in the way his hand held hers so possessively. Was she just seeing what she wanted to? Or was it all really there?

She finally tore her gaze from that picture and looked at the other, the one that included Abigail and Kip. What a fine-looking family they made!

Daisy glanced up at Reggie. "These are beautiful. I can't thank you enough."

Reggie waved away her thanks. "You're quite welcome. It was a joy to be able to take these pictures for you."

Daisy glanced Everett's way and caught him staring at the pictures, but she couldn't read his expression. Had he seen the same thing she had?

That evening, Daisy stood in the kitchen, preparing a light supper. Abigail had disappeared with a vague comment about rearranging some of the volumes in her library. And Everett sat on the sofa, reading through his many newspapers.

She loved this feeling of domesticity, of normalcy, of *family*.

She glanced up, then blinked and looked again.

Everett was still reading, but one of his hands was absently rubbing Kip's neck. Did he even realize he was doing it?

She moved toward him, a soft smile on her lips.

He glanced up with an answering smile. She saw the exact moment when he realized what he was doing. His hand stilled, and his expression closed off.

"No need to stop." Daisy joined him on the sofa. "You both looked like you were enjoying yourselves."

"Yes, well—"

"You actually looked like you'd done this before."

"As it happens, I have."

That admission caught her by surprise. "You had a dog?"

"Once, a long time ago."

He seemed unwilling to say more, but she wasn't ready to let it go. "What kind of dog was it?"

"A hound." He shifted uncomfortably.

"And he was your pet?"

"Not exactly." He folded his paper and leaned back. "There was a kennel on the estate where I grew up. Hunting dogs, bred and trained for it. My father was fond of hunting, you see, and insisted everything be kept at the ready for when he wanted to indulge in the sport."

There was a hardness to his voice when he spoke of his father.

"As a boy, I liked to watch the trainers work with the dogs. I was allowed to do so, on the condition I stayed out of everyone's way. These were prize hunting dogs, so there was no question of me trying to make a pet out of any of them—that would interfere with their training."

It seemed now that he'd started talking, he couldn't stop. She wondered if he was even aware anymore that he was speaking to her.

"When I was nearly seven I noticed one pup, the runt of the litter, who had a bad leg. Something about the pup's refusal to give up appealed to me, and I took to slipping him scraps of food. I always suspected Wilkes, the man in charge of the kennel, knew about it, but if so, he looked the other way."

His smile twisted. "I even named the animal. Figuring a runt would need an impressive name to offset his shortcomings, I named him Samson. But I quickly shortened it to Sonny."

She smiled at that. It somehow made the little boy he'd been more endearing.

"The trainers mostly ignored Sonny, so I was able to play with him occasionally. Sonny always greeted me exuberantly and followed me around as if I was someone special. I was even able to teach him a few tricks."

He was quiet for a very long time, but Daisy could tell he wasn't finished with his story.

"One morning," he finally continued, "I went to the kennel and couldn't find him. I asked Wilkes where he might be. It seemed my father had arrived the prior evening for an unannounced hunting trip. He'd reviewed the new additions to the kennel, and when he saw Sonny's limp, he had the animal put down."

Daisy's heart twisted painfully, and she reached for his hand and squeezed it. "Oh, Everett, I'm so sorry."

Everett wore that cynical smile again. "No need to be. It taught me a valuable lesson. Animals are just that—animals. Coddling them serves no useful purpose."

He stood and gathered up the papers. "If you'll excuse me, I think I'll carry these downstairs. There are a few stories I want to summarize for Tuesday's paper."

She watched him leave, her heart breaking for him. What a terrible, terrible thing to have happened, especially to a six-year-old. No wonder he wouldn't unbend when it came to Kip—he was afraid of feeling that same hurt again. Did he even realize why he'd built that wall?

Well, there were cracks in that wall now, and she aimed to make sure she and Kip pushed right through them and tore that wall down.

After supper, Abigail decided to retire to her room early, to do some reading before going to bed.

Everett watched as Daisy worked on some mending to one of her shirtwaists. That reminded him—he'd have to see that she bought some additional clothing. There was no need for his wife to go around in nearly threadbare garments.

Threadbare was a good word for his own emotions at the moment. Why in the world had he volunteered that story? He had never once spoken of Sonny in all the years since it had happened, had nearly blocked it out of his own mind. Yet she had pulled it from him with no effort at all.

Such loss of control was disconcerting. He had to resist this pull she had on him, or he would lose himself entirely.

And he might as well start now. Because there was a matter that required immediate attention. He cleared his throat. "I have something I'd like to discuss with you."

Daisy looked up, a question in her smile.

"Now that the wedding is behind us," he explained, "it's time Abigail went back to Miss Haversham's school to finish her education. And I'd like for us to present a united front when I speak to her."

Daisy set her mending aside, giving him her full attention. "Do you really think this is for the best? She enjoys being here so much."

"Her infatuation with Turnabout and all things Texas will fade in time. But the sooner she returns to Boston, the less painful the break will be."

"I didn't mean being here as in Turnabout, I meant being here as in being with you. She loves you, Everett, and she wants to spend time with you."

"There will be time for that once she completes her education."

"You're going to break her heart if you do this."

He expected these sort of melodramatics from his sister, but not from his wife. "Nonsense."

"Whether it's your intention or not, she'll see this as a rejection."

"Then we'll need to make it clear to her that it's not."

She gave him a steady look and seemed to be undergoing some kind of internal struggle. Finally, she straightened. "I never told you the full story of the time I spent with my grandmother—mostly because it's personal. But now I think I should explain it to you."

He leaned back, intrigued in spite of himself. "I'm listening."

"I guess I should start with some background." She fiddled with her collar. "My grandmother—Grandmère Longpre, as she had me call her—was what one would call a *grande dame*." Daisy made an airy movement with her hand for emphasis. "She was the daughter of a wealthy and socially prominent New Orleans family. Her husband died long before I was born, but before he passed, they had two children together, my mother and my uncle, Phillip. I'm told the family had ambitious plans for my mother's future. They anticipated securing a marriage for her with the son of another prominent family to add to their already considerable consequence."

She grimaced. "Unfortunately, at least in Grandmother's eyes, before they could make it official, my mother fell in love with an itinerant peddler and ran off and married him. Grandmother promptly disowned her."

Everett was very familiar with being disowned, though in his case, he had never been properly "owned" to start with.

"So years later," Daisy continued, "when my mother took ill and had to return home, you can see it wasn't a decision she made easily." Her expression hardened. "And Grandmother made her pay for what she saw as the humiliation my mother had heaped on her and on the family name."

Everett guessed that Daisy, even as a very young child, had been made to pay, as well.

"As for me, I was viewed as little more than a mongrel half-breed child. I told you I spent much of my time in the kitchen—that's because I felt much more welcome there than in my grandmother's presence."

He wanted to comfort her but wasn't quite certain how. He moved to sit beside her on the sofa, and apparently that was enough. She touched his arm and thanked him with her smile. "I know, unlike how my grandmother felt toward me, you truly love Abigail and are trying to do what you think best for her. But, Everett, you need to let her see that. Or you risk having her feel like I did—unloved and unwanted."

He felt some sympathy for what she'd endured, but surely she could see this was different. "Abigail knows I love her."

"Perhaps. But she also needs to knows that you love being *with* her and that you care about what makes her happy—not what she can do to make you happy. There is a difference."

What did she mean by that? "That's not what this is about."

"Isn't it?" This time *she* touched *his* arm. "Perhaps I'm wrong. But if nothing else, Abigail needs to know, without a doubt, that she doesn't need to earn your love, because she already has it."

She stood. "Please think about what I said. And if you can find it in you, pray about it, too. I'm going to bed now. Good night."

Everett stayed where he was, thinking over what she'd said.

Sending Abigail back to school was the right thing, he was sure of it. But perhaps he did need to sit his sister down and make certain she really understood why he felt that way.

And even though he was certain Abigail knew how deeply he cared for her, he supposed it wouldn't hurt to tell her so.

Everett knocked softly on their bedroom door. When there was no answer, he quietly opened the door so as not to awaken her. To his surprise, however, Daisy still sat at her dressing table, brushing her hair.

And what glorious hair it was. It was the first time he'd seen her hair unbound, and he definitely liked what he saw—thick, wavy tresses, the color of fresh-planed oak, rippled down to the middle of her back.

He tore his gaze from her mesmerizing hair, and their eyes met in the mirror. He felt an almost physical connection stretch between them.

Slowly, he moved forward, and their gazes never wavered.

He held out his hand for her hairbrush. "Do you mind?" His voice was thick, nearly unrecognizably so.

Her eyes widened, but she silently handed him the brush.

He began to draw it through her tresses, enjoying the soft feel of it, the way it seemed almost a living thing in his hands, playfully reflecting the candlelight, coyly sliding through his fingers. He inhaled the faint rosewater and lavender scent and thought he'd never smelled anything so fragrant.

As he worked, he was aware of her watching him in the mirror, of the increased rhythm of her breathing, of the warmth radiating from her.

This woman, this *lady,* was his wife. She was a gift, not a burden. Why had it taken him so long to see it?

After a time—heartbeats, minutes, hours, he had no idea—she took the brush from him and stood, facing him.

He took her chin in his hands. "You are so lovely," he whispered. "You are even more beautiful tonight than you were on our wedding day."

"No one's ever called me beautiful before," she whispered.

"And yet you are, strikingly so."

Her eyes had a luminous quality, but he saw no fear in them. He bent down and very gently kissed her. This kiss was different from the previous one they'd shared. What had started as gentle exploration suddenly turned into something much more. Her arms went around his neck and clung to him. Everett's own pulse jumped, and he tightened his hold on her.

Everett felt an exhilarating mixture of victory and capitulation. He felt an urgent need to protect her and claim her and cherish her, all at the same time. At this moment, if she'd asked him to walk through fire, he couldn't have refused her.

He lifted his head, but she gave a little whimper of protest and tugged his head back down. He didn't need further encouragement.

When they finally separated, he took her hand and led her to his bed. To his joy and relief, she not only went willingly, but wearing a shy smile on her face.

Chapter Twenty-Four

The next morning, Daisy hummed as she made breakfast. Today she felt well and truly married. And she had hope that their life together could be as marvelous as God intended for a proper marriage to be.

Everett had said such wonderful things to her last night, had made her feel so cherished and special. She hadn't known he could be so gentle, so tender.

Then she grinned. He would probably be affronted by such descriptors. But the cynic had a soft side, and she'd seen it now.

She heard Everett exit the bedchamber and glanced over her shoulder to give him a smile. "Breakfast will be ready in two shakes."

He returned her smile with a very self-satisfied one of his own. "No need to hurry on my account. I'll have a cup of coffee while I'm waiting."

Abigail padded into the kitchen from the other side of the building, Kip trailing behind. "Something smells good. Do you need any help getting it on the table?" Then she looked from one to the other of them. "Well, you two certainly seem in a good mood this morning. What's going on?"

Daisy felt her cheeks grow warm, but tried to keep her tone nonchalant. "And what's not to be happy about? It's a beautiful day outside, and we're all healthy and well provided for in here. Besides, aren't you opening your library this morning?"

Suitably distracted, Abigail began chattering excitedly about her plans for the library's opening day.

But Daisy caught the look Everett gave her, the one meant only for her, and the happy humming continued in her soul.

Everett headed downstairs right after breakfast, the smile still on his lips. Who would have thought being a family man could feel so fulfilling? Daisy, with her generous heart and sweet courage, had definitely opened his eyes to the good things to be found in his current situation.

Maybe she'd been right about other things, as well.

But for now he needed to put aside all those less-than-productive musings. He had a lot of work to do—the paper was scheduled to go out in the morning.

Everett worked steadily until midmorning, when Lionel stopped by to deliver the bundle of newspapers that had come in for him on the morning train.

Once he was alone again, Everett absently sorted through the various editions, more focused on the sound of Daisy's humming than the headlines. He decided it had a happier-than-usual, very satisfied ring to it this morning.

Then he straightened as he found an envelope addressed to him mixed in with the papers. He opened it, and immediately his focus narrowed to what he held in his hands. This was it—what he'd been waiting for all these months— an offer from a large newspaper concerning a reporter position. They wanted him to spend three weeks working on staff with the understanding that, if they liked his work, the job was his.

Which meant the job *was* his. He knew he could pull this off.

St. Louis might not be the location he would have chosen for his comeback, but it was a good, solid step on the road there. Finally, he could get back in the game and take his rightful place. He could shake the dust of this backwater from his shoes.

He climbed the stairs, wanting to share the good news with Daisy. She might still have a few qualms about moving, but surely she'd be happy for him and get over that soon enough.

He found her alone in the kitchen. Abigail was no doubt in her library.

"Oh, hi," she said when she saw him.

There was a new softness in her smile, a lightness in her tone that made him feel ten feet tall. They were closer now—surely that would make it easier for her to understand. "I have some good news."

Her smile broadened. "What is it?"

"The editor from the *St. Louis Banner Dispatch* has asked me to try out for a reporter position."

He hadn't truly expected her to jump for joy at the news, but neither had he expected the flash of utter dismay he saw in her expression before she suppressed it.

He tried again. "This is what I've been waiting for. It's not Philadelphia, but it's a definite step up from Turnabout."

She made a sharp gesture with her hand. "Don't say it like that. There's nothing wrong with Turnabout." She took a deep breath. "And anyway, bigger doesn't necessarily mean better."

He ignored that comment. "Accepting this position will

mean we can move to a city with many of the amenities Turnabout is lacking. And I can return to being a reporter, not a typesetter and press operator."

Her expression turned wistful. "But we're happy here, aren't we?"

He took her hands, hoping the physical connection would help her understand. "And we can be just as happy in St. Louis."

She didn't pull away. Rather, she gave his hands a squeeze of her own. "Think about everything you'll be leaving behind—dear friends, a home that we've made our own, the *Gazette*. The people in Turnabout have come to expect the newspaper twice a week. Not only that, some folks have even said they're looking forward to that restaurant I want to open someday. How can we leave all of this behind?"

Did she truly understand so little about him? "We'll make new friends. Someone else will step up to take over the *Gazette*. I'll even train them. And we'll live in a finer home—one that you can furnish and decorate however you like."

Her lips set in a stubborn line. "I don't want a finer home. I'm happy with this one." She took a breath. "Say we do move—then what? Is St. Louis just another stepping stone for you? As soon as you find a more prestigious job in a bigger city, will we move again?"

Best to get this all out now. "Perhaps. But moving is nothing new to you. I don't understand why you're being so stubborn about this."

"I told you before we ever got married, I left my father partly because I wanted to set down roots."

"It's not as if we'll be itinerant drifters. The only time we'll move will be when we can improve our situation."

He felt her stiffen at his use of the phrase *itinerant drifters,* and she slowly withdrew her hands.

"Improve it by your definition, you mean."

"By any reasonable person's definition."

"So now I'm not a reasonable person?"

"In this particular instance, no."

He saw her struggle for control as she took another deep breath. But her next words were said civilly enough. "And what about Abigail? Will you keep uprooting her, too?"

He frowned. "Of course not. As we discussed yesterday, she'll go back to Miss Haversham's to finish up her education. Once she's graduated, she will, of course, live with us until she finds a suitable husband."

Daisy's eyes narrowed suspiciously. "A *suitable* husband? What does that mean?"

"It means that her husband should be a man who can take care of her and provide for her both financially and socially in the manner that she deserves." This conversation seemed to be going down all the wrong paths.

Her expression settled into one of sadness and disappointment. "You still don't understand, do you? Being happy isn't tied to things or to status. It's tied to loving and being loved."

Everett tried to take back control of the conversation. "The matter of my sister's future husband is one we can discuss at another time. Of more immediate importance is the fact that I've already decided to take this position. I'll leave for St. Louis on tomorrow's train and go through the three-week trial period. Afterward, once the offer is official, I'll come back to settle affairs here and take you and Abigail away from this place."

She met his gaze steadily, her lips set in a firm line. "And if I don't want to go?"

Would she really take such a stand? But he couldn't

let her see how desperately he wanted her to accompany him—he would never beg, not even of her. "Then that will be your choice. I've already made mine."

Daisy returned to the stove as Everett stiffly marched down the stairs. How could her world have changed from such sweet joy this morning to such bitter disappointment now?

How could Everett be so blind to what was right in front of him? There was such richness and sweetness to this life if he would but take hold of it. Did his ambitions, his need to prove himself someone far superior to the castoff his parents had treated him as, have that great a hold on him?

If only she could believe that this move would be enough to satisfy him, to make him content to finally settle down. But she had seen the hunger for bigger and better in his face as he talked about what the move meant to him.

God, I know I should praise You in life's valleys as well as its mountaintops, but sometimes it's just so hard to follow through on that. Help me to see Your purpose in this, or if I can't, to at least make peace with the circumstances by remembering it is in Your hands.

The prayer settled the churning in her gut somewhat, but there still remained one big unanswered question.

Should she stay or go?

Predictably, Abigail did not take the news well. She protested that she'd just opened her library and it was already doing well. She warned that she would run away again if Everett sent her back to school. She pleaded that she couldn't bear to leave her new friends. And she cried over the idea of being separated from Daisy and Everett.

But to Daisy, the most telling of her protests came when

she asked Everett what she had done to make him want to send her away.

Through it all, Everett kept saying it was what was best for her and that if she could stick with it for just one more year, then she would be done with it once and for all. He also pointed out that learning to finish what one started was a valuable lesson that would stand her in good stead throughout her life.

Daisy found herself caught between the two of them, though her heart was in Abigail's corner. She did her best to comfort the girl and promised there would be lots of correspondence and that the number of visits, in both directions, would increase.

Everett raised a brow at that, but she looked him straight in the eye, silently challenging him to contradict her.

In the end, he shrugged and let her promises stand.

That evening, they worked together to get the newspaper ready to go out. While they still worked smoothly together, Daisy found none of the joy in it that she had before.

When she saw the small notice he'd made for the front page, stating the printing of future issues of the *Gazette* would be temporarily suspended, she protested. "I think I've learned enough to get the *Gazette* out for you while you're away."

He raised a brow at that. "I appreciate the offer, but it's not really necessary. I'll start putting out feelers for a new owner—I know several individuals who might be interested. Once I return, we can settle the matter and then the paper can resume."

"I *want* to do this. Granted, I won't be able to put out as substantial an issue, and my articles won't be as well crafted as yours, but I can manage to get something acceptable out." She raised her chin up a notch. "Wasn't it

you who said running a newspaper is making a promise
to your patrons that they can count on you to deliver what
they want to read about, week in and week out?"

He studied her thoughtfully. "Are you sure?"

"Yes. And Abigail can help me. It'll give her something
to occupy her mind with these next couple of weeks." *And
me, as well.*

After another long moment of silence, he nodded. "Very
well. I'll change the notice to indicate it'll be an abbrevi-
ated version while I am away."

Feeling she'd won a much-needed victory, Daisy went
back to work, determined to quiz him on all of the aspects of his job she was still fuzzy on. That, too, would
give them something less emotional to focus on for the
rest of the evening.

Chapter Twenty-Five

Everett left his hotel room and headed for the *Banner Dispatch* office. The latest copy of the *Turnabout Gazette* had arrived yesterday, and he'd pored over it. Daisy was doing a surprisingly good job keeping it going. And her voice was coming through loud and clear in the stories. It was almost as if she stood beside him discussing these local happenings. The stories she printed had more of a down-to-earth, colloquial tone than the stories he'd written, but he knew that they would be all the better received by the locals for it. There was less outside news in it than what he normally included, but what she did include was handled well.

She'd included a letter, and here, too, her voice shone through. It seemed Mrs. Humphries, mother of six, was expecting again, and Lionel, down at the train depot, had hired Noah Foster to help out. She also reported that Eileen Pierce, a widow with something of a notorious reputation, had stopped by to see if Abigail would purchase some of her books to place in the library. That had given him some pause, but Daisy, in her typically generous fashion, had said it appeared the widow needed money but was too proud to ask, so she'd given Abigail the money to make the purchase. There was also some personal news.

Her father had arrived in Turnabout a couple of days ago. All of Everett's protective urges surfaced, and he keenly regretted that he'd not been by her side to face the man.

But there was no hint that this had been a difficult encounter for her. In fact, she'd invited her father to move into the spare bedroom at their home, with the understanding that he was welcome to stay, so long as he didn't drink or gamble. Still, Everett knew how deeply Daisy loved the man, which meant she could so easily be hurt again.

But soon this interview period would be over, and he could be with her again. Tomorrow would mark the end of the three-week trial run. And all indications were that he had succeeded. He and the senior editor had had a long talk when he arrived about what happened in Philadelphia. Everett hadn't attempted to sugarcoat any of what had happened and his own culpability. But he'd also assured the man he'd learned from that mistake and that it had made him all the more zealous to get to the truth of a story.

Afterward, he'd been given a number of assignments— everything from covering minor social events to major breaking stories. And in every case he'd come through with flying colors—that wasn't braggadocio, that was fact. He'd enjoyed those assignments, enjoyed being part of a larger newsroom again, enjoyed pursuing stories that were meatier than births and barn raisings, enjoyed the satisfaction of seeing his byline on a front-page story.

He'd also been in touch with Miss Haversham, and she had assured him that she was prepared to accept Abigail back right after Independence Day. Additionally, he'd found a nice townhouse that would be just right for him and Daisy to move into. The kitchen was furnished with a new stove, and the place had electricity and all the other amenities to be found in a big city. It even had a nice backyard that would be perfect for both her dog and her kitchen garden. In time, she could not only grow accustomed to it, but enjoy making the place her own.

Yes, everything was coming together perfectly.

So why wasn't he more excited?

This was exactly what he'd hoped for and worked for since leaving Philadelphia, and it had happened faster than he'd dared believe it would.

But all of Daisy's talk of friends and community and setting down roots had insinuated itself into his mind, into his very being. For all of his worldly polish, it was something he'd never had before, something he hadn't really thought he'd needed.

Yet these past few weeks, when he'd come home to his empty apartment in the evenings, he'd had lots of time to think things over.

One of the things he realized, surprisingly, was that he missed having some messiness in his life, the kind of messiness Daisy and Abigail were so good at. Routines and orderliness were all well and good, but they were rather sterile and uninteresting if there was nothing to shake them up occasionally.

Another quite profound understanding hit when he realized that every time he sat down to a meal, he found himself pausing, waiting for Daisy to offer up her prayers of thanks. Those sincere, conversational, personal prayers, along with her everyday examples of forgiveness and grace, had also made their way into his being, had rekindled a spark he thought long dead. He found himself longing for the kind of relationship she had with God, the kind of relationship that was close and personal, not tied to some vague theology. And he was making progress with that. He'd begun reading his Bible again and offering up his own prayers.

Then other, smaller awarenesses hit. He found himself missing that daily chess match with Adam and the greetings on the street from people who really knew him. He found himself saddened at the thought of Abigail not being a part of his day-to-day life, at not being nearby when Adam and Reggie welcomed their new baby into the world. And if he were to be honest with himself, a small part of him even missed putting out the *Gazette* twice a week. When had his world changed? And why hadn't he noticed it before now?

There was a question he needed to answer right now, though—while he was almost certain Daisy would follow him, did he really want to pull her away from everything she'd built for herself?

A peace settled over him as he realized the answer to that question.

So what was he waiting for?

Chapter Twenty-Six

Daisy was making notes on the latest story she was writing for the *Gazette*. This one would feature Abigail and Constance and the great work they were doing with the lending library. Everett was due back in two days, and she wanted to make certain he wasn't disappointed with the job she'd done in his absence.

She didn't want to think about what would happen afterward.

His letters had been filled with news of the places he'd seen since he'd arrived in St. Louis, and the sites that she would enjoy visiting when she moved there. He even mentioned the many fine restaurants she could visit. And he'd told her of a townhouse he'd found that they could move into, pending her approval. At least there was that.

He was trying to do what he could to make this move more attractive to her. That showed he wanted her to be happy.

As for her dream of opening a restaurant, he'd never lent much credence to that, anyway, so it hadn't factored into his plans for their new life. And she'd already resigned herself to shelving that dream even if they stayed here, hadn't she?

She'd done a great deal of thinking and praying on the matter since Everett left. And she'd finally decided that she would make the move with him and do it cheerfully. It did no good to mope and pout. This was his dream, and it wasn't right of her to try to sour it for him.

Her only worry now was how to convince him to reconsider his plans for Abigail. The girl had definitely blossomed in the time she'd been here. And she loved her brother so much—did he see that?

Leaving would break Abigail's heart, and Constance's, as well. Every time the two girls discussed how to turn the new library over to Constance alone, tears began to flow.

On that score, unfortunately, she could see no happy ending. Even if she convinced Everett not to send Abigail back to Boston—which she was determined to do—Abigail would still be moving to St. Louis and away from Turnabout.

Daisy pushed that unhappy thought away. She tried to focus instead on some of the blessings that had come into her life these past weeks.

First, she'd received an answer to the letter she'd written her grandmother. Except it had come from her aunt Marie. Uncle Phillip's wife had informed her that her grandmother had passed away two months earlier.

Daisy had felt an unexpected sadness at that news. While the two of them had never been on friendly terms, her passing meant that there would never be a chance for them to mend fences.

But the rest of the letter had proved to be warm and gracious. Aunt Marie wished her every happiness in her marriage and assured her that both she and Uncle Phillip would be delighted to have her and Everett come visit whenever they liked.

Almost immediately after the letter arrived, her father

had shown up. She'd been shocked at his appearance, for the first time realizing he was getting on in years. And the kind of life he'd been leading was taking its toll.

She wanted to provide him with a home and the care he needed, but how would Everett feel about that? Surely she could convince him that there was room for her father in this new life he had planned for them.

And perhaps one more…

Reggie walked in just then, a sense of purpose in her step.

Daisy smiled, ready for a distraction. "Is there something I can do for you, or did you just come by for a visit?"

"Actually, neither." Reggie had a look of concern on her face. "I noticed a commotion at your place when I passed by, and thought you might want to check it out."

"A commotion?" Daisy was already heading for the door. "Did something happen? Are the girls okay?"

Reggie gave her a reassuring smile. "They're fine."

"Then what is it?"

"It would be best if you saw for yourself."

More puzzled than ever, Daisy quick-stepped to her place and pushed the door open. She stepped inside to see both girls and Kip staring at her with expectant expressions.

Daisy looked around, but didn't see anything out of the ordinary. "What's going on? Reggie mentioned something about a commotion."

Abigail made a sweeping motion toward the back of the building. "It's over in the storeroom. You should go take a look."

There was something odd about the way the girls were looking at her. She slowly crossed the room, glancing back at them just before she reached the doorway. Their smiles reassured her it wasn't anything serious, but she still had no idea what was going on.

Daisy reached the doorway, then stopped dead in her tracks.

Everett stood there, an uncertain smile on his face. "Hello, Daisy."

Her mind immediately started racing. What was he doing home already, and why was he here instead of at the newspaper office? Had he not gotten the job?

She stepped farther into the room, then halted again when she noticed what was behind him—a shiny new stove with a huge red ribbon on top of it.

"Everett, what? I mean, I don't—" She took a deep breath, then gave him a huge welcome-home smile. "Hello."

He moved aside and nodded to the stove. "Don't you like it?"

"Of course I do. It's the biggest, shiniest, most beautiful stove I've ever seen. But what is it doing here? What are *you* doing here? I thought you weren't coming home until Thursday."

"I got homesick."

Homesick? For Turnabout? Or for her? Her pulse quickened, and she tried desperately not to read too much into his statement. "Did you get the job?"

"Mr. O'Hanlin offered me the job, and at a higher pay than I'd expected."

"Congratulations." She tried to put as much sincerity into that word as she could.

"But I had to turn him down."

Hope leaped inside her, threatening to steal her breath. "You did?"

"I did. Because I realized something. Something you tried to tell me but that I wasn't ready to hear, until now."

She couldn't have dropped her gaze from his if her life had depended on it. "And what was that?"

He closed the gap between them and took her hands in his. "That it's not where you are that matters so much as who you're with. That family and community and roots that go deep are very important to a person's ability to thrive. And that one should never discount the dreams of others, especially those they love."

Love. Did he really mean that?

He stroked her cheek. "I know I've been arrogant and thoughtless and every kind of fool, but I hope you'll give me one more chance to get this right. I want to build my life with you right here in Turnabout. I want to turn the *Gazette* into the finest small-town newspaper there ever was. And I want to stand by you as you follow your dream to open that restaurant you want."

Daisy leaned her face into his hand as she looked into his eyes. She couldn't remember ever being happier. "Oh, Everett, I want those things, too—but only if I can share them with you. I do love you, you know, more than I can bear sometimes. And I've missed you so much these past weeks."

He gathered her in his arms and gave her the kiss she'd been longing for. It was a long, wondrous moment before they came up for air. They were both breathless, and she could feel the pounding of his heart keeping time with hers.

"Now," he said as he slipped his arm around her waist and led her toward the door, "before we forget where we are, let's go tell Abigail we're not moving, and neither is she." He gave her waist a squeeze. "Because family should stay together."

Daisy smiled at that. She had begun to suspect that their family would be increasing by one member early next year.

But she would wait until they were alone again to share her news.

God was so good. Who could have guessed when she arrived in Turnabout that He could bring forth so many blessings from such inauspicious beginnings?

Daisy knew in her heart that she'd finally found the place she'd always longed for, the place where she could feel she truly belonged.

It was right here in Everett's arms.

Epilogue

Daisy stood at the stove dishing up the last slice of meat loaf, along with some new potatoes and corn. The last of the rabbit stew had disappeared ten minutes ago. After she served this plate, she would be down to chicken soup and cold ham. She'd never dreamed so many people would show up for the opening day of her restaurant. It seemed almost everyone in town had walked through those doors this morning.

She'd just finished piling on a hearty helping of vegetables to go with the meat loaf when she felt a pair of arms snake around her waist. She let out a little squeak of surprise, then carefully set the plate down and rounded on her husband. "Everett Fulton! You almost made me drop this plate, and it's my last slice of meat loaf."

"I have faith in your dexterity, my dear." He leaned down and planted a kiss on her cheek. When he stepped back, one arm remained around her waist. "Last slice of meat loaf, is it? Far be it from me to say I told you so, but it looks like you're doing a booming business."

Daisy raised a brow. "That came about as close to an *I told you so* as you can get without actually saying the words." Then she smiled. "It's no doubt just the newness of it that's brought all these folks here today, but it *is* exciting, isn't it?"

He grinned down at her. "No more than I expected." Then his expression turned serious. "You look flushed. Why isn't Abigail in here helping you?"

"I look flushed because it's hot in here. And Abigail has her own business to attend to. I think she had six new subscribers to her library already this morning." Daisy was as proud of Abigail's accomplishment as she was of her own. And it was fun to see how the two businesses complemented each other.

"Besides," she added, "Pa has been helping me this morning. He's out front now, keeping an eye on things and refilling glasses as needed."

"Just promise me you won't overdo it," Everett said as he placed a hand gently on her stomach, as if to protect the precious new life growing there. "I can hire you some help if things get too busy around here."

She gave him an exasperated frown. "I'm healthy as a horse, and near as strong. I will *not* have you treating me like an invalid for the next seven months."

"Not like an invalid," he countered. "Rather like the precious person you are. And as the light of my life and the mother of our future child."

Everett watched as her expression went all soft and her cheeks flushed prettily. And just as he had every day since his return from St. Louis, he silently thanked God that Daisy had come into his life.

Because of her he had a family now—a true family. People he could love unconditionally and who he knew truly loved him in return.

And that was all the status he needed.

* * * * *

*If you enjoyed this story by Winnie Griggs,
be sure to look for the next book
in her TEXAS GROOMS series, coming in
October from Love Inspired Historical!*

Dear Reader,

Hello and thank you so much for taking the time to read Everett and Daisy's story. It's a story I've been wanting to tell for a very long time. And it was such fun to be able to revisit the community of Turnabout, Texas, and all the wonderful folks who inhabit it.

On the surface, Daisy and Everett were two completely different people. Everett is very much a by-the-book, appearance-conscious person with his whole life mapped out. He's also cynical and quite certain he knows what is best for him and for those around him.

Then along comes Daisy, a free spirit, more concerned with connecting to people—all kinds of people—than with appearances. And far from being cynical, she looks at life through big rose-colored glasses.

It was really fun, and sometimes very emotional, bringing these two very different and lonely people together and helping them to find their happily-ever-after. I hope you enjoyed reading their story as much as I enjoyed writing it. And stay tuned for the next book in this series, which will feature Chance Dawson.

Wishing you much love and blessings in your life,

Winnie

Questions for Dicussion

1. What did you think of Daisy's decision to strike out on her own and on foot?

2. What did you think Everett's motives were for helping Daisy that very first time? Do you think his reasons changed over time?

3. What do you think Kip meant to Daisy and why?

4. Why do you suppose Everett was so opposed to Daisy's plans to start her own restaurant? Do you agree with his reasons?

5. Why do you think Everett was so opposed to his sister coming to Turnabout?

6. What did you see as the differences and similarities in Abigail's and Daisy's motives for "running away" to Turnabout?

7. Based on what you saw in this book, what is your opinion of Chance Dawson? (His will be the next story in this series.)

8. Why do you think Everett was so focused on leaving Turnabout?

9. How did you feel about Everett's attitude toward Kip? Did this change over time?

10. How would you describe Everett and Abigail's relationship at the beginning of the book, and how did it change, if at all, by the end?

11. Do you think it was important for Everett to go to St. Louis and pursue the opportunity offered? Why or why not?

12. What did you think about Daisy's eventual reconciliation with her father? Did it ring true?

13. If you read the first book in this series, *Handpicked Husband,* did you feel the characters featured in both books remained true to character?

REQUEST YOUR FREE BOOKS!

2 FREE INSPIRATIONAL NOVELS
PLUS 2
FREE
MYSTERY GIFTS

Love Inspired
HISTORICAL
INSPIRATIONAL HISTORICAL ROMANCE

YES! Please send me 2 FREE Love Inspired® Historical novels and my 2 FREE mystery gifts (gifts are worth about $10). After receiving them, if I don't wish to receive any more books, I can return the shipping statement marked "cancel." If I don't cancel, I will receive 4 brand-new novels every month and be billed just $4.74 per book in the U.S. or $5.24 per book in Canada. That's a saving of at least 21% off the cover price. It's quite a bargain! Shipping and handling is just 50¢ per book in the U.S. and 75¢ per book in Canada.* I understand that accepting the 2 free books and gifts places me under no obligation to buy anything. I can always return a shipment and cancel at any time. Even if I never buy another book, the two free books and gifts are mine to keep forever.

102/302 IDN F5CN

Name _____ (PLEASE PRINT) _____

Address _____ Apt. # _____

City _____ State/Prov. _____ Zip/Postal Code _____

Signature (if under 18, a parent or guardian must sign)

Mail to the Harlequin® Reader Service:
IN U.S.A.: P.O. Box 1867, Buffalo, NY 14240-1867
IN CANADA: P.O. Box 609, Fort Erie, Ontario L2A 5X3

Want to try two free books from another series?
Call 1-800-873-8635 or visit www.ReaderService.com.

* Terms and prices subject to change without notice. Prices do not include applicable taxes. Sales tax applicable in N.Y. Canadian residents will be charged applicable taxes. Offer not valid in Quebec. This offer is limited to one order per household. Not valid for current subscribers to Love Inspired Historical books. All orders subject to credit approval. Credit or debit balances in a customer's account(s) may be offset by any other outstanding balance owed by or to the customer. Please allow 4 to 6 weeks for delivery. Offer available while quantities last.

Your Privacy—The Harlequin® Reader Service is committed to protecting your privacy. Our Privacy Policy is available online at www.ReaderService.com or upon request from the Harlequin Reader Service.

We make a portion of our mailing list available to reputable third parties that offer products we believe may interest you. If you prefer that we not exchange your name with third parties, or if you wish to clarify or modify your communication preferences, please visit us at www.ReaderService.com/consumerschoice or write to us at Harlequin Reader Service Preference Service, P.O. Box 9062, Buffalo, NY 14269. Include your complete name and address.

LIH13R

The pavement outside the Kansas City airport radiated heat
even though the sun had already sunk below the horizon.
Tate held his seven-year-old daughter's hand a little tighter
and squinted against the dying sunshine to read the signs
hanging overhead.

"That's it down there," he said, pointing. "Baggage
Claim A."

Lily Farnsworth was the last of six new business owners
to arrive, each selected by the Save Our Street Committee of
the town of Bygones. As a member of the committee, Tate
had been asked to meet her at the airport in Kansas City and
transport her to Bygones. With the grand opening just a week
away, most of the shop owners had been at work preparing
their stores for some time already, but Ms. Farnsworth
had delayed until after her sister's wedding, assuring the
committee that a florist's shop required less preparation than
some retail businesses. Tate hoped she was right.

He still wasn't convinced that this scheme, financed by a
mysterious, anonymous donor, would work, but if something
didn't revive the financial fortunes of Bygones—and soon—
their small town would become just another ghost town on the
north central plains.

Isabella stopped before the automatic doors and waited

for him to catch up. They entered the cool building together. A pair of gleaming luggage carousels occupied the open space, both vacant. A few people milled about. Among them was a tall, pretty woman with long blond hair and round tortoiseshell glasses. She was perched atop a veritable mountain of luggage. She wore black ballet slippers and white knit leggings beneath a gossamery blue dress with fluttery sleeves and hems. Her very long hair was parted in the middle and waved about her face and shoulders. He felt the insane urge to look more closely behind the lenses of her glasses, but of course he would not.

He turned away, the better to resist the urge to stare, and scanned the building for anyone who might be his florist.

One by one, the possibilities faded away. Finally Isabella gave him that look that said, "Dad, you're being a goof again." She slipped her little hand into his, and he sighed inwardly. Turning, he walked the few yards to the luggage mountain and swept off his straw cowboy hat.

"Are you Lily Farnsworth?"

To find out if Bygones can turn itself around,
pick up LOVE IN BLOOM
wherever Love Inspired books are sold.

LIEXP7823